Sarah's Second Chance
©2021, Patricia Clifton

This book is a work of fiction. References to real people, events, establishments, organizations, or locals are intended only to provide a sense of authenticity and are used fictitiously. All other characters, and all incidences and dialogue are drawn from the author's imagination and are not to be considered as real.

Sarah's Second Chance. Copyright 2021 by Patricia Clifton. All rights reserved. Printed in the United States of America. No parts of this book may be used or reproduced in any manner without written permission except in quotations used within articles of reviews.

Published by Book Baby Publishing Co., Pennsauken, NJ. Information request may be sent to info@bookbaby.com. Books and e-books may be purchased from major book retailers.

The author may be contacted at her page on Facebook.

ISBN (soft cover) 978-1-09835-711-5
ISBN (e-book) 978-1-09835-712-2

Sarah's Second Chance

Patricia Clifton

Chapter 1

Sarah's Marriage

Glenn surprised Sarah when he called to say, "I'm back in town, I've missed you...I need to see you right away." Glenn's charming voice caused a sweet grin to ease across her face and her heart to quiver.

With a surge of excitement Sarah hurriedly worked her morning schedule, so she could meet Glenn for lunch. Shortly before 11:00, she grabbed her purse, ran from her office as she finger-combed her Beatles style haircut and slipped into the elevator in the nick of time.

With only a short walk, Sarah beamed with excitement as she stepped hurriedly up the tall steps to the charming Morgan House Inn, and whiffed the comforting fragrance of fried chicken and casseroles filling the air. As the host opened the massive wooden Victorian doors with etched glass panels, she became mesmerized by the 1890's splendor inside. Tables covered in white cloths, set with vintage china and flatware filled the elegant dining room, that lent to an enchanted mood. She felt a lift in her step, as though she had entered a captivating daydream.

"I'm here for lunch with Glenn Brooks."

"Yes, please follow me."

Sarah appeared stunning in her colorful Lilly dress as she crossed the dining room with a light quick step and was seated. Across the table from her, Glenn leaned forward, grasped her hand, and said, "Will you marry me?"

With his flash of words of the sudden proposal, her breath caught in her throat. A thought that made her feel stifled. She coughed and with an empty feeling while holding her breath, waited for his next statement…wondering what that might be, or was she expected to give an immediate answer to his pending question which seized her with surprise.

"You know we're in South Carolina," he went on to explain. "Why don't we go to the clinic for a blood test this afternoon, and then the courthouse tomorrow morning? I've fallen in love with you and feel I can't live another day without you as my own." He leaned forward, as his baby blues glistened. "I don't think we should wait any longer. You couldn't be more perfect for me and I sense the feeling is mutual."

The feeling of shock caused something in her heart to hesitate. "I love the sound of your words," Sarah whispered. The uncertainty of this rushed proposal caused her to question his statement but soon found herself intentionally ignoring that feeling deep inside. She drifted into thought, *He is everything I could want in a husband…a hard worker, affectionate and enjoys life.*

In a wavering daze, Sarah rearranged her seafood salad as she slowly ate three bites and placed her fork aside as she looked at Glenn. She saw him wolfing down his ham sandwich appearing confident and seemingly with no thoughts of the proposal. She smiled as his confidence created a feeling of admiration inside of her for this strong man.

Sarah was thrust into reality as the Morgan House server asked, "Would you like to order dessert? Today we have peach cobbler and triple chocolate cake."

While caught up in the dream of his proposal, fueled by the fervor of excitement, Sarah heard herself say, "Yes, I will marry you."

The waiter's stunned face lit up. "Looks as though you will need celebration glasses of champagne and a slice of triple chocolate cake."

"Yes, bring it on…it's going to be a good day," Glenn smiled and squeezed Sarah's limp hand.

* * *

Their wedding vows were spoken the next day before the Justice of the Peace and two witnesses from the office next door. Sarah's excitement was churning, sparked by her enthusiasm for her knight in shining armor who hurried her off in his Marina Blue Camaro. They drove immediately to Sarah's apartment and spent the afternoon and evening loving on each other.

Well before the sun rose the next morning, Glenn was growing restless, and yearning for his space. He thought, *it is early Saturday morning, I wonder where my little secretary might have wondered off to last night. I'll slip into the den and give her a quick call.* Glenn delighted in their conversation while hearing her excitement and was looking forward to waking Sarah.

Sarah awoke with a feeling of enchantment by her sudden marriage to the man of her dreams. "I feel wonderful, but I need to call my parents and best friend," She whispered as she folded back the warm covers.

"That can wait…I need you now," Glenn said with an alluring smile.

Later while having coffee, Sarah discussed with Glenn her marriage explanation for her parents, and he casually agreed.

His response was, "Yeah, yeah, that sounds like a good thing to say. I've never met your parents, but that will work."

Sarah was shaken when he didn't offer encouragement as she relived her account of their whirlwind wedding, and he didn't even say he would talk with her parents. She felt disappointed. *It seems the one who was always laughing and smiling…the one who was romantically playful with me has gone into a shell*, she thought.

* * *

For lunch they strolled in the warm sunshine to a local seafood diner a few blocks away. Sarah's excitement was obvious by the way she placed her arm around his waist or held his hand or elbow and whispered in his ear. She laughed as she pointed out to Glenn the new fall collection of coats while wiping perspiration from her brow.

They ordered a meal of shrimp-rolls and fried flounder. As Sarah tasted a second helping of the succulent flounder, Glenn said something that shocked her to the core.

"I've had a number of girlfriends in my lifetime. Even one of your friends winked at me several times when we had dinner at the Creek Cafe. I remember numerous ones who were good to me and we got along fine. Some I had to teach a few things, like how I want to be treated and what I expect from a woman. There are a few things you will have to learn."

Sarah gasp as a lump of fish caught in her throat…she coughed as her eyes stretched wide…cleared her throat of the choking feeling as salty tears flowed and a sweaty hot heat covered her body. Sarah could not believe her ears…on the second day of their marriage to hear him say something like this. *To speak so openly of his past girlfriends, and to describe them as an object that's expected to satisfy his needs. It feels as though he now has me and is telling me his game plan while he encases me with his perfect web.*

With a bewildered feeling like being stabbed in the heart, Sarah stared at the tired waitress behind the counter and said, "What have I gotten myself into?" Her heartbeat trembled as a heat swept over her body and Sarah knew she was about to faint. As her vision began to blur, and her thoughts began to waver she whispered, "If I pass out… who will help me? Maybe the lady behind the counter…"

Her eyes dimmed as the burgundy Naugahyde covered banquette cushion rushed up to meet her, and everything went black.

* * *

Early Monday morning they arose with anticipation. Glenn left for his long drive to Augusta for work, while Sarah's last week on the job was to complete Mr. Martin's office project. The final items had to be unpacked and placed. She wanted the project finished before moving at the end of the week from Charleston to her husband's apartment in southeast Georgia.

Saying goodbye to my friends at work…with thoughts of being a recent college graduate…leaving my first job…having to rebuild that passion in a new location is growing bittersweet. Sarah had hoped their marriage would leave her heart warm, but instead uncertainty filled her thoughts.

Her marriage and how she always wanted to be the good wife with an affectionate homelife, was her dream, but the change in Glenn crippled her. She had always seen his over confidence as a virtue, but now it came across as arrogance that frightened her.

Sarah thought, *hopefully when I get moved in and take care of Glenn like a good wife would do, things will be better.* "Mom always said, you marry for life…if a problem exist you work it out…or you just make the best of it. Can't embarrass the family with a divorce." A quiver washed over Sarah as she rethought her quick decision to get married.

At the time of their marriage, Sarah had known Glenn for almost a year and had fallen deeply in love with his caring warm nature. She fondly remembered *that warm day in late September our paths accidentally crossed as I was leaving Mr. Martin's office, but I was stressed and hadn't noticed his kindness, until he called that night. He reminded me of his gentlemanly ways as he had opened doors and carried the heavy carpet sample books to the elevator.*

After Sarah recalled his kind help, she agreed to meet Glenn the next day. *The instant I saw him I was mesmerized by his handsome good looks and graceful charm.*

That September day we spent several hours on a shaded bench at the marina park listening to the shrimp boats unload their bounty as we shared our life stories. Glenn mentioned several times how he had bragged to Mr. Martin on my color selections and his choice of a beautiful decorator.

* * *

With an unsettled heart filled with anticipation, Sarah drove herself to their apartment in a town south of Augusta. She had given several pieces of her furniture to friends and placed the remainder in storage. She took what few personal items she could pack in her Volvo coupe.

Sarah saw the disarray of Glenn's apartment and changed the sheets, washed several loads of his clothes, and took out the trash. She prepared a delicious candlelight dinner that had to be warmed because Glenn arrived home late.

That night as Sarah stepped into the shower, she began to think, *He acts as though he's not excited to see me, I feel intimidated by his moodiness, but I want everything to be pleasant because I can't imagine losing hope…so soon. I want to make things work but his sharp responses hurt, and his passion is mechanical, as though he's mowing the grass.*

* * *

Sarah was thrilled to find a temporary job at a local department store, because in this small rural town there was no such thing as an interior decorating agency. She made friends quickly with the regular clientele and began building rapport with other employees in the nearby stores. She soon became a valued employee noticed by her employer. Sarah enjoyed her work and treasured the friendships she made, especially getting to know Carrie.

Sarah and Carrie were having lunch at the local drugstore, and Sarah was feeling put-down. She spoke aloud with trust, "Glenn bragged about his high paying job when we dated but I'm finding my little check is more important than at first I thought." Sarah was careful about mentioning their personal business, but she was angry with him for begging her for every cent she had. "He doesn't let me have access to any money."

* * *

Glenn called home from work often saying he was working on a major project. With authority he spoke, "I have to stay late for a planning meeting and hope to be home by 9:00. Maybe it won't last late into the night but if I need to spend the night in Augusta, I'll call."

"You stay often…I'm sure your supervisor is taking notice of your extra work," she said with encouragement as any good wife would do. It was easy to fake her understanding over the phone, but she was discouraged by his late-night work schedule.

For dinner, Sarah made her usual meal when alone…bought chicken salad with a glass of pinot grigio. She sat at the table but felt sad seeing the empty chairs, so she moved to a stool at the counter. Sarah pushed her food around the plate and ate each tasteless bite by memory. Her thoughts wavered as she focused on Glenn, *when we were dating, I was impressed by the way he spoke and acted. I laughed heartily at his tales of humorous antics. My heart had danced to the rhythm of his charming words, and the more he spoke the deeper into the rabbit hole I obviously tumbled.*

Sarah thought of the changes in her life and wished for the husband she thought she knew…the one she thought she could trust, respect, and admire. "I feel alone, rejected at home with nowhere to turn…my parents would have no understanding of my marriage troubles. They would be ashamed of me and forced to apologize to their friends for my mistake."

"I feel as though I'm in an unstable situation. My intentions were to be the best for him but now it seems what I thought was best isn't best anymore," she mumbled as she stumbled off to the bedroom… alone again.

* * *

A few months later, Glenn came in the backdoor from work, whistling, and said, "Guess what?"

My mind thought of a lot of things, but not this one. I heard what he said and looked at him with unsuspecting disbelief.

"I've been house shopping in Augusta, and I've found the perfect one," he said with certainty.

Sarah was in shock and wondered whether they could afford a move, and it upset her to think of leaving her new friends, especially the sweet older lady who worked nearby and had befriended her in a motherly way. Though silently devastated, she agreed to his plans and soon they moved into the new house.

The house was gorgeous. Sarah loved the spaciousness and the smart new furnishings they bought. She thought often of the friends she left behind, especially her motherly friend, and her companion Carrie.

* * *

Months later as Sarah prepared for Glenn's office Christmas party, she bought a gorgeous navy-blue crepe dress with a delicate sparkling shawl and got a flattering haircut. She felt pretty when they entered the Victorian ballroom at the historic Bon-Air Hotel. Sarah felt enchanted as Glenn strolled her around the room, and his local sales crew circled them as he introduced her.

"Guy's, this is Sarah. Sarah this is my faithful work crew," Glenn stated with authority.

"Hello, it's nice to finally get to meet you all," she said with a smile. "The hotel and Christmas party are festive and lovely…I'm honored to be with everyone."

The guys smiled and complimented him on his beautiful wife, all except Mike. Sarah's eyes shifted to him several times as she noticed his silence and the way he stared at her as though trying to figure her out. As Glenn whisked Sarah away, she looked back at Mike who was looking at her over the rim of his drink.

Mike whispered softly, "What's this wholesome, beautiful young lady doing with a jerk like him? She appears timid…an easy target for Glenn. He'll trap her and destroy her with a slow death…I fear for her."

* * *

Glenn's dominance along with his harsh demeaning language escalated, and not long after Sarah was hired by a high-profile interior design showroom, he demanded she quit her job. "We have a new home, and you need to be here taking care of it," he said. "Besides one of those smart young guys at work might cozy up to you." That was his arrogant, but insecure reasoning.

"This job was much like my job in Charleston…which I loved," Sarah confided to Carrie as soon as she was alone. "I'm sorry, I'm having to quit…"

With painful hesitation Sarah heeded his command and left the job she loved. She didn't want to upset Glenn. The isolation robbed her creativeness, and she began to feel less confident. It seemed his belittling comments were oftentimes more than she could bear.

His late-night meetings, lingering phone calls, and rushing out to meet clients at all hours, created questionable feelings for Sarah but… "As the good wife would do to play the game, I always encouraged Glenn to enjoy himself."

Several months after quitting her job he surprised her by saying, "In order to save money, we need to sell your car." He strongly said, "You need to clean the house, keep my clothes washed, pressed, and my starched shirts hanging in the closet with the left sleeve facing out. I forgot to mention, I have that club meeting tonight, I'll grab dinner downtown."

Sarah remembered, *I looked at him with astonishment, and with a fear of his anger. I didn't say a word…removed the dinner settings from the table and started putting away the meal, as I thought even less of him. I spilled beet juice on my shorts that were now a size too large and already spotted from wash-day bleach. I looked at my old, stained clothing and thought how they match my tired broken feelings.*

* * *

Carrie was Sarah's source of comfort and she was looking forward to their lunch meeting because Sarah needed to confide to her friend. Carrie's wisdom and common sense were encouraging to her fragile ego. While sharing a dessert, Sarah mentioned, "I do have a neighbor who is kind to me and will ask me to go with her to lunch, or shopping. I always go because it's my only outing, and she knows I must be home early to have Glenn's dinner ready," Sarah shared. "Thank you for coming by and picking me up."

"Stay close to your neighbor…she means more to you than you think," Carrie said as her penetrating eyes looked deep into Sarah's understanding eyes.

* * *

Several summers later at the company picnic, Mike unexpectedly met Sarah in the hallway of the office complex. He greeted her kindly and Sarah stopped to chat a moment. The conversation ended with Mike saying with an intense look into her eyes, "If you ever need help, just let me know."

With a clear understanding of his sincerity and concern, and with knowing someone knows the situation she was in, Sarah felt a small measure of comfort. Sarah looked directly into his eyes and said, "Thank you, I understand…I will remember your offer."

Glenn had been watching. That evening he questioned Sarah endlessly as to why she was talking with Mike, and he demanded she never go near him again. "I have the right to demand this, you are my wife, and I control what you do."

With overwhelming disbelief, Sarah felt forced to agree, but in her heart, she was thankful knowing Mike was aware of her situation.

As she was lying in bed that night, she began to seriously question things. *I'm basically alone. Glenn has refused to visit my friends in Charleston, and seldom mentions visiting my parents. When he does visit, he's always aloof and never offers complimentary comments to my parents or makes positive references to our marriage. His main interest is telling them how important he is as a district sales representative.*

* * *

Time was passing, and Sarah was feeling hopeless while struggling to survive Glenn's dream killer ways. It was taking its toll on Sarah physically and emotionally. She continued to struggle at not giving up on her marriage, because she wanted to be a successfully married woman, and did not want to be an embarrassment to her family. The beliefs and reactions of her parents implied they would not give her the emotional support she needed to leave Glenn. Her self-worth was destroyed to the point of not seeing her way out.

Even though Sarah felt rejected and battered, she continued to satisfy his demands while her will to go on was fractured. She saw her future as bleak, but continued to attend the company parties, respond to each of Glenn's requests and tread lightly in his presence. She struggled through exhaustion to please him as she saw her disheartening future through a shattered heart.

"I've spent years coddling his ego, and wearing the mask of happiness, but his toxic abuse has worn me into a depression I can't pull free of," Sarah whispered as her bent frame staggered into the kitchen.

A next-door neighbor couldn't reach Sarah by phone and decided she needed to make an impromptu visit. She found Sarah trembling, weak and in a confused state of mind. She knew Sarah needed help and called 911, after not being able to reach Glenn.

Under emergency conditions, Sarah was admitted to the hospital for an evaluation, and after several weeks of treatment was diagnosed by Dr. Freeman as having reactive depression hampered by malnutrition and an overall degenerative condition.

After weeks of shock treatments and talk therapy, he determined Sarah's depression was a result of her controlling husband, and her fear of shaming her parents.

After consulting with her husband and with Sarah's description of his behavior toward her, Dr. Freeman saw Glenn as having characteristics of a demanding narcissistic personality. His manipulation and control of Sarah's life, his targeting of her to come into his trap with marriage, and the way he praised her in public and without warning flipped to belittle her in private were signs of a narcissist. Sarah could be in a dangerous situation, and this hospital stay could be a clear sign of danger to come.

Dr. Freeman's treatment plan for Sarah was to rebuild her confidence by helping her believe in herself. Through talk therapy and medication, this was accomplished. "Sarah, I'm your trusted friend with whom you can confide and contact anytime. Please call if you feel you might be in trouble." Dr. Freeman feared that when she went back into the home, she more than likely would be faced by the same deadly toxic situation.

Chapter 2

Sarah awoke in her quiet bedroom at home and realized she was alone. She laid in the warm bed and thought of the plan she had gone over before falling to sleep last night. "I have decided for my safety and sanity, I must leave my husband. His control of me with his belittling ways and threats of violence are destroying the person I feel I am and want to be. With my peak years waning I feel I deserve more than the worthless feeling his intimidation causes, I deserve peace of mind."

"He's away today so I'll discreetly search his home office for investments, tag receipts and the previous year's income tax returns and make copies. Money...I'll need money, I have none...I'll start searching and hiding what I can find. I know if he catches me planning something, I'll be in trouble. The shock would make him start hiding cash and transferring his funds to offshore investments. I know his obsession for protecting *his* money," Sarah mumbled as she headed to the kitchen for coffee.

"I need to call Dad's lawyer," Sarah mumbled as she took the first sip. "I'm sure he can give me valuable information on what I should do. His encouragement will help me stay strong as I search," She said as she opened the kitchen door to the back porch and felt a cool breath of air flow past.

As soon as Sarah told the lawyer her business, he began to ask questions. "Sarah, tell me about your marriage?"

"Well, sir, I married with total commitment, but that promise is wavering. Over the years I've disregarded abusive incidences thrown in my face. Early in our marriage, I overlooked finding condoms in his wallet, later a close friend at work had a baby who grew to have similar physical characteristics as Glenn, and his many relationships with other women that just didn't seem right."

"I've tolerated his ways by putting-up a front that the union was perfect. Often, he made me feel, I was the reason for his flirting, if he had an affair, it would be because of me, and I harbored the blame for his unpredictable behavior because he made me feel I was responsible. I suffered through the mental abuse of his open flirtations and of suspicious activities that didn't include me. I've had enough of his verbal abuse and frightful physical threats…I need to get out of this because it's getting worse…I deserve a peaceful life."

"Yes Sarah, I agree with you. You will need to list all assets along with the information you already have. You can send your information to me along with a fifty-dollar retainer check or cash in your case. I will file it if you decide to go further. Sarah, be careful."

* * *

The culmination of Glenn's selfishness and her forgiving tolerance came to a head when she discovered the UPS package of cigars with pink bindings, addressed to Glenn, hidden in his home office desk drawer. A rush of burning fire seared her face. "He's fathered a girl," Sarah mumbled as a heat flushed her body.

Sarah's heightened anger pushed her until she forcefully asked, "Where did the pink banded cigars come from?"

He stammered a bit, paused, "From a friend organizing an advertisement for GQ magazine."

My frozen smile in response to his blabbering masked the words I was feeling. I feared to boldly challenge him because I knew his tactical games. He would immediately degrade me and show his control by making me turn away. His tactics are cruel and insensitive with sharp words always on the tip of his tongue. I must be quiet and walk away to hold on to my sanity, Sarah thought as it felt her ribs would crush her heart.

Sarah felt a desperate need to talk with someone, so she called Dr. Freeman's phone and left a message, "I pretend not to see his ways because his presence is hard to bear. To question anything only brings on another lie I must accept. The lies and questions have taken its toll on my feelings toward my husband and our suffocating marriage. Currents of cold anger stir, as feelings of distrust make me physically ill with disgust as I struggle to find my way out."

* * *

While struggling with the problems of her homelife, Sarah cared for her aging parents…her father had Alzheimer's and was later diagnosed with cancer.

As Sarah's dad realized he was failing and needed extra help, also realized she needed a vehicle, so he gave her the old but reliable Suburban. He also shared with her instructions on locations of important papers and his thoughts for investments. Sarah made detailed notes and personally contacted his lawyer because she could see her dad declining rapidly.

In the final year, the chemo and radiation treatments were made to his body without him understanding why. Sarah thought, *it's sad to watch Dad emaciate into a pale-faced shell of a man.*

Sarah saw her mom's judgment was failing. *Mom was adamant as to not placing dad in a care center for fear of having to go there herself and having to give up her membership to The Club and her Cadillac keys. Both hold symbolic meaning to her, but now have lost their importance.*

Hours of phone calls from her mom, doctor visits and urgent trips were taking its toll. Sarah, with sleepy eyes and a furrowed forehead patiently continued to aid her mother's direct request.

* * *

During a lunch visit with Carrie, Sarah confided, "I talk with Glenn about my parents, knowing I was setting myself up for his selfish comments. I would find myself wanting to say more and my lips would separate…even a syllable of a word might roll out of my mouth, but I turned it into a cough. He was hurtful with the few comments I made. I've learned from his ways how to survive…I couldn't say all I wanted to say," Sarah mumbled in a low voice to Carrie.

"I'm afraid of showing my true feelings for fear of getting hurt…I moan into my pillow at night, and my shower has become a refuge. My sadness, mixed with words and tears, are quietly washed into the drain. I wanted help from a caring companion, but after so many years of trying, I have given up for fear of Glenn's egotistical nature. I feel sad and alone because his demanding ways has built a wall between us," Sarah quietly spoke as tears glazed her eyes.

With a painful stare that weakened into a frown she said, "He can easily break my spirit when he looks down, closes his eyes, rolls his lips, and slides his teeth together in a side-to-side grinding fashion.

Then his tone of voice and attitude changes into, 'How can I make this simple for the dummy?'"

"He always looks so noble and powerful, so as a survival tactic I won't speak or look at him in order to protect myself from the '*you are stupid*' look." Sarah with an exhausted appearance confided to Carrie, "Carrie, I have enjoyed our lunch, but I'm afraid I've put a gloomy cloud over our visit. I'm sorry…I needed to talk."

* * *

As Sarah drove the familiar roads home, she thought, *its dreadfully mundane to follow this path that leads to the place filled with heart ache that never ends.* "My life is leading to sadness."

Sarah entered the code for the gates to open, she thought, *all this once meant something, but now I see my mental health is the price I'm paying…It's not worth the cost.*

Sarah entered the quiet house and went into her kitchen with a feeling of self-control until she saw the island and a flashback of the night before flooded her thoughts. Glenn was frightfully upset when she asked his opinion on relocating her parents.

He gave her 'the look,' banged his fist on the counter and said, "You look at me when I'm talking to you. You want to do what? Where would you move them? Oooh no, not here or in a house near-by. That takes money and it will be hard to get your mother to agree. You do what you want…whatever you do, is fine with me, but don't count on me to get involved with anything concerning her. By the way…I won't be home until late this evening, client meeting."

Sarah quickly dropped her head and slipped into her humiliated posture as he slammed the door. Life was a heavy load…Sarah had lost sight of hope. She was cognizant of her daily life but couldn't see things turning around to anything more than what it was. She needed her husband to be someone she could talk with and could receive positive encouragement from, especially during this stressful situation with her parents.

Sarah ate another square of coffee cake along with two more cups of coffee. She felt sick to her stomach and hurried to the bathroom as she held her napkin tightly over her mouth. She threw up until her empty stomach was gagging tiny droplets of water that mixed with her tears. She was drenched with sweat and wiped her face with a damp cloth.

Sarah looked in the mirror and felt disgust with her reflection… quickly turned off the light…she felt her chest jerking as tears welled up. While standing in the dark…she cried with sorrowful rage.

She eventually wilted into her chair as a sharp pain of bitter hurt raced through her body and her tears were dried by an angry heat. With silenced authority she said, "That's ok, I'll have time to call Carrie, buy that expensive pocketbook at the mall, or bake a pound cake for the Simms family. Attend your, so called meeting, I have plenty to occupy my time." Only knowing she would spend her evening sitting in front of the television watching reruns of Law & Order on the USA Channel, while sipping a glass of wine. Sarah would be looking forward to seeing that handsome character Elliott Stabler find and obliterate the egotistical bad guy.

As she vaguely watched television, her mind drifted to situations that had given her grievous sleepless nights. Sarah became angry as her eyes began to droop and she couldn't stay awake to watch Elliott's final scene as the wine drifted her off into a restful sleep.

* * *

Out of sheer anger and deep frustration she thought, *I feel I might explode if I can't say something in confidence to a trusted confidant.* She called Carrie early the next morning, and in an unpredictable manner as soon as she answered, burst forth saying, "Carrie, I'm so alone."

"Sarah, after our last lunch, I've been worried and concerned. I know how alone you are. Now tell me, what can I do to let you know how much I care?"

"I'm not sure, now. I just needed to express my desperation. I need to change my life. I must tell you some things."

Sarah remembered, *years earlier Carrie without knowing had brought me out of a deep depression. She was always telling me how special I am and that she loved me. I was confused and unable to internalize Carrie's kind expressions. I learned to repeat her words in conversations and found it emotionally uplifting, to say complimentary things like my friend.*

"I learned a valuable lesson from you about sharing feelings, reaching out and trusting a friend. I saw our friendship growing into a trusting relationship. Thank you, Carrie," Sarah said knowing the sweet value of her friend. "Soon, I want to talk a while and tell you my plan."

* * *

Sarah's father's illness grew worse as his organs began shutting down. He eventually drifted into a catatonic state of contented sleep. Her father's death coupled with her mother's increased frailty and her untrustworthy husband brought Sarah to the lowest emotional level she had ever been. Her plans were put on hold as she stoically made it through her dad's funeral.

With little help from anyone, Sarah came to realize it was up to her. She knew she was alone and shattered…somewhat glued together like a cracked eggshell. She often wished she could disappear and rest, but she had to keep easing along.

* * *

Sarah's days were a blur and she looked forward to the door slamming as he left the house each morning. "Knowing I have some precious time alone, time to putter in the house while drinking my coffee in peace is comforting. I'm longing for solitude or is it time away from Glenn I need," Sarah mumbled as she stirred her coffee while looking out the kitchen window into the distant unknown. "If the rains would stop..." Her thoughts were cloudy gray like the break of day, and the pains zipped through her head like the razor-sharp lightning that split the dreary morning sky.

A self-improvement book Sarah was reading recommended living one day at a time. She saw it as a simplistic suggestion that wouldn't work in her complicated life. She thought, *I have others to deal with and my own situation is breaking me down. How can I not plan and worry about tomorrow?*

With a fresh look at her life Sarah took a deep breath and spoke aloud in a muted tone, "To keep peace with my husband, I've lived the life he demanded, and in order to satisfy the expectations of my parents, I've lived the life they required, and the life others have demanded of me. My dream is to be free of severe emotional distress and live the remainder of my life in peace and quiet. I'm getting older and my time is running out." Sarah boldly spoke with emotion and confidence in her voice.

Sarah seldom shouted, but on this dreary day her excitement got the best of her...she yelled into the open room, "I have the gumption to survive...to help relieve some of my stress, I will try taking one day at a time." With the thoughtful compassionate care of Dr. Freeman, Sarah began her struggle to normalcy.

With a positive attitude and a determination to change, Sarah breathed deeply, and said in a rich tone, "I've made the decision to do what's best for me and medically right for mom."

* * *

Sarah was excited to find an assisted living home less than thirty minutes away. The administrator said, "There's a bridge group, and afternoon tea and scones, along with other activities. I recommend setting up a guest visit to show you and your mom around the facility."

"That sounds wonderful. I think she would love being in a beautifully decorated apartment and having delicious chef prepared dinners with the ladies," Sarah said to the administrator.

During their visit Sarah used finesse and encouraging words to her mom concerning the center. "Mom this reminds me of the afternoons you spent at the club playing bridge or having lunch with the girls." Sarah was satisfied with what she saw and wanted to believe her mom was pleased.

"Yes, I think I remember those days," her mom said with a contented smile of approval.

With the guidance of an administrator, her mom was moved in and settled into their routine. The finances were handled by a draft, so from that point on she was cared for in the best possible place and Sarah never heard the word *money* mentioned by anyone.

After spending a pleasant day of adjustment for her mother, Sarah found respite in her car as she dropped her shoulders and breathed a sigh of relief. She spoke confidently aloud, "This day has been a good one, I hope all of her tomorrows and mine will go as well."

With assurance Sarah drove home to face an agitated husband. His first comment was, "What's for dinner, I have a meeting this evening at seven with Niki, my new secretary. You should meet her… she has a fantastic personality."

Sarah thought, *I bet she does,* but quickly erased those thoughts because she was determined to not let him get under her skin…by now she knew him well.

"I have to discuss my business trip schedule and conventions with her. I'm sure I'll need for her to travel with me on occasion," he said with an intimidating smile as he looked directly at Sarah.

Sarah thought, *this conversation is so typical of you…I feel empathy for Niki…I hope she's not naïve when it comes to dealing with you.*

As he was leaving the table, he took one more jab at Sarah. "I just noticed how your hair is graying, and your face is wrinkled, you're getting old. My my, have you looked at yourself lately…your hip bones are poking out like a sick cow."

Sarah cringed, and thought as she went about stacking the dishwasher with the dinner dishes, *he wants to upset me, so he'll feel justified with being with his secretary tonight…I can't let him get to me, I have to remain strong.* It was a relief to Sarah to hear the back door close and watch the two red blurs of his mustang ease out of the driveway and disappear into the darkness.

As Sarah sat in the quiet den, the phone rang. It was her accountant calling to say several special deliveries had arrived at his office and would like to see her the next day at two o'clock to share the holdings information.

Sarah excitedly said, "Yes, I will be there." She practically ran to the shower to wash her hair and select an outfit for tomorrow's meeting. All evening she found herself smiling and dancing as she thought more about her future than of her current situation.

* * *

Sarah's accountant found a letter addressed to her that her dad had discretely folded into his will. It expressed how he knew the pain she was under but praised her for trying to make the best of things. He wrote, Y*ou're the beneficiary of my estate, so treat it as security for you and your mom. I'm giving this to YOU with my blessings.*

Sarah cried as her heart filled with joy, knowing her dad knew and understood her marriage circumstances.

After the meeting on impulse Sarah left a message for Dr. Freeman. "I didn't know until now that my dad perceptively knew what was going on in my marriage, and this was his plan for my financial security and my way out."

"You can see your future, can't you Sarah," he called to say.

Her response was, "Yes, yes I can, and thank you."

Chapter 3

For years Carrie had mentioned the phrase "making memories." Sarah had no profound knowledge of the meaning of Carrie's statement. She thought about her life, "I didn't want to remember things." Sarah's eyes had forgotten how to enjoy watching a dramatic fall sunset or smelling the freshness of the air after a summer rain like Carrie often mentioned. Sarah was making no memories in her life, but with Dr. Freeman's encouragement and Carrie for a model, Sarah clearly saw it was time to look forward.

Carrie heard a painful rumor and because of its suspicious nature and Sarah's frail appearance, decided to give Sarah a call. She gently encouraged her, but never let on she knew anything. Carrie suggested they meet the next day at the Inn on Telfair.

It was a beautiful sunny winter day, and Sarah was excited about meeting her friend for lunch. The Victorian mansion made a dramatic statement in its maintained classic appearance. The grand entrance was lovely, and the dining rooms were filled with warmth and hominess. They were seated in the main parlor near a fireplace with its elegantly carved mirrored mantel. Potted palms gave their table for two a feeling of privacy.

Sarah needed her friend, and it didn't take long before her feelings for Glenn purged, and what she said reinforced what Carrie had always thought of him. Carrie's heart quivered as she listened to her friend's stories of his abuse while she choked from tears fired by anger.

"Recently we helped our friend with her wedding, do you remember how Glenn degraded me in front of the caterers."

"I remember the one in charge looking at you then Glenn as if wanting to say, 'this girl has worked tirelessly, and you think you have the right to come in here and yell at her.'"

"I wasn't sure what he was thinking," Sarah said in a low voice.

"He felt for you but couldn't say anything. You left quickly for the restroom so Glenn would stop yelling. I remember your posture was rigid, as you turned…your expressionless appearance frightened me and in a weak voice you said, 'I think I'm going to have a break down.' Then tears began to well up in your eyes, akin to a wounded animal and I knew you were in trouble."

Carrie took her hand as each saw the other through tear-stained eyes and said, "I knew something like that would happen, that's why I told myself I would be with you that day. I knew you would need help."

Sarah said in a trembling voice, "That night when I got home, I told him it was over…I had had enough and was leaving. He told me, 'you're not leaving me, I will see to that,'" Sarah spoke with a frightened voice.

Carrie, knowing the binding abusive trap Sarah was caught in, encouraged her to remain in close contact with Dr. Freeman.

Sarah made several phone calls to Dr. Freeman who kept her thinking positively. He continually encouraged her to a point where she could maintain a confident outlook. She had the faith, will and determination to believe in her future and thrived on the thoughts of a new life...her life.

* * *

At 2 a.m. Sarah was awakened by her cell phone ringing, Glenn's supervisor Mike called to say Glenn had been in a serious accident in Dallas, and his secretary would make reservations for Sarah to fly to Texas. At this point he had no information about Glenn's condition.

Sarah quickly said, "I can be at the airport in three hours, so try to book a flight around six o'clock, if possible."

"I'll let you know something soon," Mike kindly said.

Sarah quickly threw a few pairs of jeans and several sweaters into her suitcase. She ran to the clothes dryer and grabbed a gown and underwear. She went into her closet to find her tennis shoes, but in her haste took a pair of bedroom shoes and forgot to go back for the extra pair of walking shoes. She filled her carry-on bag with make-up... remembered her meds, a curling iron, and stuffed in a windbreaker.

Her phone rang, it startled her, but she calmed as she saw it was Mike. "I'm sorry to have to tell you this, but..."

Sarah braced for the worst, *Glenn must have died*, she thought.

"Are you there, I thought you should know this before you reached Dallas. Glenn was severely injured in a car driven by a long-time female friend of his. She died at the scene. I'm saying this because I don't want you to get to Dallas and hear all of this."

"All of this, yes I'm sorry, but I'm not surprised," she said as her voice tapered to a whisper. "Not surprised at all."

As Sarah said good-bye, the pain and anger rose inside and she spoke aloud with rage, "Why am I feeling so obligated to care for this arrogant, misbegotten, selfish mongrel of a man who never had respect for our marriage or for me as his wife. Why should I feel the obligation to play the part of the good wife any longer?" she said with questioning.

After some thought she said, "But I must go…it's my duty…what will people think."

On the way out the back door, Sarah grabbed her computer and the cell phone charger. Without stopping to attend to much more and in an unexplained frantic rage mixed with anger and emotions, she threw her things into the back of her Suburban.

"The years of his betrayal and the hatred of his treatment of me, generated by his current actions are sickening." As she got into her SUV, anger heated her body and she yelled, "Why…I'm growing old, I'm physically tired and emotionally sick…why has this happened? Haven't I suffered enough?"

As she ran back to lock the garage door…a strong gust of wind blew a heavy mist of rain into her face and she felt the cold water running down between her breasts. Her face was drenched, but there was no time to go back to dry off. "I'm honestly afraid if I go back inside, the horrid stress of all this might make me choose to not leave," Sarah said as she grabbed the garage door frame to support her trembling knees.

In the gray pouring early morning rain Sarah with her arthritis acting up, left for the airport. The sky was full of dark rumbling clouds and often a flash of lightening frightened her into reality. She quivered from a sudden chill. "Is it the frigid rainwater that wet my shirt that has me feeling cold and listless or Glenn? I feel sickened by the circumstances and controlled by a world that's smothering me physically and emotionally," Sarah mumbled in this time of bewilderment.

Mike sent an e-mail, "Hello Sarah, you'll need to check in at Delta. Your ticket is for flight 109, Gate 4 at 6:15 to Dallas. Sarah, call often to let me know Glenn's condition, but please let me know how you're doing. I don't like you having to face this alone. I have a call into the Dallas company branch for someone to check on you each day. Take care and know I'm sorry."

It was a struggle to park her car, unload her luggage, and get her boarding pass. She wanted to cry out for help. She looked for someone to make desperate eye contact with, but everyone was hurrying here and there and had no time for her.

Sarah finally boarded the plane and made it to 15B and wasted no time in going limp as she fell into her seat between a grumpy looking businessman and a mother with a young baby. The exhaustion had enveloped her.

Her only contentment was in knowing the lady would be busy with her baby, and the man to her left with the furrowed brow would be occupied with his New York Times. That feeling brought a measure of relief.

During the flight, her reflections often jumped from past pains to this present disaster. Sarah couldn't help but imagine what she would likely have to face in Dallas.

Her body shuttered in anger and lost in thought while considering her circumstances. Sarah's thought, *I'm not surprised by what has happened. I remember hundreds of times closing my eyes to situations and turning and walking away. I thought it was letting him know I was ashamed of his behavior, but instead he acted as though I was hiding from the truth, and it gave him permission to continue with his shenanigans.*

I vividly remember attending a party...Glenn was making advances to a woman while they danced...then followed her. I pointed out to our friend what was happening as my husband was about to enter the bathroom the woman had just entered. I was surprised watching this taking place in front of me, but our friend confronted him, and Glenn decided not to go inside. Disgusting scenes like that were the norm.

Even with this trip I was suspicious of his activities. He bought new underwear and lounging pajamas. A trending magazine had listed husbands buying underwear as a top tip off they're having an affair. Several times during the week I called his room and got no answer, even at three in the morning…that was another tip off.

The most shocking lately was when he returned from Denver. Sarah saw him step out of the shower wearing his wet T-shirt. A leading magazine had stated what that meant.

That night I waited for him to go to sleep, turned on a tiny flashlight, lifted his pajama top…gasped in amazement at the fresh parallel claw marks on each side of his back, and imagined the particulars leading up to this kind of scrape. My rage and anger became violent, and for a split second I thought of things beyond a rational thought pattern. I wanted to scream. The tears burned hot against my face as I squeezed my eyes shut. With thoughts of raging anger Sarah twisted in her seat, as she felt the strained muscles of her grimacing face.

I hurried from the room because his peaceful snoring was an annoyance. I loaded my camera with low light film and slipped into the bedroom, lifted his top and took several pictures. One included a portion of his face, so there would be no denying it was him. I made my way to the office and for several hours thought…

A jarring noise disturbed Sarah as the baby beside her began to cry, she quivered and realized, *I'm on the way to Dallas*. She took a deep breath, felt her chest hurting as she realized her fingernails were curled into the seat cushion. She dropped her head as uncontrollable tears began to flow…she blew her nose, wiped her eyes with the pretense of having a cold. She regained her composure, looked to the left, and he was looking into her eyes. A faint smile came over her face because *he might have been watching me for a while, and knew my heart was hurting,* she thought.

By the time Sarah found her bags at Baggage Claim and exited the airport, she was physically exhausted. She zipped her raincoat and waited on the platform for a cab. The stranger who sat beside her whistled and kindly motioned for her to take his cab.

Sarah smiled her first to what became her last heartwarming smile of the day. Thank goodness her cabbie was friendly, and his pleasant voice soothed her as she prepared to face what awaited her at the hospital.

Sarah entered Glenn's unit in a run-down state of mind. She glanced at her husband while trying to understand her ambivalent feelings. *Here I am in Texas to straighten out my husband's nasty deeds,* she thought as her empathy began to fade. Her anger rose as she stopped at the foot of his bed…*I must overcome my feelings and approach him with a wifely attitude. The doctors and nurses are looking,* she thought.

What Sarah didn't know was they knew the circumstances that caused this. The dead mistress was a social butterfly, so the newspapers were filled with details and Glenn's story had been in all the news reports. The doctors and nurses knew more about Sarah's husband than Sarah, which caused them to be empathetic to her needs. She was a victim who also needed their support…the one who was silently suffering.

That night as Sarah reached her room and turned on the television, she was lambasted by the facts of the accident. The reporter opened with, "A former Dallas mayor's wife was the driver of her car last evening that ran a red light and was broadsided. She died at the scene. Her body will be sent to the crime lab for testing. A male passenger who had a long relationship with the deceased was taken to Memorial Hospital where he is listed in critical condition. They were returning from an evening out after attending the Texas Cattleman's Convention."

* * *

Glenn was in intensive care for four weeks of endless days of surgeries to repair internal injuries and set broken bones. During the second week the swelling in his brain was down and time would determine the degree of its recovery. Later, he was awakened from a medically induced coma into semi-consciousness. Eventually he was moved into a private room. Several weeks later, he was well enough to travel with assistance, and transferred to a hospital closer to home.

Often Glenn's colleagues dropped by after work. Sarah was uneasy having to listen to his buddies paint a pretty cover-up picture of Glenn and all his shenanigans. Glenn would moan at their stories, but it was unclear if he understood what his friends were laughing about.

One night with a feeling of withheld frustration Sarah looked at Glenn as he lay sleeping, and freely whispered, "The most blatant of your co-workers comes by often, eventually I'll quietly tell him, I know how it really was, and he doesn't have to cover for you anymore." Eventually his colleagues stopped coming around as their conversations had changed from seeing Glenn as their mighty hero, into seeing the results of his life.

Sarah always looked forward to Mike's visits. He seemed to care for Sarah and always brought her good news, with words of encouragement. Over coffee and a muffin or lunch in the hospital cafeteria, their friendship grew as their conversations became more at ease.

Recently during lunch, out of the blue and with a somber look on his face Mike said to Sarah, "I remember the first day Glenn came in and told us about you. It was a Monday morning after his sales meetings in Charleston. The first thing he said was 'I've met the girl of my dreams.'" Mike remembered the concern he had for the girl, because Glenn came in every Monday morning talking about his rendezvouses with women.

A flashback flooded Mike's thoughts *as he remembered how Glenn referred to Sarah as being bought and paid for. I own her, he often said. Even after their marriage, Glenn hinted and bragged about his casual encounters.* "I was often sarcastic with Glenn because of his pride, and I saw you as a kindhearted lady who was treated carelessly."

Her head dropped as she rubbed her forehead…closed her eyes as her shoulders drooped and Sarah took a deep breath. "Carelessly," she mumbled.

"I'm sorry, Sarah, I said too much…I didn't mean to upset you."

"You didn't, it's just so much has happened, and I've kept it to myself because I thought after what my mom had led me to believe and the trending magazines stated in the late fifties and sixties…all marriages were male dominant, and I was to be the submissive wife. When the mental abuse began to escalate, I became trapped, because I continued to try and be the perfect wife like my mom and the magazines described. Because of the embarrassment of failure, I put up a front that the marriage was fine, but you knew, and I always thought you knew something."

"Yes, I knew, and I silently supported you."

"My phone is beeping…let me check this. The doctor will be in the room soon, I must go," Sarah said as she stood.

Mike stood as he laid his napkin on the table. "Sarah, I admire you for supporting Glenn under the conditions I know you've been under." He stepped forward and put his hand softly on Sarah's arm, and kindly said, "If I can ever help you through emotional, financial or just someone to vent to…then please call me."

"I will…this gave me a chance to talk honestly and openly. We'll do this again. Thank you," Sarah said as their honesty brought a glassy look of sadness to her eyes.

He eased her near as he patted her on the shoulder. The warmth of his hand never faded as she learned to recall the feeling during the lonely weeks ahead.

* * *

"After Glenn was transferred to the rehabilitation center, I returned home to stay. When I entered the house, I was aware of its peacefulness, and stood to let myself enjoy the fragrance of home," Sarah quietly spoke to Carrie.

"The sound of water flowing in the shower and the feel of its warmth was wonderful because I was ready to wash the hospital smell from my body. I sat in silence and enjoyed a bowl of Cheerios for dinner and a glass of chardonnay before bed," Sarah humbly said.

"The fragrance of my bed linens was like a fresh spring breeze, and I stretched and adjusted my body into a comfortable position and drifted into a restful sleep. My room was bright with sunlight when the phone rang and awakened me to a wrong number. I lay quietly enjoying the feeling of my bed's warmth, the soothing tranquility of silence and the healing effect of sleeping late," Sarah joyfully spoke as Carrie willingly encouraged her to talk.

* * *

When Glenn reached his plateau, he was discharged, and the homecoming was somewhat bittersweet. Glenn was conscious but had no recollection of the accident and often Sarah wasn't sure he knew where he was or who she was.

Her thoughts of the accident and now his condition completely diminished her view of the marriage. Their love for each other had become tarnished over the years, so now Sarah took care of him because of their marriage contract.

He remained in a separate room from Sarah's in a hospital bed or a wheelchair, with countless medications regulating his body. His pads were changed, several daily baths were given, and his stomach tolerated soft foods. The home health nurse came daily, and the physical therapist came twice a week to exercise his legs. Both legs had been broken in the accident along with his right arm and hip. Because of the head trauma, Glenn's reasoning and thoughts were not clearing and might not ever clear.

As Sarah listened to the heart monitor, she tacked a few cards on the board at the end of his bed, as her thoughts drifted, *I'm looking at this sleeping shell of a man remembering the sham of the life we have lived. Now I'm seeing this crumbled man in a different light…I feel the release of the hold he had on me…as the weight of his control is lifted away.*

* * *

Sarah called Carrie and confided to her, "It's been well over a year and I don't see much improvement. I don't think he will ever be able to treat me in the way he once did. I've noticed his eyes narrow…his lips tighten and mumble as he looks at me, but he can't form his words. I'm sorry to say, but it might make caring for him easier if he can't speak or reach for me in anger like he treated me in the past…but sometimes he looks directly into my eyes as though trying to say something. I want to think he's wanting to say, 'I'm sorry.'" Sarah's words were spoken with a feeling of tired honesty.

"I'm sure you're in a stressful situation, but there must be a measure of contentment that has your mind at peace…at peace with the knowledge that you are free from his hold."

"Yes, I do feel that peacefulness…my life has come a long way…I don't have to pretend anymore, I can be myself without fear from him."

Carrie honestly supported Sarah and understood the false front she had been required to put forth during her marriage. Carrie's loyal touch with reality saw the change in Sarah as they both realized Glenn's condition and how it was his personality that brought this on himself.

Sarah appeared as having complete concern for her husband but only Carrie, her husband Ben and Mike knew the truth. They talked about the hurt and pain caused by Glenn's years of emotional abuse. Through reassuring conversations with each of them, Sarah breathed a breath of new life.

* * *

Glenn never gained use of his body and his brain remained in a fog. He spent most of his time in bed as his health was in declined. It wasn't long before a respiratory infection made him extremely ill. Glenn was treated with antibiotics, that didn't seem to be working. Before the medication could be changed, he became painfully weak, and was rushed to the hospital but died before the EMT's had barely left the house.

On the day of the funeral, Sarah awoke in a muddled daze of exhaustion and the feeling of the change in her life that she so desperately wanted had happened because of his destructive nature. Sarah whispered her conclusion, "I'm sorry it had to happen this way.

As Sarah was viewing the casket, she found herself talking to Glenn, saying things she wanted to say during their marriage but was stifled by his over-powering fearful threats. "During the years after the accident, I revisited our marriage struggles, and thought of the difficulties trying to make it work with your arrogant narcissistic behavior. It had taken me years to discover your character had a known list of behavioral symptoms with expected results. Maybe a doctor could have helped…if we had known, or if you would have gone. I wish our life could have been better because I always felt bogged down by the struggle. I'm sorry to have to say this, but now I feel the load has been lifted and I have hope."

Sarah's words are mixed with tears and a smile, and as she rejoins Carrie and Ben, she knows this change in her life will be dealt with positively. She sees her ailing mom as a priority, but she realizes her spirits need to be lifted.

During the long ride to the family cemetery Sarah had time to reflect. *This community knew Glenn as financially generous and eager to help. They didn't know him when he was on his own at conventions, or at home behind closed doors. I hope I can forget his harsh abusiveness and the times he grabbed me in violent anger.*

Sarah felt ambivalent as she stood in the misty rain and intently stared at the burial site. *I know over time I'll get past this horrific period in my life. I hope I will also be able to escape the flashbacks and scars you left me with.* As Sarah placed a rose on the mound of dirt, she mustered one sentence, "Now I will go forward with my life."

* * *

Sarah's thoughtful next-door neighbor along with aid from Carrie arranged to have Glenn's room cleared and thoroughly cleaned during the funeral service. This was a welcomed surprise, because Sarah was already dreading walking into the quite house and seeing the stacks of diapers and medical supplies. She smiled with appreciation as the fragrant fresh air surrounded her instead of a clinical antiseptic smell which she had thoughts of facing with regret.

She and Carrie hurried to his room and found instead of the hospital bed a beautifully made bed with fresh flowers on the nightstand. Sarah became emotional as she said, "The dreaded reminders have been replaced by lovely things, and what a relief to know the years of lying are over." Carrie held her hand in comfort, and Sarah composed herself as family and friends arrived.

* * *

The next week, Sarah faced a brisk wind to keep an appointment with Glenn's lawyer to probate the will. As she parked, she thought, *life is often like the weather*. "Sometimes we have to face a strong wind, but we must hold on to the tiny memory of the warm spring days, so we can survive," Sarah mumbled as she switched off the car.

It took Sarah weeks to clear-up the paperwork. "I cried during my trips to the lawyer's office. I grieve for the years of mental abuse, and the stress of those years is over-powering. I will get through this, and I know there's a bright future. I will be alright...I won't have to walk on eggshells. I can breathe and do things without fear of his anger. I'm feeling like a worthy person once again," Sarah remorsefully shared with Dr. Freeman.

* * *

The most devastating situation came late one night when Sarah received a phone call from a woman, claiming to be Glenn's common law wife with whom they had a daughter. She asked if their daughter was mentioned in Glenn's will, if not she would contest it and demand her share. She went on to tell Sarah how she knew Glenn was the father. Her story was devastating because some of her facts were familiar to Sarah. After the call while feeling frustrated, Sarah had flashbacks of the mental anguish Glenn had left in his wake.

Sarah felt the need for an appointment with Dr. Freeman. After listening to Sarah's dilemma, he advised her, "Realize the façade you built was to protect your husband from family and friends, and now you have no need to protect anyone except yourself. If anything should arise concerning the child, it will be considered as gossip, and if it is the truth, then it will be handled by a lawyer. That part of your life is in your past."

He stressed for her to take care of herself. "The more you grow as a confident lady, then the more you have to offer the people around you, and the more friends you will attract. The more you attract with your charm and knowledge, the broader your friendship base will grow, and in turn you will grow familiar to each of them. You must figure out your likes and develop a passion for each. Soon you will notice a positive change in yourself. You will become more self-assured. You have suffered, but you can go on now with your life not his," Dr. Freeman said.

Sarah miraculously held herself together and the estate was settled. She had the most trouble handling the personal affairs associated with Glenn's life. With the help of a lawyer and a private investigator, they discovered the girl was not related by blood. It was a scheme put together by the girl's mother.

When the girl was a toddler, Glenn had spent time at their house. She came to think of Glenn as her father, and her mother encouraged the dream. Sarah was relieved to hear she was not legally responsible for the child but felt empathy for her due to the lifestyle Glenn had created around her. She breathed a needed sigh of relief when that was resolved.

Chapter 4

Embracing a New Life in a New Location

Within the year, Sarah's mother died, and Sarah found herself alone in the city. This gave her a chance to make a major decision in her life. After much thought, Sarah decided to move from her home filled with reminders of her past to the peacefulness of the farm…located near Carrie, and Sarah knew how important her friend had become in her life.

Sarah got to know Carrie's cousin Lucy, and they enjoyed spending time together. Lucy was more outgoing and was always discovering a new wine, searching out a new restaurant or traveling to interesting places.

While the three of them were sampling a glass of Italian Pinot Grigio, Lucy spoke of a trip to Newport, RI she and two of her friends were planning. "Sarah why don't you come along with us?"

Sarah was shocked that someone had invited her to go on a girl's vacation. Her lack of confidence caused by years of isolation made her feel she would never be chosen or chosen last in the games of life.

"I'll think about it. I've always dreamed of going to the historic town of Newport," as shyness controlled her appearance.

"Don't think about it…say yes. We'll have a wonderful time," Lucy said with certainty.

Carrie said, "Sarah, I know you'll have fun…I'll be glad when I retire."

The invitation came with a propelling force into a reality of which Sarah had no clue on how to handle, but an opportunity she wanted to take. "I'm excited to be included in your group," Sarah said with an inward determination to survive her lack of confidence.

Several places were mentioned as possible sights to see. A harbor cruise of the Narragansett Bay was a priority. Touring the historic mansions on Shoreline Drive and to walk the cliffs trail behind the houses along the waterfront were an essential part of the trip. Also, there would be eating out and shopping.

With thoughts of traveling to places she had dreamed of seeing, Sarah grew excited about being with Lucy and her friends. Lucy was good at looking after other people, and Sarah was thankful for her help and not resentful. She had given Sarah a general idea of the clothing and things needed, and Sarah seized this chance to get rid of her dismal rags by taking them to the second time around shop.

In preparation for shopping, she purposefully sat in the mall watching to see what ladies her age wore. It was refreshing to be able to freely pick colors and pay for beautiful things, with her money. She was a hesitant shopper who questioned her selections, and sometimes thought, *the cashier must be laughing at my purchases*. Shopping eventually changed from being intimidating into an adventure.

* * *

Early on, the girl's sense of adventure was intimidating to Sarah who had never been away from home like this. She eventually identified with a friend and began to imitate her responses and gestures. Soon Sarah began to laugh and feel comfortable. It was a tiny thing to many, but it was an achievement for Sarah.

For dinner on the second night, Sarah lifted her head with confidence and smiled as she ordered the meal she wanted, "I would like a Spring Mix Salad with Champaign dressing, Lobster Cream Pasta with the Black Truffle sauce…and another glass of Chardonnay."

With a feeling of humble achievement, she looked to her left and found Lucy's smiling face staring at her with an approving expression. Lucy mouthed the words, "Excellent choice."

With a slight smile, Sarah scanned the table and thought, *there is no one to tell me one glass of wine is enough or stop laughing or think about what it's costing.* She exhaled and grinned with relief as she turned to the pleasant friend sitting next to her. Sarah beamed inside as she understood *each moment as a new hurdle to cross with grace.* "I appreciate each of you for making this new adventure rewarding," Sarah said with dancing thoughts of her changing life.

Life was exciting and here she was making memories. The ladies were encouraging to each other, and Newport was a refreshing change from the way she had been living. The town was alive with a historic past and was bubbling with new experiences directed to the future… much like Sarah. The sun was bright, the world was fresh and new, and Sarah was looking at it through new eyes. Like a rose sprinkled by the mist of the New England harbor town, Sarah began to blossom into an amazing dynamic woman.

The waterfront was alive with activity and as they boarded a schooner for a harbor tour a young shipmate extended his hand to assist Sarah. "Welcome aboard, my lady." He was an employee of the nautical touring company, but to Sarah his extended hand warmed her and brought a quick smile as she looked into his dark Italian eyes. Often during the tour, he playfully winked at her as he offered bits of trivia about the bay. The tour was educational but as Sarah listened, she became entranced by his charm and often missed parts of his presentation about the wealthy industrialist who built homes there.

As she departed the gangplank, her eyes were in search of her young admirer. She thought she had missed him, but on the crowded wharf below she spotted his coal-black hair and then his sweet face. As she approached, he took her hand smiled and said, "Have a good evening, my lady."

That night at dinner the ladies made plans to tour several mansions the next day. Sarah was excited about seeing the industrialist homes.

Lucy said, "The sun has kissed Sarah's cheeks…she looks radiant."

Inwardly, Sarah was ecstatic about the special male attention on the harbor tour, and now the compliments from the ladies about her complexion. "Thank you, it has been an inspiring day," Sarah said as she felt special.

Lucy recognized the change. Sarah's face began to have a look of excitement instead of her usual look of fear and uncertainty.

The next morning as she walked through the historic homes, Sarah was happy to offer her friends additional information about the furnishings. "I remember studying descriptions of table and chair legs and had used them in my short decorating career, particularly in Charleston." A flashback of her career cut short by her controlling husband caused her to quiver. Sarah quickly replaced that hurt with a smile while enjoying life.

* * *

The following weekend after the group returned from Rhode Island, Carrie called and invited Sarah to a birthday gathering for her sister, Kim. They were to meet at a nearby restaurant for dinner in a low-keyed atmosphere with only close family and friends.

Sarah thought, *I enjoy the peaceful contentment of living on the farm, especially since a sweet stray dog showed up at my house. His sweetness has given me a new friend. At this point in my life peacefulness and contentment are all I want. I appreciate living near my dear friend, new friend Lucy and now Bob.* "I'm looking forward to the party. I enjoy you and your family, and Lucy and her husband Charlie," Sarah happily said to Carrie.

Carrie called later to suggest for Sarah to meet at their house and ride to the party with her family. This gave Sarah a chance to confide in Carrie. "Lucy is insisting I meet her cousin Jim. I don't mind meeting someone, but that's all I care to do. Please watch and give me an escape if you see it's not going well."

Lucy had grown up with Jim and they had a close relationship. His wife had died years earlier after a long fight with ovarian cancer. "Lucy thought it would be nice for me to visit with a true survivor, but I'm really not looking for anyone to talk with nor am I interested in a true survivor. I'm working at my own pace, but respectfully I will go along with Lucy's wishes," Sarah said to Carrie with some trepidation as she finger-combed her hair.

* * *

Jim was light-hearted and fun. He always had a smile on his face and the crowd was delighted by his treasured family stories. Sarah smiled warmly and enjoyed herself, but often closed her eyes as past terrors streamed through her mind. After dinner she walked outside with Carrie while the others were having coffee and dessert.

At times Sarah felt sad or happy with friends, but alone. She was searching for her place. "I really needed to get outside. I should be happy with everyone full of conversation, but I have this growing feeling inside that keeps telling me I shouldn't be happy."

Carrie took her hand, "Sarah, so many things have happened to you through the years. Each thing took away a piece of your happiness. It's natural for you to wonder about feelings and question every move you make. You're going through a process and eventually you will begin feeling wonderful… with no questioning of yourself. I know what's inside of you, and I know you will eventually be alright."

"Carrie, I couldn't have made it this far if it had not been for you. You keep me pointed in the right direction. You know me and I feel you knew what was happening early on…long before I thought anyone had a clue. I thank you for watching over me…I love you."

"You're rebuilding yourself and one day soon you will say, I feel different, I'm rebuilt," Carrie said with confidence.

"You have always been an encourager and have always found the best in me." Carrie and Sarah hugged knowing their bond of friendship was stronger.

It wasn't long before the others came outside, and Jim was delighted when he saw Sarah and Carrie talking. A smile formed as he admired Sarah standing in the glowing light of the moon.

Some well-wishers left for the evening, but this intimate group of friends gathered in a small cluster of Adirondack chairs and talked. The moon was full, and the evening was crisp, but refreshing. They touched on a variety of subjects, starting with the weather and politics.

Eventually Kim spoke, "I would like to thank my circle of friends for their kindness through the years. Thank you for coming to my birthday dinner." Your friendship, and encouragement means more to me than you know.

After a while and in a somewhat shy tone, Sarah in turn thanked everyone for the support they have given her. "I couldn't have made it this far without your reassurance." As she made a circling motion with her hand and scanned each face she said, "I hope we will always be there for each other."

Jim watched her as she talked and became entranced by her beautiful smile as he thought, *what a charming, graceful lady? With her soft-spoken gentle nature, I'm sure she would be a pleasure to spend time with…talking or listening to music or walking hand in hand. She's special and loved by so many friends.*

The girls, Lucy, Kim, Carrie, and Sarah hugged and shed a tear or two as they walked arm in arm to the parking lot along with cousins and friends where they hugged and said their good-byes.

As the friends said farewell, Sarah turned and unexpectedly found herself facing Jim. In awe they stared at each other and said nothing as the noise of the group muffled, and their thoughts became tunneled.

Nervously, words softly stammered from Sarah's lips, "Jim, it was nice meeting you. You talked with everyone, and your words were humble and sincere, as your cousin Lucy had described you."

Jim took her hand and said, "Thank you," as he nervously massaged her fingers and said, "Your hands are cold my dear. Maybe Carrie has a blanket in the car." Jim unconsciously touched Sarah's shoulder, and out of sheer adoration for her strength and positive attitude gently embraced her. He instantly had an urge to protect Sarah in a comforting way.

Sarah looked down as she said, "My hands are always cold." As Sarah's face lifted in the light of the moon, he looked into her beautiful dark brown eyes and felt an astounding attraction. "I'll be alright, but thank you…have a good night, Jim."

He observed her shyness and encased her hands with his. "I enjoyed the evening with you all and good night to you, Sarah," he said as his smiled broadened and his eyes twinkled.

Jim's feet became unplanted from the earth as Lucy tugged him toward the car. He whispered, "I thought you wanted me to show Sarah my strength, instead she has shown me the willingness of her heart grounded on her caring friendships. I think she is full of more sincere love and concern for others than anyone I've ever met. She has shown me real courage. Even I shed a tear. I really feel blessed by being here tonight."

On the way to Lucy's house, Jim expressed his feelings about the evening. "My evenings are often spent in large places with lots of noise and elevator music. I travel to places where no one speaks of kindness and appreciation. I think I'm missing the closeness of friends and family. I could see and feel it tonight. I need to change my life… rearrange my priorities."

"Carrie has told me a lot about Sarah and according to her, Sarah has been through some painful times because her husband treated her like crap through most of their marriage," said Lucy.

"Carrie said Sarah was strong and has always worked things out during all of her turmoil or possibly did a good job pretending everything was alright. She seemed to think clearly, even though she was suffering," Lucy said assuredly.

"What did he do to treat her wrong?"

"The usual things men do when they act like dogs, but in this case with anger. Her marriage was truly an emotional ride because of his arrogant narcissistic ways," Lucy said with bitterness.

"That's sad to hear," Jim said as he reflected on his own life and thought about Sarah's sweet spirit.

"She's a fine lady who needs to be treated with respect and dignity," Charlie said.

"You're right dear… she does deserve to be respected. Also, her parents died soon before and after her husband. Their lives and illnesses also brought on additional stress."

When they arrived at Charlie and Lucy's house, Jim thanked Lucy for inviting him to go with them. "This has truly enlightened me." Jim kissed her cheek and shook Charlie's hand. "I'll see you guys again soon, and if you go out with that same group of folks, then please let me know, I would like to be included."

"We will. Good night dear."

Charlie quietly whispered to himself, "I bet you would like to go, but Sarah's too sweet for you. Hope you don't start hitting on her."

During the night, Jim thought about his life and spoke aloud candidly about his thoughtless behavior. "I've spent years and money foolishly looking for something. I've thrown my money around and had numbers of relationships I've carelessly used and discarded. I must turn my life around and become a part of a caring relationship with a gentle companion."

The reality of his life hit as he questioned himself aloud, "Do I have the ability to show honest understanding to someone as sweet as Sarah or am I stuck with a life of searching." He wondered, *do I have the innate ability to change and will I be able to break away from the fast-paced lifestyle I've depended on for so long.* "What about my age and physical health, I must be several years older than Sarah…I know in my mind I can be a contributing partner…but what if she isn't interested in an older man like me. I don't think my money will persuade her because she's not impressed by a life the way mine is now," he said.

"I once lived a respectable life and had a family that meant the world to me, but my wife's sickness was a turning point as I listened to the wrong people and found excitement in bright lights, with all it had to offer. I identified with that outgoing lifestyle as my friends and family slipped away while thinking of me as a pleasure-seeker instead of the humanitarian I once was."

Jim's night was restless as he thought of Sarah and her struggles in life. He thought of his own life, *I desperately want someone special to love. I want to be loved and trusted, and I desperately want the love of my family.* He and his three children had been somewhat estranged for the last ten years. *I must change and hopefully that change will eventually include Sarah.* Finally, with contented thoughts he fell asleep.

Jim awoke thinking about his life. For me to have the life I treasure I must change because I won't find that treasure in the way I'm living now," he said with sincerity.

He thought more about Sarah and his need for a kind companion and her need for a trusting partner, neither of which he was sure he could provide or was worthy enough to accept. "The only thing I'm sure of after being with Sarah and her friends…my life is headed in the wrong direction. I know Sarah and her kindness, is my answer. Lucy can help me. Let me call her," he said with feelings.

"Lucy, I have something to ask you. I can't stop thinking about Sarah. I thought my life was somewhat complete until she walked into it."

"I had a feeling your call would be about Sarah."

"I would like to see her again. Not to intrude, but I would like to get to know her. She is just so beautiful, kindhearted, yet unpretentious. I would like to be in her presence."

"Remember she's fragile, but I'll think of something…if you betray her in any way, I'll be upset with you."

"I know you girls are protective of her, but I honestly feel I need her in my life. I won't push myself on her…I need to listen to her…I need her strength. I sure want to turn over a new leaf and I see Sarah as my helper. At first, I thought she needed me, but after the restless night I had…I realized how lost I am…I need her."

"Well Jim, I've wished for a long time you would turn back to the good-hearted cousin you once were. I feel you're sincere, so I'll help you."

As their conversation ended, Lucy realized she had to do something, but what. "Jim has a terrible reputation for short uncommitted relationships, and I don't want to set Sarah up for another one of his disasters, but he seems sincere. He really does need to settle down, because deep down he is a real renaissance man," Lucy mumbled as she closed the book she was reading. She had to think of something fast, because they were leaving in four days for a cruise on the Mississippi River.

"Maybe a casual dinner party will work. Yes, a Riverboat Feast to celebrate our pending trip," Lucy whispered aloud. From there, her mind started to plan the event. She thought of the guest list. "Carrie and Ben for sure, of course Sarah and Jim, Becki and Keith, who operate the marina, and a few others. We'll have a Southern bar-b-que, a couple of salads, string beans and raspberry tea and a pitcher of Southern Mint Juleps. That will be perfect."

"Jim, I think I have it worked out. Are you free for dinner at our place at Barefoot Cay on Tuesday night?

"Yes ma'am, I can be there any time you say and bring anything you need."

"Don't you still go out on Tuesdays?"

"I usually do, but like I said, I must turn over a new leaf, and I've already started."

"We're leaving at the end of the week, so I thought we could have a theme party centered on our riverboat trip, but all for your benefit."

"I'm hoping it will."

"Now, let me call everyone. I'll be in touch."

"Thanks a million, *cus*...Love you."

Charlie was holding the newspaper in front of his face and listening to their conversation. "Are you sure, you're doing the right thing for Sarah...pairing her up with Jim. You know his track record with relationships and his extra-curricular activities," Charlie said.

"He seems sincere in wanting to change and he sees Sarah as a positive influence in his life. I agree with him and feel he will be better...this time. You never have liked Jim and now that he's showing interest in Sarah, you're all upset."

"I'm not upset. I just don't want to see Sarah get hurt by that squanderer."

"Down deep, I really don't think he's like that. Since his wife died, he has been lost in his struggle to survive. He has sunk low, but maybe now he sees the error of his ways. I have to help him, but I'll keep my eyes open and protect Sarah if things start to go wrong."

"I'll keep my eyes on him, also," Charlie said in a muffled tone.

Lucy called Sarah who was a little hesitant to attend the dinner because she had seldom visited in their house. Her reluctance came from her insecurity. After Lucy said it would be mainly family celebrating their Delta Queen trip...she accepted.

"What would you like for me to bring?" Sarah asked. "Oh, I know, I have a great recipe for a Carolina Trifle."

"A trifle sounds perfect, a true southern dessert for our Delta Queen gathering."

Carrie was excited about the party and volunteered to bring her famous Cajun Pasta Salad. The neighbors, Becki and Keith graciously offered to bring the Mint Juleps, since Charlie was clueless about making the drink. Lucy asked Jim to pick up the chipped pork and two Bar-B-Que chickens.

* * *

On Monday morning, Sarah went shopping. It took her a while to find the perfect summer outfit, but she eventually bought a fuchsia paisley gauze print top with mid-length sleeves, and a white Bohemian inspired gathered skirt. She thought it would go along with the theme of the dinner party. She would have avoided this outfit a year ago, but now found it flattering for her blooming personality.

Her favorite southern style restaurant was in the mall, so she stopped for one of their delicious chicken pot pies. She sat quietly and drank a relaxing cup of coffee before ordering, and let her mind linger over her purchases…she smiled when she thought about the turquoise sandals with the silver trim. She shook her head as she imagined herself wearing them with the bold flowered summer dress. "What was I thinking? Did it really look good on me or did the sales lady say that to increase her commissions?" Sarah anxiously whispered.

In her self-imposed doubt, Sarah reached into her pocketbook for a book of encouraging phrases by Dr. Wayne Dyer. She tried to keep herself built up, because sometimes she was her own worst enemy. Shortly before the waiter came to take her order, she closed her eyes for a time of meditation as her thoughts lingered on what she had read.

"Are you ready to order, ma'am?"

"I'd like chicken pot pie, and a glass of water. Thank you," she said as she handed him the menu.

Sarah continued to read the quotes and bits of wisdom from the book *Ten Secrets for Success and Inner Peace* she carried as a go to thing during awkward alone situations and this was one of those times. Sarah seldom entered a restaurant and to be alone felt intimidating. Today was a new hurdle for her, so she put the book away and held her head up while she straightened her blouse, refolded the napkin and rearranged the silverware. She glanced at the bud vase and noticed the silks needed fluffing but decided not to bother with that.

As she spooned the first bite of the warm pot pie, she closed her eyes and inhaled a long draw of flavors. She reclaimed her peace of mind and excitement for life as she savored each morsel of her meal and enjoyed the tranquility of being alone.

A while later the waiter came over and said, "Ma'am, let me refill your coffee and water, also would you like to order a dessert?"

"No thank you, I'm fine. This will be all."

"The gentleman at the round table across the room in the corner has already paid for your lunch."

"I'm sorry, who paid for my lunch?"

"The gentleman in the green shirt at the round table."

Sarah looked over as Jim lifted his hand from the table and slowly waved to her.

Her smile lingered as she returned his wave and quietly repeated the words, "Thank you," as she nodded in appreciation of his thoughtfulness.

Her smile was evident as she fumbled in her wallet. "Let me give you your tip."

"Oh, he took care of that also and quite generously I must say."

"What a pleasant surprise. I enjoyed my lunch and I hope you have a blessed day."

"Thank you, ma'am, come back to see us, and bring your friend," he said as he motioned toward Jim. "Be sure to ask for Steve."

"Thank you, Steve. I'll ask for you…maybe we will be returning." she said with a smile.

Jim was having lunch with a group of men, so Sarah didn't go over to thank him personally. She looked his way until he looked up in her direction. Her lips repeated "thank you" and she waved gently as her smile broadened, to which he acknowledged her with a nod and a smile.

While driving home, she couldn't stop thinking of Jim and his unexpected act of kindness. She had never had anyone do something so special. She smiled broadly as a remembrance of his face became implanted into her memory.

* * *

On Tuesday Sarah made her Southern Carolina Trifle, pressed her outfit, and took a short afternoon nap. She planned to arrive at Lucy's two hours before the other guest. She wanted to have time to catch her breath and become comfortable. Sarah also wished to help Lucy with the final food preparations.

Sarah felt comfortable in the kitchen with Lucy because Lucy took the lead. At this time in her life, Sarah appreciated a self-assured leader.

During their conversations Lucy casually mentioned that Jim was coming.

Sarah smiled as she remembered him from her first introduction at Kim's birthday dinner, but she remembered him best from yesterday. "Oh, let me tell you something exciting about Jim."

Lucy was all ears when she heard the words "tell you…about Jim" as her eyebrows arched, and an O-smile parted her lips…*something wonderful has happened between them. Something she had not heard that was kindling their relationship.* Her eyes widened as she looked into Sarah's eyes and listened with interest.

"I was at Fredrick's in Bellville having lunch. After my meal, the waiter came over and said my bill had been paid by the gentleman at the corner table. I looked and Jim waved. He smiled the sweetest smile."

"He did."

"Yes, it was the sweetest surprise," Sarah said as she whipped the Cajun dip mix into the sour cream.

Sarah smiled broadly and Lucy noticed her as she waltzed around the kitchen while preparing the other food. She seemed to be light as a feather as she talked about Jim.

Sarah was glad Jim would be there tonight. Her first thought was, he's not a stranger and his sense of humor will be pleasant. "Jim has a great personality," Sarah said as she reached in the cabinet for a couple of wine glasses.

Lucy thought with a delightful feeling, *Wow, I think Sarah has been smitten without me even doing anything.*

As they finished their preparations, Lucy poured glasses of Merlot and they moved to the screened back porch to enjoy the spring breeze. The fragrant Ginger Lilies were in full bloom and the tiny blue Forget-Me-Nots stood sparkling against the Brown-Eyed-Susan's dark green leaves.

The wine is working its tranquil magic and if anyone asked the question, then the answer would be …and all is right with the world, Sarah thought as she enjoyed feeling as a confident woman.

To their surprise, Jim opened the patio door. Lucy looked at him, then at Sarah, and then back to Jim. He had the same idea about helping Lucy with the early preparations and asking Lucy a few questions about how he should proceed with Sarah. He came early not knowing Sarah would be there, but when he saw her, his eyes lit up with innocent mischievousness.

"Hello ladies," he said in his deep voice with a lovely smile on his face. His expression was contagious, and they burst into excitement at seeing him. They quickly turned and walked from the corner of the porch where they had been watching the hummingbirds on the fragrant Confederate Jasmine vine. Lucy led and Sarah followed. Jim's eyes skimmed Sarah with admiration as she looked up to make fleeting eye contact.

He gently clutched each one's upper arms and hugged and kissed them on the cheek. Sarah wilted to the strength of his tender grasp and the dampness of his lips as he kissed her. She closed her eyes as his breath exhaled on her skin.

It was her first embrace and kiss from a man in several years, and the feel of his warm touch lingered. She shyly chanced a glancing look up into his grayish green eyes then looked away. He realized her demureness, and quickly reached to touch her arm as a sign of reassurance and confirmation of her importance to him… that brought a smile to her face as she glanced fleetingly into his eyes.

"The Bar-B-Que is on the counter…Lucy, I think I'd like to try a small glass of wine like you girls are having?"

"It's good to see you, Sarah…you look great. Come, let's sit here."

"It's nice to see you as well."

"Is the food prep finished, and are you girls resting while enjoying a glass of Lucy's famous Merlot?"

"Yes, we were looking at her lovely flowers…and also talking about their up-coming trip."

"Here's your wine, Jim," Lucy said as she turned to go back into the kitchen.

"Thanks…come and sit with us. By the way, where's Charlie?"

"Charlie went to a neighbor's house…he's gathering fresh mint and having a lesson on making a Mint Julep. Let me finish inside. You guys just sit and talk, I'll be back," Lucy picked up her wine glass, glanced at Sarah and turned toward the kitchen with the intentions of shuffling a few dishes around and finding busy work while giving Jim time alone with Sarah. In her mind she knew Jim was excited, but she could only imagine how nervous Sarah must be with having to make small talk.

"That color looks nice on you," Jim said as his eyes scanned Sarah.

"Thank you, I wanted to tell you how much I appreciated you buying my lunch yesterday."

"You're welcome. You looked as though you could use a little pick-me-up. I wish it could have been at a time when I could have joined you, but we were discussing another job at the coast near St. Mary's."

"What kind of projects are you working on?"

"Presently we're building a covered repair shop at a boat yard which will accommodate large yachts. It's a mammoth undertaking, but so far everything is on schedule. We're also pricing a floating dock that attaches to a covered pavilion."

"That sounds like a big project, also," Sarah nervously said.

"Yes, but enough about me, what were you doing in town yesterday?"

"An exciting day, I went to the grocery store, to buy gas, and then Betsy's to shop," she said as she waved her hand in her direction.

"Well, your day was worthwhile because you certainly found the perfect outfit."

Jim leaned forward in Sarah's direction. He took on a more serious look and said, "A few weeks ago when we attended the birthday gathering for Kim, I noticed the relationship you have with your friends, and it's apparent that you all have a strong attachment."

"We have grown close through the support we've given each other. They are my dear old and new friends. A true friend will love you always and add special meaning to the seasons of your life," Sarah recalled.

"That's true. What great philosopher said that?"

"It was just something the wine made me think of, so I suppose the philosopher was Merlot." They both laughed. "I should go inside and help Lucy," Sarah said.

He quickly touched her forearm, rubbed it with his thumb and said, "Please stay. She likes to throw a party, so whatever she's doing will make her happy. Besides, who would want to give up sitting on the porch. The temperature is perfect, the birds are chirping, and the conversation is great…who could ask for anything better?"

Sarah reached out and said, "Now what great philosopher said that?" And they both smiled.

Later Lucy and Charlie came out on the porch. Charlie was wearing a straw plantation style hat that was fitting to the riverboat theme. Jim commented and suggested he take it on the trip.

"Sure," Charlie said somewhat sarcastically.

Charlie wanted to make a toast to everyone, so Jim and Sarah started to rise from their chairs. Sarah was a little wobbly…Jim reached out to steady her, and quickly ran his arm around Sarah's waist in a gentlemanly way. "A little too much of Lucy's famous merlot," Jim said sweetly.

"You've been sitting too long and sipping on an empty stomach," Charlie said.

"Why don't you two go for a walk in the garden and get a little fresh air. The walking will clear your head," Lucy said.

"Let me do our toast first," Charlie exclaimed.

"Ok dear, go ahead."

"Here's to life, lived humbly with dear friends to celebrate all our memorable occasions and many more to come."

"Here, here," they all said hardily as they raised their drinks and took a sip in agreement.

"Take these crackers… now go walk…and Jim, take care of Sarah," Lucy said.

Jim looked back and winked.

Charlie turned and whispered, "Lord, please watch over Sarah. She's much too delicate for this guy."

Jim observed Sarah as she maneuvered the garden paths. He saw her as an incredibly beautiful lady who had not been appreciated for her amazing uniqueness. Her dark brown eyes drew her to him like a magnetic field that silently reaches out and circles its equal. As Sarah stepped toward him, he instinctively reached out to her. Their eyes met and for a fleeting moment she looked at him…then quickly glanced away. He recognized her sweetness, but also saw an intelligent woman with feelings and emotions.

After a while Jim said, "The guests are arriving… we should go inside," as he held her delicate hand.

"Must we?" she said in a whisper without realizing she was speaking.

"Perhaps we will do this again."

She shyly looked at Jim, "I would like that," but thought, *why did I say that.*

Jim had forgotten how to care for a gentle lady and spoke cautiously as he realized his circumstance. He second guessed his words and movements with Sarah because he earnestly wanted to make the best impression with her. He saw how Sarah made the simple things of life, like flowers, birds, and unexpected laughter more enjoyable. It had been a while since he had appreciated these things, and the feeling it created was evident in his excitement.

As soon as they arrived inside, Lucy grabbed Sarah by the arm and said, "Come help me, I'm in a panic."

Sarah glanced at Jim with a look of, *I was enjoying myself, but I must help Lucy.* Sarah said, "Thank you for the walk, but please excuse me."

He quickly nodded as his eyebrows tightened. With reluctance he let go of her arm.

Lucy dragged Sarah to the kitchen then into the Butler's pantry which she was using as a prep area. She gave her a glass of wine and said, "Enjoy this as you help me place the food."

She handed her a tray of Hot Mexican Salsa Dip and nacho chips to place on the kitchen island. Sarah bumped into Charlie as she rounded the corner to the kitchen and he asked, "How did the walk go?"

"Like a dream," she said as she looked back at him and winked as she continued to walk toward the island.

Charlie's feelings changed from admiration to agitation as he turned toward the pantry and spotted Lucy cursing at the cucumber sandwiches. The sandwiches were flopping over as she hurriedly tried to fill the ceramic platter, they had bought in Mexico last year.

He hurried to her because he feared he would see it flung against the wall at any minute.

As Sarah placed the tray of chips and dip on the island, Keith the neighbor shifted behind her and asked, "What do you have there?"

"…Corn chips and dip, help yourself," she said with a smile.

"I believe I will… say, are you related to Charlie or a friend?"

"I'm a friend."

"Do you live around here?"

"…near Bellville."

"Yep, I'm familiar with Bellville. I've been through there many times."

"I actually got to know Charlie and Lucy through a mutual friend," Sarah said.

"Come by the marina sometime and I'll line you up on a fishing expedition."

"I'm not much of a fisherman, but I'll think about that."

With a broad smile, she turned, and her focus fell on Jim with his eyes locked dead on her. He forced a tiny smile as his eyebrows lowered into a questioning gaze.

Was he watching me? I haven't done anything wrong, but his brief grin said he was upset, she thought, *maybe, it was a touch of jealousy toward Keith. Yes, that's what it was.* Her heartbeat quickened, and her excitement was aroused as she looked back at Jim while smiling her tiny smile.

Before entering the pantry, she arched her back and felt as confident as any elegant lady. She felt admired. *How about that,* she thought, *me causing someone to be jealous. It's refreshing to think someone cares enough for me to show a spark of concern.*

Lucy spoke much as a tired drill sergeant, "Here darling, run this tray to the island and then check the ice bucket on the counter. Charlie, bring the ice to the cooler under this table and then take this pitcher of Mint Juleps to the bar and hurry back. We can have this done in five minutes, hurry."

Sarah went to the other side of the island and placed the platter of sandwiches next to the Spinach cheese ball. She turned quickly to check the ice and ran into Jim. He reached out and caught her waist before they collided. Her reaction was to touch his shoulders but eased her hand to her side instead.

"Lucy has you running. I thought I better get over and see if I could help you. What can I do?" Jim said as he enjoyed the perfumed fragrance of her skin.

"Check the ice bucket at the bar and help Charlie, he's looking for ice in the garage. Help him make up another pitcher of Mint Julep. Thank you so much," she said with a long gaze held in Jim's direction.

Jim continued to hold Sarah as he listened to her instructions. "I'll do that… slow down a little or Lucy will work you to death. I know her well," Jim said as his hand released his gentle hold.

Sarah's eyebrows danced as she looked at him and touched his arm. "Don't forget, please bring that small bowl of mint sprigs for our guests to garnish their drinks."

Charlie had already made a pitcher of simple syrup for the Mint Julips, and began giving instructions to Jim like an old pro. "First Jim, muddle the mint, use this little bowl and thing."

Jim quickly expressed, "Do what to the mint?"

"Just mash it a little to release the mint flavor. Then put a cup of sugar syrup in the pitcher, add a little muddled mint. Add at least two cups of Tennessee Bourbon and one bottle of sparkling water. Stir and taste, and pour me a taste, also."

After Jim finished muddling and making two pitchers of drinks, he poured shot glass samples for each of them. "Good job Jim, I'll take this pitcher out if you'll bring the other one and the garnishing mint." After several samplings, Charlie and Jim were in good spirits.

"After you take this out, start another pitcher of Mint Julep. I think that's all we'll need because I plan to serve dinner in about forty-five minutes," Lucy said boldly to Charlie.

"Sure, I'll be glad to," As Charlie's wink brought a smile to Jim's face.

Sarah was leaving the kitchen with a dish of pickles when Jim walked past. He whispered, "Meet me in the pantry in a few minutes."

"I will," was her quick response.

Sarah entered the pantry and Jim was braced against the counter as he finished stirring the pitcher of drinks. When he turned and saw her, he smiled the most heartwarming smile and lightly touched her waist. He complimented her on her calm demeanor as she patiently assisted Charlie and Lucy. "You never seemed frustrated in that race to get everything done. What's your secret?"

"There's no secret. I choose to be calm and not let myself get frustrated."

"I didn't realize it could be a choice. I thought people were just born patient, but patience can be learned?"

"The choice is to not be impatient. Just try it…when you get in a tense situation, tell yourself, not to get upset."

"I'll work on that. You're so unique."

"Thank you for the compliment and you're not so bad yourself," she said with a wink as she turned to leave.

He reached out to take hold of her, but missed, "Don't leave so soon."

"I need to find Lucy, and you my friend, have had too many Mint Julep samples," she said with a grin and a twinkle of amusement.

Jim watched her leave and shook his head, "What a special lady. Watch it now… your old self is creeping in and you can't let that happen."

The folks mingled and talked as they enjoyed the appetizers. After a while, the island was cleared, and the dinner plates and utensils were put into place. A colorful ceramic platter of southern BBQ was added along with a yellow bowl of string beans. A pewter bowl of tossed salad and another with broccoli pasta salad were also added.

Charlie and Jim filled glasses with ice for the guests to decide on sweet tea, fresh squeezed lemonade, or water. Charlie said as he patted Jim on the shoulder, "Maybe that's our last job for the night. Now we can relax."

It was a lovely festive dinner and Jim was always close at hand to assist Sarah. They talked often and honestly enjoyed each other's company, as they discussed his marine construction business and his many family connections. He was raised in a humble homelife and was now managing his own successful company. Jim was intriguing and always pleasant with a smiling face.

After the meal Sarah cleared the island and stayed in the kitchen a few minutes to help Lucy get things somewhat organized. They enjoyed their last swallow of wine and laughed as they remembered the rush while setting up the appetizers.

Sarah had a soft lift in her step and a pleasing smile as she worked. She returned to the dining room and placed the dessert plates and forks in a pleasing arrangement on the server. Lastly, she carried out the Carolina Trifle she had meticulously made.

"Sarah, you're zipping around the kitchen getting things done like you're floating on air," Lucy said.

"In a way I am. It's been a long time since I've laughed and enjoyed being with people. This has been a wonderful evening. Thank you for asking me to be a part of this," Sarah said as she hugged Lucy.

Sarah and Lucy hugged again as they joined the other guests, and it was a delight for Sarah to see everyone enjoy the trifle. Lucy beamed as Jim stood to seat Sarah as she took her place beside him.

Before she was comfortable, Sarah spotted Charlie coming through the pantry door and quickly got up to help him.

"Sarah, how about trying a Mint Julep, I just made a fresh pitcher to use as a night cap for a few folks," Charlie said as he balanced the pitcher and a Bud as he struggled to catch his straw hat as it slipped over his eyes. They laughed as Sarah pushed it back.

"Thanks Sarah, I don't know what I'd do without you," he said as he kissed her cheek.

From across the room, Jim saw Charlie's show of affection and a sharp pain of jealousy raced through his body. He wanted to be the one to kiss her cheeks. In midsentence he lost his train of thought as his back became rigid, his eyes narrowed, and his lips drew into a hard line.

Sarah looked up to find him looking directly at her, as her laughter with Charlie turned into a look of confusion. For the second time tonight she wondered about Jim's look, *is this my past life returning? I don't know him well enough to interpret his responses, and I have no idea the intentions of his friendship. I will be observant because I won't let myself be controlled, not again, but if it's his way of showing concern then I'll handle that at the appropriate time.* As she rejoined everyone at the table, she thought, *I'm sure I'll be discerning until I'm comfortable in his presence. Until then I'll have to wonder, if it was a sign of intended possessiveness or could it possibly be passion?*

Sarah was pleased with the comfortable way she felt being near Jim. Her concerns eased as the two of them shared bits of information, and she saw Jim as wanting to be a friend.

Jim never made any advancement to Sarah other than to assist her on several occasions during their walk and to particularly help her down the long front steps as she departed from the house that evening.

As Jim walked Sarah to her car, he gently held her elbow. They enjoyed the pleasant scent of the salt marsh air and the warm coastal breeze.

"I hope I didn't bore you tonight with conversation about my work and family."

"Oh no, I enjoyed hearing your life story."

"I'll follow you home if you would like, since it's late, and you don't have a D D," he added.

"No need for that, I'm feeling fine. I was careful after the little incident on the porch and the walk we took helped me get myself together. I'll call Lucy when I get home but thank you for your thoughtfulness."

He gently hugged her and kissed her below her ear lobe, and said, "Lucy had you working…you didn't have time for refreshments or much to eat."

"I really didn't need or want anything else…I have three containers of food, so I won't have to cook much this week." With reluctance, she slowly let her hand move through the tender clutches of his fingers, and as she turned to get into her car, he gently grasped her hand to hold her a moment longer.

"Your fingers are warm tonight."

With a broad smile she turned and looked into his eyes, "You remembered."

"Of course, I remembered."

She smiled sweetly as she looked into his twinkling eyes. "I enjoyed the evening."

"So did I. Good night, Sarah and call when you get home."

As Sarah drove along the darkened highway, her thoughts turned to Jim. She knew he had awakened her emotions. Her feelings ranged from tremendous excitement over the attention Jim had given her, to the dark depressed side of how her husband had treated her. Her feminine side enjoyed Jim's refreshing personality, but she knew she wasn't ready to share her life with anyone, no matter how sweet they appeared.

Jim went inside to talk to Lucy and Charlie, and to wait for Sarah's call. He entered the den in a tranquil daze and sat heavy on the sofa while in deep thought. Sarah was raging in his thoughts and tugging at his heart.

"How do you think the dinner party went?" Lucy said trying to pull him out of his trance.

"It was the best. I appreciate what you guys are doing to help me. She is wonderful, fascinating, and intriguing, and oh so sweet."

In about twenty minutes, Sarah called. Lucy, with a knowing look on her face handed the phone to Jim. He smiled as he answered.

"Charlie," Sarah said.

"No, this is Jim."

"What a nice surprise," Sarah smiled at the thought of talking to Jim.

"I answered for Lucy. She's busy wiping the counter and Charlie's on the sofa."

"I'm home and everything is alright. I enjoyed the evening and getting to know you…and thanks-a-million for walking with me in the garden."

"It was a tortuous task," he said with a nervous laugh, "but I enjoyed every minute of it." Sarah laughed and smiled at his humor. "Maybe we can all get together soon."

"You are kind…thank you for remembering. Please, tell Lucy how much I enjoyed the evening and I'll call her tomorrow. Good night Jim."

"You have a good night, Sarah, and I will always remember." He slowly, unknowingly, slipped the phone down to his heart and closed his eyes for a few seconds as he exhaled.

Lucy watched him, and knew he was at a turning point. As Lucy looked at him, she formed a new image of Jim. His manner had changed. He was soft and gentle as he spoke, not boisterous like he had been at times in the past. "Charlie said Jim was living the fast life and had to act that way to stay in tune with that lifestyle. Now he really looks like the old familiar Jim, the one I have loved all my life. You know since the birthday gathering, I haven't heard of him partying and all he talks about is working," Lucy whispered to Carrie.

Lucy thought about Jim's life. *When he was a young boy his father died at war and after high school Jim was drafted into the Army and sent to Vietnam. He quickly went from a handsome charmer into the real theater of war. As soon as he was discharged, Jim started college, finished, and went to work with his brother. Soon got married, and it wasn't long before the babies started to arrive.*

He worked hard all his life, was committed to his job, his children, and an ailing wife. In their later years, as the children had moved away and started their own families, Ann became ill with ovarian cancer and died. The children quickly revolted when they saw their dad throwing caution to the wind. Maybe now he is seeing life with a more mature set of eyes.

Chapter 5

Jim felt proud of his interest in Sarah as he talked with friends and unearthed several personal facts about her. The most important was she was not seeing anyone and had politely rejected all potential suitors. Jim thought, *with my family connections, I might stand a better chance than anyone else…at least I will count on that.*

Jim's heart began to swell as countless people described Sarah as honest and generous with the sweetest most caring nature. He thought, *why haven't I heard of her before now? I thought I knew all the ladies in the community, and then it occurred to me, she is different from the ladies I know. Sarah is described as a lady of virtue.*

He saw on Sarah's church marquee that a community wide anniversary reception was scheduled for one of his distant cousins. Jim immediately thought *there's a good chance I can visit with Sarah as well as with my relatives.* "I'll definitely go shopping for a new spiffy sport coat and loafers for the event."

After talking with Sarah at the reception he knew he had to think of a way to be with her in an unassuming manner. Jim knew Sarah was a great cook, but he couldn't call and ask for her Carolina Trifle recipe. "I must call Lucy for advice."

Lucy, with a keen interest in helping Jim said, "Sarah's a talented decorator. Her farmhouse is beautiful, and she helps others make improvements to their homes."

"That has to be the starting point to build our relationship," he said with joy. "My house has not been changed in years, so where should I start."

"Try the den…that will be the easiest starting point," Lucy cleverly said.

He looked at the den's depressing dark paint, and the drapes were worn with a spider condo at the top. In the years since his wife died, he hadn't noticed how the room had deteriorated. The stack of newspapers beside his chair had been there for months and the shuffled junk mail on the kitchen island needed throwing out. He looked at the carpet and shook his head. "How did I let this happen?" he mumbled. "Maybe the den would be the starting point. First I have to clean this place before I can ask Sarah to come over and help me decorate anything."

After a week of cleaning and hauling off trash, he decided, "Now I'm almost ready to make the phone call," he said aloud as he scanned the den and kitchen. That evening while watching *Out of Africa,* his thinking was dominated by thoughts of Sarah, *as he saw similarities between her and the character Karen Blixen. He saw Sarah as strong as Karen while having to overcome a philandering husband and a loss of her own identity. Sarah as with Karen had grown into an attractive woman with strong managing skills. Karen's compassion for the people around her paralleled the care Sarah gave her friends. They suffered tremendous loss and emotional pain and both ladies rebounded, and he adored their strength of character. Karen eventually fell in love and Jim was hoping also for that parallel.*

* * *

Sarah was feeling restless as she realized her heart was empty. She remembered Jim's friendship and how it made her feel womanly. Carrie, through the years had taught her how to love and enjoy people, and Sarah was beginning to appreciate that comfort as she thought of Jim.

It was a loving friendship with Carrie that saved Sarah from emotional tragedy. Now the constant guilt and questioning of her validity in life was less severe and she was feeling freedom from the pain of past marital controversies and tensions. Carrie taught her, through example, that love with a generous spirit and care for others would help eliminate her self-doubt. As her heart was excited, she noticed the negative feelings of her past were fading.

Jim's thoughts of Sarah were influenced by her character and her strengths. *She appears to be honest, thoughtful and for sure unpretentious. She's been through a lot but remains brave.* "I've seen her uneasy at times, but never weak and coward like. She works hard and I admire that. On the outside she's beautiful, but inside her heart is humble, caring and compassionate.

"To be with a gentle honest person would be comforting and more rewarding than trying to keep up with expensive dinners out, country club dances and touchy, feely, fair weather friends. I've got to call her and hear her voice," Jim said with determination.

Jim without hesitation called Sarah. "Hello Sarah, how's the weather at your house?" *Wow, that was a dumb lead-off-question,* he thought.

"It's a bit over-cast but the weather forecaster said it will possibly clear by late morning. How is it at your house?"

"...about the same as yours. Let me ask you something, the rooms in my house are looking drab, and Lucy said you're a fabulous decorator."

"Fabulous?" Sarah said with a nervous chuckle.

"Yes fabulous. I wanted to ask if you would consider coming over and give me some pointers on a few changes."

Sarah enjoyed decorating and was always generous to volunteer her time to help others. She had long since left the business, but her creative talents were always ready to share. "Sure, I will be glad to help you."

Her sudden yes answer put her into a state of shock as she realized what she had done. She would be alone with him. Her mind was flashing...*are you crazy, as it filled with what if thoughts,* as she tried to carry on a conversation. "When do you want me to come over?" she calmly found herself saying as her palms became clammy.

Jim wanted to say, now, but knew he couldn't. "How does your schedule look for tomorrow afternoon, would two o'clock work?"

"That's great...if you have any magazine pictures, paint colors or thoughts about special areas, then we can incorporate your inspiration ideas into the plan." Sarah spoke in a professional manner, as she thought of being alone with Jim. Her husband intimidated her, destroyed her self-confidence and here she was agreeing to an appointment with Jim. She wouldn't have Lucy to depend on...what would she say?

"I'll jot down a few thoughts. Do you know where I live?"

"Yes, Lucy told me," Sarah nervously said.

She knows where I live, he quickly thought. "Then I look forward to seeing you tomorrow."

After their conversation ended, she began to pace. She thought about being in the house with Jim and the palms of her hands became moist, "What have you gotten yourself into this time?" Sarah began to panic and decided she had to call him and cancel. "I haven't been alone with a man in years, especially a kind considerate man like Jim. No, I can't be that paranoid. I need to go through with this...I must move on with my life and venture out on my own. I'll be alone with him. What will I talk about, oh why did I agree to this?"

As she calmed her thoughts became more positive, but later that evening her fears of leaving her comfort zone overwhelmed her, and she telephoned Dr. Freeman's answering machine to tell him the good news of accepting her first job in a long while, but also to mention her fears.

Jim was nervous, also. He wanted her there first because he cared for her. "I want to share some quality time with Sarah, but under the pretense of needing a decorator. I'm fascinated by her, as a caring acquaintance who has won me over with her modest humility. Whatever it cost to change the den will be worth it," he spoke aloud as contentment gave a peaceful feeling.

* * *

Lucy had given Sarah explicit directions, and as soon as Lucy mentioned the iron gates and stone columns, she knew exactly where Jim's house was located. As she drove along the country backroads, she thought, *I've passed the entrance many times and wondered who lived behind the massive iron gates with the stoned columns and iron fencing.*

"Wow, the entrance is neatly manicured," she vocalized with excitement. She noticed various shades of green foliaged shrubs forming graceful curves along the stately entry and massive groupings of red Knock-out Roses adding color. A narrow planting of Blue Salvia following the curve of the driveway added a spark to the planted beds and blooming clumps of white Sweet William dotted the edges. Sarah thought out loud, "This is a patriotic flowerbed." Sarah remembered Lucy describing Jim as a man who cared for his country and his fellow man.

The gates opened and Sarah drove the concrete lane…she observed the rolling hill pastures, streams and ponds disguised by hardwood trees in a natural setting. Native flowering trees and shrubs filled the mature forest. The driveway curved through a maze of landscaped gardens accented by the regional magnolia, dogwoods, and azaleas, and soon the structure came into full view. As she focused on the house and yard, her breath was taken away by this beautiful historic mansion located in such a quiet picturesque location. She felt somewhat intimidated by its grandeur.

"This house looks amazing…I had no idea Jim's home would be like this," Sarah spoke as the reality of being there jolted her out of her overwhelming amazement.

She noticed her palms dampened and could hardly contain her emotions concerning their meeting. Her fears of being alone with Jim created a sweeping heat that burned her cheeks. She was glad she wore something simple and cool to hopefully mask her weak knees and quivering heart.

Sarah had struggled through a marriage filled with pain and had not yet allowed herself to trust a male figure, especially now a man who was showing signs of a friendship. Her nervous anticipation predicted a disaster, and she wasn't sure if she needed to cry or crank up the band, but her true desire was for a congenial afternoon of planning.

When she stopped her Suburban near the front walk, Sarah noticed it was ten till two. She twisted in her seat to grab her leather tote while holding her notebook. A nervous fumble and a catch on the floor mat caused her to drop everything, and the tote's contents spilled in her seat and on the driveway. As she fumbled to retrieve her cell phone, tape measure, drafting pencils and what seemed to be a hundred pieces of loose change she whispered, "I hope that fiasco was out of sight of the house."

To hide her nervousness, Sarah unknowingly breathed out an exasperating breath, and went limp as she propped against the driver's seat. She quickly tucked her notebook firmly under her arm. She stood and looked toward the house for signs of movement, took a deep breath, wiped the sweat off her upper lip, fluffed her shirt and started the long walk to the front door.

As Sarah unlatched the white garden gate and began to meander down the brick walkway, she mumbled, "The plantings of gorgeous blooming flowers are outstanding, and the contrast with the deep green lawn shaded by the enormous live oak trees in the far corners of the yard is dramatic." A refreshing summer breeze caught her by surprise, and she breathed deep.

The magnificent mansion was a remarkable Georgian style home possibly built in the early nineteen-hundreds and appeared to be meticulously maintained through the years. Sarah imagined the grand parties and stories it held within its walls.

Jim opened the massive four feet wide solid oak nine panel door before she could ring the bell. He took her hand, kissed her cheek, and welcomed her in as he said, "Warm."

She exhaled and smiled a knowing smile. Sarah instinctively put her hand over his and looked at him with reserved delight.

"Come in, my dear. I have been looking forward to this all day," he said as he closed the door while still holding her hand. "Please just make yourself at home. Feel free to look and make any suggestions you want. The house needs a fresh look, as you can tell."

She quickly looked away from his penetrating eyes and began to glance at the entrance hall as if to send a signal, it was time to start talking about decorating. Without delay she began to pick up clues to his needed improvements, so that she could move into why she was there without having to make small talk. She had a fear of their meeting drifting into awkward speechlessness.

Her extreme anxiety made her feel as though she was entering a dangerous forbidden territory, but with her eyes wide open and with two small steps she ventured further inside. The entrance hall was spotless and spacious with a beautiful curved wooden balustrade stairway that gave an elegant first impression. She noticed the furniture was worn and could use a facelift. The lampshades on the console table had taken on a frayed stained look, and the antique Persian rug needed cleaning. She quickly caught an unseen glance of how impeccably Jim was dressed and made a mental note that *the room needed more of an update than he needed.*

She purposefully avoided looking directly at him as he talked because, she was afraid of breaking into a drenching nervous sweat. She thought *how embarrassing that would be if my face turned red and sweat drops formed on my upper lip or the tip of my nose.* Sarah feared looking visibly nervous. "I love old homes" she said as she spotted the 10inch crown molding and a large pier mirror oddly gracing the wall behind an oversized wooden dining room chair.

"Do you live here all by yourself?" W*hat a dumb question. I know he's by himself. Why did I ask such a thing?*

He sensed her shy nervousness and made a joke about his house being a *Man's Cave* now. "Judging by the size of this place you would think a family of ten would live here, or maybe I would rent out rooms, but it's just me, now that my children have families of their own." Their laughter broke the ice.

Sarah glanced at Jim and her eyes skimmed his face before she looked at the floor. She released her shoulders and breathed deeply as she again noticed the antique Persian rug under her feet. She instantly tried to become lighter and said," I should take my sandals off."

"Don't even think about that. This house is used and enjoyed. It's been that way since it was built almost a hundred years ago. Let me take your rain jacket."

Sarah exhaled and began to feel better and had partially removed her jacket before he had a chance to assist her. Her inward and outward tensions were beginning to ease, and she felt as though she could go on with the job, instead of running for the door.

"Your home looks as though it holds a lot of history. Maybe you can tell me the story behind its grandeur."

As he laid her jacket on the English settee he said, "The house was built by my great grandfather, James William Alexander, in 1902 and my grandfather inherited the house in 1922 when James William died, and my father inherited it in the early forties before I was born," he said as he marveled at her interest in the house.

As Jim turned and lifted his hand to direct her into the den, she observed *his sharp creased khaki pants and recently purchased knit polo shirt. Whoever had ironed the shirt had not pressed out all the new shirt fold lines.* He half turned and said, "I would like for you to look at the den."

She glanced at his face and noticed *his greenish twinkling eyes and beautiful smile,* with a fleeting observance, *of how nice he looks,* streamed through her thoughts. She had been in his presence a few times, but *today his eyes have a clear sparkle like she had not seen before and his entire face beams,* she thought

"The last time the den was remodeled was about twenty-five years ago…it's time to make furniture changes, paint and whatever else you suggest," as he turned their eyes locked.

His eyes noticed her over all youthfulness. Her face glowed not as a drab mid-sixty-year-old, but with the glow of compassion, enthusiasm, and excitement. He admired her appearance.

"Yes, I think we can make some changes to freshen your den."

He noticed her white cotton eyelet blouse with the top three buttons unfastened, and as he looked past the opened collar, his eyes rested on the hint of a lace camisole that showed as she gracefully moved into the room. The open blouse gave notice to a small sterling silver chain with a silver pendant and turquoise stone hanging from her delicate neck as it gracefully lay against her chest. His eyes studied her every chance he got.

"And these silk flower arrangements need replacing. I've used the air compressor to blow the dust off too many times…it looks a little unorganized."

"Now that's a manly way to clean house, I like that method. It's not beyond repair. A lot of this can be reused with no problem. Would you like to make a few simple furniture changes this afternoon, just to see what you like and start the process of making some decisions on what you might like to keep and what you need to change?"

"Oh yes, I'm ready to start something."

"Let me look for a few seconds." Sarah stood in the middle of the room and quietly looked over the present layout and how it could be changed. Her eyes immediately recognized the architectural charm of rich wide moldings and door casings. The spaciousness of the room was conducive to having separate casual sitting and entertainment areas.

Jim confidently stood beside her and drew in the soothing aroma of her presence as it drenched his body with warmth, and he heard her sweetly say, "Older homes have a soul that we must observe and respect as we plan changes. The interior moldings, the architectural exterior and the antiques give your home a distinctive history."

"I do have a passion for the age of the house which has been well maintained through the years," he said with a deep appreciation of her concern for the aesthetic value and the longevity of his family home.

After studying the room, Sarah began to talk. "Here's what I'm thinking." She turned quickly to move over to the sofa and had to reach out and take hold of Jim's arm to keep from running into him. *He must be putting some serious thought into this because he seems to be in a daze.*

As she slipped past him, he noticed how she smelled faintly of sweet delicate perfume he couldn't identify. Her hair smelled fresh as a wayward curl drifted across her forehead. Her touch jarred him, and he reached out to her. Sarah released her grasp and moved around him as she continued to move toward the sofa.

"Let's think about the traffic flow and consider how you enter and exit the room from the kitchen and foyer. We also need to consider group seating and your exit to the porch."

"I never put any thought into such things. The room has always had a jumbled look, with areas that look lost."

"We will definitely look at the entire room, and consider its commanding architectural elements…the doorways, the windows and the fireplace. When you start to think about furniture placement, it can get a little tricky, first we need to decide what works best for seating and traffic flow. With the sofa as it is now, puts people and feet in the flow of the room. You might consider changing the sofa over to this area near these gorgeous windows," Sarah used her graceful hands as she talked.

"You're right. It will be better by the window."

"The sofa should float out a few feet, with a sofa table and lamps behind it. A medium size chest and lamp could go here next to your chair and this round center table at the other end." As Sarah moved in front of the new sofa area she said, "You have plenty of room to have an upholstered coffee table covered with a tightly woven fabric to serve as extra seating as well as a place to prop your feet."

As she walked to the other side of the room, he couldn't help but notice her long slender legs and how her skinny fitting jeans hugged the shape of her body. He became infatuated by her gracefulness as she pointed out the placement of a large chest in place of the present sofa.

She moved with the flowing grace of a ballerina as her arms lifted to show the suggested width and height of the chest. With an elegant pirouette, she looked at Jim and their eyes locked as a tiny smile formed with a look of enthusiasm that filled their faces.

With an intense look Sarah continued to speak and point out furniture placement. "This area would be perfect with lamps and a major piece of artwork or an ornate antique mirror hanging above the chest. The walking path would be less congested, and you would also end up with additional storage," she said as she moved to the other side of the room.

"I like that idea…it would give storage, and would look nice," Jim spoke in his low southern drawl as the vision of her walking from place to place replayed in his thoughts and created a sudden quiver.

As Sarah used her hands to point out placement of furniture and accessories, and to emphasize needed changes, Jim became fascinated by her gracefulness. He enjoyed the way she spoke with confidence as she took command of the room. She challenged him to think in a way he had never been required to think before.

"Would you like to move this sofa over to the window area? I brought some moving pads in case we wanted to move something."

"Sure…let me call Henry to come help us. He's busy cutting the grass, but this won't take long."

The three of them moved the sofa and placed a small chest and lamp between the sofa and Jim's chair. A lovely antique center table was placed at the other end of the sofa.

"This will be all we can move today, but I have some thoughts about changes in the television area. Now let's look and talk." Sarah said as she lifted her right hand and gracefully opened her palm and curved her fingers in his direction.

"What about a glass of water, wine, coffee, coke?"

In a deep train of thought, she said, "Water is fine."

Jim went into the kitchen and fixed two glasses while Sarah studied the room.

"Come over. I'll sit on the sofa and you in your chair, so we can try out the new vantage point."

He placed their glasses on coasters and settled. "Let me move up a little, I can't see all of you," he said as they slipped his recliner forward. "I like this…being close to the guest."

"If you keep the lamp on the back side of the chest, then you can keep your remote here and your drink coasters near the front."

"This will work," he said.

"This placement puts the main functioning piece of furniture, the sofa as a focal point in the room against these gorgeous windows. Then we will build around it with accent pieces."

While they were seated, Jim took the opportunity to ask a few questions. "How long have you lived in this area?"

"When I got married, we lived in a town nearby for about three years before moving to Augusta. We lived there for about thirty-five years but owned a farmhouse and a few acres of land nearby. After my husband died, I moved to the farmhouse and have lived here about 18 months. I'm trying to rebuild my life."

"My wife died several years ago. I had a hard time accepting her death and did everything possible not to face what had happened. Starting over was difficult for me."

"I'm sorry. The surviving spouse often lives in a confusing world of loss, and unsure about how to handle things. It's easy to make an unwise decision but thank goodness for second chances." The nervousness Sarah once had was now gone, she felt more at ease and enjoyed their conversation. She listened instead of trying to out-think him and predict his next question. "Now, I have some other thoughts."

Gee, she's reading my mind, he thought as he quickly looked around at her. "Alright, what are you thinking?"

"This room is quite large, so it can be designed with two seating areas. The area nearest the foyer entrance, with the warmth of the fireplace is more personal and intimate. By restraining the massive size of your room into two areas, will give you a chance to personalize each area, but tie them together with color. The warm colors will create the cozy feel."

"Intimate, yes, I like intimate," Jim said.

"Intimate, as warm with an inviting ambience," Sarah spoke with a glowing smile.

"That sounds even better."

"Beside the fireplace, I visualize two leather wingback chairs flanking the right side and a small, upholstered settee on the left. This would serve as a conversation/reading area. With this beautiful wall of books on either side of the fireplace, it will be a great place to sit and read or just carry on a cozy conversation. A low chest can be placed between the wing chairs for holding perhaps a cup of tea and a good book can be within easy reach."

"I like that…previously, I thought of that area as unused space because I tried to use the entire room as one space and that got lost. Now I can see how the entire room will be useful."

Then Sarah turned and walked toward the entrance to the den from the kitchen and turned around. He couldn't help but watch her walk away from him. He noticed her slender legs with tanned ankles.

"Now let us look at the room's new focal points. When you enter the room from the kitchen," she said, as she motioned for him to come over, "you first see the window and the future sofa area." While standing directly behind him and with her right hand placed gently on his right shoulder, she reached her arm out in front of him and framed the sight line with her thumb and index fingers.

He reached out and gently held her wrist and moved her hand into his line of vision from his chair to the end of the sofa. "I can see what you're talking about." The mere touch of her arm on his shoulder and holding her delicate wrist created a strong emotional excitement for him.

"This chair and sofa area must be spectacular. We have to make this an incredible impact area because it's the first area you see when you enter the room from the kitchen."

"Yes, you're right. Let me look at that again."

Then she pressed his shoulder a little and directed him to the foyer/den entrance. "When you enter from the foyer and look to the right, you see, what could be your future television viewing area." In the same manner as before, she framed this area with her fingers for his viewing. "Then from the sofa area, look to the left of you in front of the fireplace would be the relaxing conversation area I described."

Jim held her wrist and repositioned her hand in the direction of the far wall. "I like viewing the room like this," he said as he moved her arm around to slowly encompass the entire room. "It really helps me see just the specific areas you're referring too.

"These are important visual areas, so we have to make them pop with color with something spectacular. We need to add an anchor piece of furniture here. This must be filled with something bold and exciting. This will be where you will add the pizzazz," she said as she found her hand gripping his right shoulder.

"I like the sound of bold and exciting, but I especially like the word pizzazz. Let me look at the sofa area again." He deliberately moved her hand into the sofa line of vision. "I understand…it helps to view the room like this," he said as he enjoyed holding her tapered wrist. "Looking at the entire room at once is overwhelming."

"With the few changes we made today, your room looks more open and inviting. Now we will decide what you want to do and how we can take care of everything. Do you have a wish list for the room?"

"I'm sure I would like new carpet and a new sofa and maybe a chair for me. The window curtains are as old as the last remodel about twenty-five years ago, so I'm sure new ones would be better. What do you think?"

"I agree with that and I know a local place where we can find many of the items you'll need. The furniture store I like has beautiful well-made furniture and accessories. Also, a lady who makes window treatments for their customers. For the construction, I know Jonathan Baker well. He comes to my house quite often to repair things or just help me with odd repair jobs."

"I trust your opinions and I respect the people and places you already know. I also have a paint chip I've kept for about fifteen years. I've always liked this shade of green."

"This will help with the direction you want to go." He purposefully touched her fingers as he handed Sarah the chip and their vision locked.

"I noticed the original gently worn pine floors in the entrance hall. Is there hardwood under this carpet and would you consider going back to wood with area rugs to define the two areas… with a wide area in between for accessing the porch," she said as she pointed out each cluster.

"Yes, there is wood here, and I would strongly consider the change."

"Wood has a more sophisticated look, and I thought it would give your room a more updated feel and would integrate beautifully with the nostalgic feel of the home," she said as she pointed to the oversized bookshelves and coffered ceiling.

"An updated look sounds fine with me. I could use an update around here," he said with a smile.

He noticed her eyes again as she smiled that intriguing tiny smile. They were as dark as the black waters of the Ebenezer River on a winter morning. He thought, *her eyes bring back the memory of a brown-eyed girl I longed for in my past.* Sarah held his gaze as he stared at her with an intense look. They continued to talk about the room's antique furnishings, and as often as he could, Jim would stand close enough to brush her arm or touch her fingers.

"With the charm and age of your home, and with these beautiful antiques, I feel you need to stay with classical traditional furnishings. The furniture you buy has to compliment your antiques and keep a balance between the old and new and between luxury and easy living." she said as she went over to sit on the sofa. As Sarah sat and crossed her legs, he noticed her slender tapered ankles and delicate black sandals with mother of pearl trim. "I thought at first the sofa could be saved, but it seems to have a few broken springs and it's really not the right style for the room. We can easily replace this with something better and more traditional."

"What do you mean by traditional?"

"This sofa has rolled arms with a rounded pillow back that gives it a modern look. I think a more classical sofa, something with a small amount of exposed nail heads and soft lines in a deep rich color would add to the room. We're looking for that, come in and sit down, piece of furniture."

"As we get older, comfort becomes a luxury. You want to balance the elegance of fine timeless fabric with the ease of casual living. You want something with style and definitely not trendy." Sarah used her arms and hands to emphasize the sofa arms and her hands rubbed along the fabric seats as she mentioned the need for a rich color. Her hand movements added to the descriptive words she used and quickly caught his eye.

Her femininity was evident as he noticed the lace camisole showing during her hand movements. "That sounds good to me. That old sofa has gone through kids and grandkids." Jim said as he moved back to his favorite chair and sat down. His thoughts tried to remember the last time kids or grandkids had sat on that sofa. Unfortunately, not much since his wife's death, and now that his daughters have quietly avoided him. He was glad to see Sarah gracefully seated there but was sorry it had to be on the cushion with the worn edge, and the wayward springs.

As he repositioned himself in his chair, Sarah quickly noticed his shiny new loafers, no socks and tanned ankles and said, "I think a comfortable, leather reclining wing back chair would look good for you." *Oh no, he caught me looking at him,* she thought, as she gracefully motioned with her hand in his direction.

He nodded in agreement. "It has to be a comfortable chair with maybe room for two. I might need some room for cuddling, I mean sleeping," he quickly added.

Her eyes widened and darted with a quick glance at him and a slight gasp as she put her fingers over her mouth. Her eyebrows raised into a peak. She broke into a shy, but somewhat devilish smile, and then quickly looked away as she shook her head. "It sounds as though we might need to look for furnishings in a spicy color palette to go along with the soothing green you like," she said as she raised her eyebrows and looked at him out of the corner of her eye.

He saw her glancing eyes cut in his direction. *Oops, I think I shocked her with my comment,* he thought, *because I sure got a reaction from her.*

Sarah dropped her head and rolled her shoulders toward Jim as she re-crossed her legs and shook her foot a few times unknowingly in his direction. With a straight face, she said, "Of course, we will keep that in mind. The client should always make special requests for what they want in the room. If we can't find a double reclining chair, then maybe the sofa can be reserved for your cuddling, I mean sleeping area. Does that sound alright?" She patted the sofa and started a new train of thought.

"Sounds good to me," he said with a smile.

Sarah shook her head, smiled as she stood and walked away. He watched her and knew he got her attention in the most sensual manner. He saw her reaction and knew deep down below her fractured protective shield a delicate feminine woman was lurking.

Sarah walked over to the opening of the kitchen/den area. "Construction could be done here to close off the kitchen and just have an opening like the one going into the foyer, or if you prefer closing the kitchen off completely, French doors with a transom much like the doors going out onto the back porch. She used her hands to show where the new wall would be and the door opening. That would give a wall to put an armoire, that's a large piece of furniture with doors or an open entertainment center to hold a television and its components."

"Jonathan is knowledgeable at blending new construction flawlessly into old construction. He and I have worked together on several areas like this at my farmhouse, so I can say he's quite a talented carpenter."

"That's good to know about Jonathan. I never have liked sitting here and looking into the kitchen," he said, as he wandered over and stood beside Sarah. He enjoyed being close to her and having the warmth and fragrance of her body stir his body and soul. He wanted to rest his hand gently on her back at her waist, but knew he had to refrain.

They had brushed against each other as they moved about the room, but he was wishing for more. He wanted to put his arms around her, but he knew it was too early in his pursuit to make a move like that. In a daring move, he purposefully placed his hand on the counter as Sarah quickly moved her hands back and forth to visually draw a wall line. "The area between the cabinets would be walled up and finished off like the existing kitchen walls." She bumped his hand and moved over it and back again. He watched her eyes, and she gave him a darting look and a gentle smile as she continued to talk.

"That idea sounds perfect."

Sarah turned and leaned against the counter. "What do you think about repainting this room in a lighter shade of the green you like? Also consider painting the bookcases and trim in a fresh cream color." She intently looked at him to get his true reaction because this would be a major change that he might not have anticipated. "A medium to light shade would be different from the present dark color. Men often think a den must be painted dark, but it can be depressing, and you miss the rich moldings, windows with their commanding views and your handsome wood floors. A fresh lighter green will make a positive change."

"The wood is beautiful. Fresh paint would add a bright crisp look, but that would be a decision you would have to make, because you have to be completely satisfied from the beginning, because once the paint goes on, it's expensive to redo," she said with a questioning look.

Jim leaned against the counter beside Sarah, crossed his arms over his chest and said, "I'll put thought into that. This was my great granddad's favorite room, and he chose the wood for the molding and bookcases."

"Always in remodeling or redecorating, the emotional ties of the owner must be considered first. Then consider a fresh coat of mat polyurethane with new lighting in certain areas." Sarah placed her hand lightly on his arm and said, "Redecorating can be painful when there are memories, but we can work through it and do what's best for you and the house. Home-owners often reach a point of contentment in their homes and areas become special and need to be considered during the renovation for the room to not lose its personal intimate charm."

Jim smiled and breathed a sigh of relief because *I had decided before hand, I would agree to everything she said in hopes of having more decorating encounters. She seems to have read my mind about the moldings and bookcases because she gave me a way out. Maybe this will be painless as well as productive because she seems easy to work with.* He smiled and said, "Let me think more about that change."

"In this area, you need to consider removing the counter from jutting out into the den, then closing off this area with a door opening like that one or French doors with a transom above, then plaster and paint the walls. The new crown, base and door casings can be matched to the original. The wall in the kitchen is sheetrock so we can add a few receptacles and repaint."

"If I decide to paint, then what color do you think will look good?"

'It will depend on the color of the largest piece of furniture, and that will likely be the sofa. If you can find something in a spicy reddish shade and your beautiful green paint chip color would be a soothing wall color. Then possibly a plaid fabric of spicy red and green would be nice for other things like window treatments or an armchair."

"What do you mean when you said, what color sofa I picked out, I need for you to pick it out. All of this is frightening to me."

They both smiled and Sarah placed her hand on his arm and said, "What if we go shopping together and find what you need."

"Now that sounds perfect to me," he said as he reached out and took her hand.

"You're ready to take the first step."

"I'm ready," he said as he shook her hand in agreement.

"We need to measure the room, make a list of the major things you need and plan a shopping trip," Sarah said with excitement.

She gathered her measuring tape and notebook from the sofa and began to make a quick rendering of the room. "I'll hold the tape at the hook, and you can read off the numbers. My husband always gave me the hook end because it's the dumb end he would always say."

Jim shook his head and thought, *that is not true for you, and if he believed that, then he was clueless of your remarkable abilities.* Sarah held the tape and began to record the numbers as Jim read them off. At one point, while measuring into a corner, Sarah sat on the floor and upon rising, Jim extended his hand, which she took and gracefully stood.

"Thanks," she said as he slowly let go.

Jim enjoyed watching her work and listening to her talk. He was amazed at how Sarah was seeing things from large construction to accessorizing the furniture in small details. He was in awe of her discerning creativeness and felt completely assured she would help him in more than one way. Jim said, "I'll be ready tomorrow, if that's alright with you…about nine o'clock."

With a smile, she said, "I like an enthusiastic client anxious for a change. I'll be here at nine."

Sarah turned to the sofa and gathered her purse and supplies, "I'm really thankful for this opportunity to help you. I've been out of the workforce for a while and I've missed decorating and working with people. Your project is exciting to me, and at this time, I need excitement."

"This means a lot to me for reasons I won't say now, but please, don't leave so soon. Can I get you something else to drink? I don't have any of Lucy's famous merlot, but maybe we can find something."

"I really need to be going. I've been here three hours and it's time for your dinner.

"Good, we can find something in the kitchen and have dinner together."

With a smile on her face she said, "I want to redo this rendering, and think of other things you might need…its best I leave, I'm meeting an old friend for dinner at seven, and he's always prompt. Thank you for everything and I'll see you at nine," Sarah said as she extended her hand, and he took hold of her warm fingers but surprised her with a gentle hug.

As he understood he was the definite loser of Sarah for the evening, he began helping her gather her measuring tape and papers, with thoughts that he would be the one with her all day tomorrow. "Sarah, thank you for coming over today, because this means more than you know. Let me get your jacket…oh look… the sun is shining." As he walked her to her car, he placed his hand lightly on the small of her back and said, "I'm looking forward to our shopping trip." He removed his hand and reached forward to open the gate and then open her car door.

"Call me later tonight if you have any questions."

"Oh look, a lucky penny right beside your car door." He picked it up and rubbed it between his hands and almost said aloud, but quickly changed it to a thought, *is this an omen? I hope it brings me good luck.*

Sarah didn't tell him about her commotion and probably it was a penny she had failed to pick up. She thought, *he doesn't need to know I was shaking in my sandals when I got here.* As Sarah smiled and turned to reach out to shake his hand, she looked into his eyes with a sweet caring look and said, "Thank you and nine. Oh, I almost forgot. We need to exchange cell numbers just in case you think of something else or I have a question about the measurements."

He already had her number, but at her request, he would gladly record it again. She wrote his number on the top of her work sheet, so she could enter it after she arrived at home. She was too nervous to attempt to remember how to record it while standing in front of him.

Jim, feeling a little downcast wandered into the house. He mumbled, "I thought she was dressed so cute and casual just for our meeting, but she might have been dressed that way for her date. I didn't know she was seeing anyone. Maybe it's just something unexpected… but I'll have her all day tomorrow to myself."

* * *

After feeding the dog and watering a few drooping pots of flowers on the porch, Sarah worked in her office, completing the drawing, then placed it along with the shopping list into her leather attaché bag. She went into her bedroom, showered, and dressed in a white shirt, gray jeans, and tennis shoes for her casual dinner. She also laid out her clothes and shoes for the next day.

After returning home from dinner with Mike, she showered and got into bed. She began to read when her house phone rang, and to her surprise, it was Jim. "Sarah, do you want to ride in my truck or your SUV?"

"Your truck sounds fine to me. We might buy something we need to transport."

Sarah, I'm glad you're helping me. I will see you tomorrow."

"I'm excited about your project, also. Good night, Jim."

When he clicked off the phone he thought, *I adore her. She honestly wants to help. I can't believe this amazing person has come into my life.*

* * *

The day began early for Sarah. After her breakfast and a quick work out, she took a long shower and groomed her body with care as she thought of being with Jim all day. Suddenly a frightening chill raced over her as the flashback caused her to shake as she thought about being alone with him. She kept repeating, "I must do this, I must, I must venture out."

Sarah chose to wear her most comfortable black jeans, with a summery blouse of blue and coral flowers with black accents. Sarah's choice of casual clothes made her feel less constrained by the anticipated stress of the day. As Sarah dressed, she kept repeating, "It will be ok."

Sarah arrived at Jim's house well before nine. She wanted to let him know she was punctual, organized, and efficient at her job.

"Good morning come in my dear. I have to find my cell phone and then we can leave."

Will you look in the den? It's in the charger somewhere. Here it is. It was in the bathroom. I had it in there while getting ready because I was actually afraid you might call and change your mind about the project."

"Now why would you think that?"

"I wasn't sure you had time to fool with me."

With her gorgeous bright smile and her twinkling brown eyes, she said, "I love the charm of your home and I love your desire to keep its architectural integrity as you make some needed changes. I enjoy helping people who are genuinely excited about their improvements. I'm retired now and you seem to want my help, maybe without strict deadlines. It's easier to work under those conditions. Plus, I've been around you a few times, so it's not like going into a complete stranger's home to start a new job. I think we can make it work and I know it will be enjoyable."

"I'm certain it will work, but I wanted to hear how you were feeling this morning." He was beaming as he felt her hand.

"Before we leave, let me give you this book. It's a collection of poetry by Elizabeth Barrett Browning. You mentioned yesterday while thumbing through the bookshelves, how much you enjoy reading her poetry. The book belonged to my mother, and I would like for you to have it because you will treasure it."

"Your gift is special, but this was your mother's."

"I know, she was special, like her books, and you are special."

"Your gift is kind and thoughtful, and I thank you," she said as she touched his arm.

"Are you ready to leave?"

"I'm a bit nervous, but ready to go."

"Don't be...I'll take care of you. The truck is near the back door." In his mind he thought, *strike another one up for her. Going in the truck was a litmus test that added more assurance that Sarah was a genuinely unpretentious lady.*

They exited the house through the kitchen into the garage. This gave Sarah a chance to see other areas of the house that might need redecorating sometime in the future.

She didn't know at the time, but her answer about going in his truck was a benchmark in their relationship. Over the years, many of his female friends had turned up their nose at his request to ride in a pick-up truck. Jim at heart was a humble man who enjoyed the basics of life but knew how to live in the grand scheme his life was giving him now, but that way was rapidly changing. He never forgot his humble training as a child at the hands of his mother and grandparents. With a gleam in his eye, they were off to the city on an adventure that offered individual longings.

With uncertain anticipation, Sarah was somewhat dreading the hour and a half trip, but with conversations and nervous laughter at his funny life experiences, it soon became pleasurable. Thank goodness for Jim's wonderful personality because Sarah's nervousness was slowly fading.

They reminisced about Lucy and Charlie's Mississippi River dinner party. "I'll never forget you and Lucy and the surprised look when I opened the patio door."

"We were both so glad to see you and thanks for walking me around the garden. I can't drink wine on an empty stomach."

"You evidently don't drink much."

"I really don't. I was fascinated with our conversation and should have been snacking on crackers or something. Thanks for taking care of me."

"I will be glad to take care of you anytime. It will always be my pleasure. How was your dinner last night?"

"It was nice. I met my friend Mike at Brown's and had a delicious shrimp pasta dish. Mike is a friend who watched over me from a distance when I was married because he worked with Glenn and knew him well. Mike is my dear friend from that era."

"It's comforting to have caring friends in our lives. Is he your close special friend?" Jim asked with hopes of finding out more about Mike.

"Friends add a special level of contentment to our days. He's a dear friend because I learned to depend on him for honest feelings. We appreciate each other in a friend kind of way."

Their conversations often led into more personal thoughts about a variety of subjects dealing with their lives. Jim thought, *I will tread lightly because this for me is an introduction to someone I want to know on a more intimate level. For now, I don't want to touch on any controversial subjects.* One subject…her husband…almost brought tears to her eyes and a catch in her throat, he noticed. After a somewhat shaky answer, they intuitively in silence agreed not to go there, at least not on this trip.

For Sarah, being with Jim was an introduction into another world. After her painful years of marriage and because of her personal struggle was trying to revitalize her own identity. *I've retreated into a solitary life of the Today Show, a Soap Opera or two and Wheel of Fortune, and at this moment I'm uneasy.* She tried to breathe in a regular rhythm and converse without running her words together in nervous speech. *I'll try to rely on my experience and knowledge as an interior decorator to get me through these first few hours, but what about the hours after this,* she thought.

He sat silently for a while and thought about the things Lucy had told him about Sarah. He sensed the warmth of her gaze and turned to find her eyes locked on him. He saw sadness as she turned away and quickly asked, "What's your favorite color?"

He reached over and patted her arm and said, "Green and tan… how about you?"

"Green and tan with a splash of rusty red."

"It must be the splash that I'm missing, and that's what I need you to help me find." he said with a laugh and rubbed the top of her hand, as he noticed she didn't pull away.

"Our mission will be to find things you need, but also we will search diligently for your splash," Sarah laughed because she realized how she enjoyed his warmhearted personality.

He smiled broadly and touched her arm again and said, "I love a mission." He paused, grasped her fingers, and said, "You might not know, but I served in Vietnam. We went out on missions I wasn't sure I would return from alive. I saw the word mission as a painful word that gave me nightmares. I just realized I said the word in a pleasant way that shocked me. Now with you, I see the word meaning color and excitement, fun new things with a splash."

"The Vietnam era of our country was a frightening time for young men, they never knew when their draft number might be called, and whether being in college would defer them or not. The evening news gave accounts of such dangerous fighting conditions for the soldiers, and CBS sadly gave the death toll for the day. It was a painful time for our generation because friends were going away and not all coming back." Sarah turned to look at Jim and said, "You along with the thousands of others were always in my thoughts. Now we will make the word mission a rewarding adventure."

The phrase, 'you...were always in my thoughts' caused him to take a double take of Sarah. He thought, *no she can't be the girl my mom wrote me about...not the one I fell in love with and searched for, but never found. Her sparkling dark brown eyes and her sweet personality are characteristics my mom mentioned...no it can't be...she's too young and I'm not lucky enough to have the girl of my dreams to just accidentally be sitting next to me like this.* He looked intently at Sarah through glassy eyes and said, "Yes, we will do our best to make this a rewarding adventure."

With a smile on her face, she reached over and nervously patted the seat beside him. "At first, I selfishly wanted this to be a carefree project because of my personal need to break out of my shell, but now I see how this will benefit both of our wishes. You might have to help me because I get uptight and nervous sometime."

"I've noticed... I will help you," Jim said with a smile and briefly held her hand.

She looked at him, smiled and thought, *I didn't realize my nervousness was that obvious. I don't want him to think I'm weak, but I appreciate his awareness and help he's offering.*

The huge furniture store was packed with sofas in a variety of colors and fabrics. She carried the room diagram, furniture list and the green paint chip inside her attaché type satchel, as any efficient decorator on a shopping trip would. Jim recognized her uneasiness the minute they entered the store, he eventually touched her elbow and whispered, "Exhale." He gently squeezed her arm before letting go.

She turned to him, breathed a sigh in response to his observation and smiled. It took her a while to make the transition, but she finally could breathe calmly.

In their search, they came across a beautiful sofa upholstered in deep red chenille. She recognized it instantly as the perfect one. The color was warm, and the fabric was soft to the touch, and perfect for his wish as a possible place to cuddle.

She sat on one end and Jim sat near the middle and they both found it to be the right comfort level. Then suddenly, he kicked off his shoes, threw his heels on the opposite end of the sofa from her and before she knew what was happening had his head in her lap. She threw up her hands as to not touch her client and hang onto a thin thread of the professional decorator look.

"I think this will work. What do you think?" said Jim as he looked into Sarah's eyes.

With hands politely placed on the arm of the sofa and across the back, and with a shocked look, Sarah said in a calm voice, "I think it will work, the color and fabric are perfect, but I don't think the saleslady understands your prankster personality or that we have a bit of a friendship."

With a smile on his face and a slight grin he said "I think this is perfect, too. It feels right."

With a tight lipped, guarded expression on her face, Sarah quietly spoke, "People are beginning to look. I think we need to get up. You know, I'm supposed to be your decorator on a professional level." With a somewhat devilish smile on her face she whispered, "The sales lady is beginning to look at us out of the corner of her eye. She's not sure whether to keep smiling or run. Of course, I'm not sure either…if she runs, maybe I should plan to leave with her."

With a broad smile on his face, he stood and offered his hand for her to rise.

Without his letting go, they walked to the end of the perfect sofa, around a tall display wall, as though he wanted to discuss the sofa, but instead in his excited charm…he stole his first spontaneous kiss from Sarah.

As a heat flushed her face Sarah said with a questioning smile, "Now, what was that for?"

With his charming smile Jim said, "Just because I'm happy, and you're sooo cute when you're serious. Please don't yell at me or run for the door."

As her face blushed and her gorgeous brown eyes sparkled as she smiled that precious tiny smile and said, "I won't run, but you are surprising me."

Sarah had a soothing look on her face as they walked around the wall and Jim with a broad smile said, "I'll take it."

While searching through the store for a matching chair, they rounded a corner and simultaneously spotted the one and only special cuddling chair. She looked into his dancing eyes and he looked at her. Jim knew it was just what he was wanting. The plaid fabric was a medium tone of green and gold with a touch of deep red that matched perfectly with the sofa fabric swatch, but best of all, it was cozily designed for two. With a broad smile, he asked Sarah to sit with him and try it out.

"I'll sit and help you with your decision, but I draw the line at cuddling. That's not in our contract," she said with a quirky smile and squinting eyes.

Jim with an endearing look smiled as he thought of Sarah and her clever remark.

During their investigation of the cuddling chair, their eyes locked and each in their own way knew the chair was the perfect one.

Sarah immediately jumped up and said, "This will work."

Jim jumped up and said, "I think it will work also. We'll take it. I mean, I'll take it."

The sales lady added it to the list.

Later in the afternoon, they found two dark burgundy leather wing chairs and a tapestry covered settee to go on either side of the fireplace for the room's reading and conversation area. This completed their initial shopping list, but as they were searching, they found an additional side table and a large armoire for the television.

By accident they discovered a beautiful large antique English chest, perfect for storage and as a warm accent piece for a couple of wrought iron lamps and a hand-crafted ceramic bowl of silk greenery and fruit. As she visually placed the chest and accessories, she remembered an oil painting of a rural landscape with lambs in the foreground and the herdsman with a touch of deep red in his clothing. *That will be the perfect focal point for that area.* "That will be perfect," she said as she came back to reality.

He, not knowing what she was thinking, responded with, "Perfect" because he felt what was perfect with her was perfect for him.

Jim thought as he looked at Sarah with endearment, *I'm also seeing the room coming together, but I'm seeing other things and the room is the project it's taking to work toward my personal goal of pleasing Sarah to the point that she will consider a friendship.*

"Jim, your excitement for the room is obvious because you're smiling and adding bits of welcomed information to your decorating plan. You often point out paintings you like or a piece of furniture that catches your eye. You have also commented on items for future projects." Sarah thought, *I enjoy his excitement.*

"So, my excitement is obvious."

"Yes, and that adds pleasure to our work," she said as her eyes twinkled.

"It's three-thirty…I'm exhausted and need food. What about you," Jim said.

"There's a steak house close by that serves a variety of meals, if that's alright with you." At the restaurant, they chose to dine in a booth in the bar area. It was quieter and gave them a chance to look over the furniture list and discuss the next step in redecorating. During dinner they laughed and relived the pleasures of their first shopping adventure. Jim enjoyed retelling the story of the stolen kiss.

Sarah smiled broadly as she said, "What made you do that? You caught me by surprise."

"You just looked like you needed to be kissed. You're cute when you're serious, but you're beautiful when you smile. I told you I would help you make this a fun day."

"After the shock…I did smile…and it took away my up-tight feeling. I found myself unexpectedly laughing or smiling at your gallant personality. The entire day has been full of sweet surprises," she said as her smile filled her face and Sarah thought, *he treats me like an old friend, I like that.*

After dinner Sarah gathered her personal items, Jim reached over and took her hand, "Our project has brought welcomed changes to my life for which I'm thankful, and Sarah you're a talented lady and I'm glad you're helping with the project."

She relaxed her hand, placed her other hand over his and looked deep into his eyes. She knew his words were sincere. His expressions of gratitude were obvious, and if she had tried to talk, she might have cried because of the searing flashback of belittling pains from her marriage.

They brought home several of his small accessory finds, but the furniture pieces were scheduled to be delivered in about six weeks. This gave the carpenters and Sarah time to remove a counter that extended into the den, build the wall between the kitchen and den, and install a double French door with a transom…put in new lighting and receptacles, plaster the new wall, and paint the two rooms, and lastly the floors had to be stripped and refinished. Sarah thought, *wow, but I feel sure we can get it done on time.*

Chapter 6

They began working immediately... with Jonathan as lead carpenter, Terry as his assistant and Sarah as flunkey. The first project was to remove the furniture, store usable pieces in the living room and give away a few modern pieces. Several pieces needed to be restored.

Next Sarah packed his books and treasured mementos from the bookshelves. This gave her a view into Jim's past by packing years of Rotary Club appreciation awards and stacks of family genealogy. She noticed in his pictures whether posed or impromptu, Jim was invariably smiling with a pleasing contented look on his face. He was always circled by people young and old and dressed neatly, whether in jeans or a suit and tie.

He seemed to be generous with his time because his awards were for helping the needy in the community. While packing his keepsakes, Sarah smiled because she was mentally building a profile of a valued client, but also a personal image of a compassionate man.

After the third day of demolition, Sarah waited at the house for Jim to come in from work. She needed to inform her client of the progress and describe their plans for the next few weeks. Jim was excited to see her, because until now they had been communicating only by e-mails and an occasional evening phone call.

"I'm glad to see you. This is much better than those e-mail progress reports…even though I do enjoy our occasional evening calls," Jim said as he held her warm hand in a friendly manner and unexpectedly kissed it tenderly.

"You might not enjoy this visit, because we have to talk about paying bills and salaries."

With a smile on his face he said, "I'll enjoy talking about anything with you, my dear."

Sarah smiled outwardly, but her heart was pounding. All day she had been concerned about this face-to-face meeting. What would she do if Jim showed disappointment with the job?

They walked into the den, and with noticeable jitters in her voice, she pointed out the position of several pot light fixtures needed above the television and bookcase areas.

For almost an hour they moved around the room, as she described changes, furniture placement and colors. He followed closely and occasionally brushed against Sarah during their client-decorator waltz. He seemed to be exceptionally pleased with everything and Sarah was thankful.

At the table in the breakfast room, they discussed paying Jonathan and Terry, several tickets to Lowe's and a bill from the local hardware store. Everything was agreeable and easy to explain.

"I'm always nervous about talking over bills and payments with a client, but this has been a pleasure. Jonathan and Terry are excited about the job and look forward to meeting you."

At the end of their meeting, she gathered her papers, filed them away in her leather bag and started to rise. Jim immediately stood and asked if she could stay longer. "Maybe to talk about a…" He couldn't think fast enough to come up with the cleverest or most unpretentious reason for her to stay. He reached his hand with thoughts of grasping her arm, but that would scare her off. He let his arm fall to his side. He thought of begging, but the right thought wouldn't come. He fumbled miserably with words, so he lightly held her elbow as he walked her out the back door, through the rose garden toward the courtyard beside the carriage house.

"The roses smell sweet this evening," she said.

"It's their first flourish of blooms, so I guess they're putting on a show and it could be the early heat we're having this week that's brought out their fragrance. I have the clippers in the tool shed, and a jar, let me give you a bouquet of roses to take home."

"Thank you, that's so special."

When they reached her vehicle, parked beside the carriage house, Sarah reached out to shake her client's hand, he took hold of it and held it as he blurted out in a stammering schoolboy voice, "You always hug Jonathan, Terry and all your friends when you say goodbye to them. What about me, I'm your friend, aren't I?"

"We are friends through Carrie and Lucy, but at this point you're my client first. I know I'm not charging you for helping…because we are acquainted, but we have to treat our work relationship in a professional way."

"I really would like to be your friend first."

She smiled and said, "In time. Just leave the checks on the breakfast room table and I'll take care of everything. Thanks. I'll see you next week after you return from your trip. I'll make sure the house is locked and our trash is cleaned up when we leave on Friday. Have fun. Bye now."

"Why don't you come with me?"

With a broad beaming expression Sarah dropped her shoulders and said, "You know I can't do that…I barely know you, and besides, I have laundry to finish and Bob would miss me."

As she closed the door and cranked her car he questioned loudly, "Who the heck is Bob?"

Unable to hear the question, she shifted the vehicle into reverse and with a smile on her face, looked him square in the eyes, and waved bye as she backed into the turn-around area and drove down the drive.

Sarah was enamored by his friendliness but was fearful of a relationship, especially a work-related relationship. *What if he's fooling me like my husband did…I must be with Jim enough to see his reactions in a lot of situations before I ever consider more than this*, Sarah thought.

"Is she playing hard to get and is she serious about our client relationship. I wanted her help so we could develop a friendship…I didn't think it would be just business. I really wish I didn't have this blasted trip. I need to be close by her. Who is Bob? I thought I knew everything about her," he said out loud, as he hung his head and slowly stumbled into the house. "I just can't stand the idea of her spending the weekend with someone."

As Jim finished packing, he kept replaying their conversation and tried to think what he could do next and questioned himself as to why he didn't know about Bob.

"I'll call her often, maybe every hour. That will really mess up their weekend. No that's childish. Maybe I'll just call the house phone by mistake, and maybe he will answer, then I can find out a little about this fellow. I just wish I didn't have to go away," he said as he closed the suitcase and stuffed his airline e-tickets into his carryon bag. Before he walked out the door, he scribbled a construction note to Sarah and left it neatly tucked under the coffee canister.

As soon as Sarah arrived at home, she went to the utility shed to dip a bowl of dry dog food for her trusted friend. Her plan was to finish her outside chores, go inside for a long bath, and put on her favorite silk pj's and rest. The cell phone rang, and she looked and saw it was Jim. "What are you doing?" he said.

"I'm getting things ready for Bob."

"You didn't waste any time," he said. "Do you have time to talk to me?"

"Yes, you're the client. Hold on a minute, I've got to finish this and then we can talk."

His thoughts were raging as he imagined what she might be doing, while he waited.

She gathered her things and started talking as she looked at the wilting pot plants.

"I just thought about the check for the hardware store, I can deliver it when I get back, so just leave it on the table," he said.

"I will be glad to do that."

"Well, I guess I need to let you get back to Bob."

"That's ok...I'm through with him for the night."

"Gee, you're fast."

"Well sometimes it really doesn't take long."

His mind was thinking things he couldn't say. He thought *if I could be alone with her, I would treat her in a way she would want to be with me for hours, even days, hopefully a lifetime. Bob and Mike, these old friends from her past would soon be no competition at all.* He knew he was nearing the autumn of his years, but he was ready to put forth his best effort for Sarah.

"Well, I have to go. The checks are on the table, and I'm leaving now."

"Did you remember to pack the rain jacket you said you might need?"

"No, I didn't. Let me go back. Thanks for reminding me. Call if you have any questions, and I'll call often to find out about the construction. Have a great evening and I look forward to talking to you soon."

"Thank you for the roses and take care." Sarah found a small crystal vase, arranged the roses, and placed it on the kitchen window shelf. The fragrance immediately brought a smile to her face and she dropped her tense shoulders and whispered, "Thank you Jim."

As she laid the mail on her desk, she noticed the home repair magazine "This Old House" and thumbed through it as she poured a glass of Chardonnay. She meandered into the den to relax in her cozy recliner while she thumbed through the magazine.

It eventually collapsed into her lap as her thoughts of the day replayed in her mind. She mentally built the kitchen wall according to the plans she and Jonathan had discussed. She found a note pad on her side table and made a list of sub-contractors she needed to call. She also listed Jonathan, because she had to add some additional things to the supply list for Monday.

Sarah finished the wine, refilled her glass, and headed for her bedroom with visions of a warm bath in her Victorian claw foot bathtub. She started to unbutton her shirt and unfasten her belt and jeans. She unlaced her work boots and slowly undressed as visions of Jim flashed into her thoughts…*I wonder what he's thinking about tonight.* She gathered her silk pajamas from the dresser drawer along with a soft cotton washcloth and towel. She turned on the warm bath water and dribbled a lavender fragranced oil and bubble bath into the water. The scent permeated the room.

Soaking in the warm bubbly waters of the old, restored bathtub and sipping on the wine, her body relaxed as her thoughts drifted to Jim. She recalled the caring expressions he made that afternoon. She thought about all the times his hand slipped down her arm and squeezed her fingers as he approved of her construction and decorating plans. She thought of the times his hand rested on her shoulder, and how she was glad to let him rest it there.

Her body shuddered and a hot sensation switched rapidly through her midsection, and she felt a twinge of guilt, which was overcome by a slow physical response to the warm fragrant bath water and her thoughts turned to pleasure. Sarah finished her glass of wine and thought of how *I didn't pull away from him and his warm fingers felt good next to my skin.*

She said aloud, "I miss his touch, but I will use discreet judgement, and not totally discourage his charms. I haven't overcome my past. The pain from my husband's abuse haunts me and causes an unsure feeling. I'm working at getting past those feelings, but until then it would be unfair to befriend someone when my emotions are not settled."

Sarah applied her nightly face and body creams and dressed for bed. She wrapped herself in a warm chenille robe and imagined things which she quickly abandoned and tramped off to the kitchen for a bowl of Cheerios and milk. *He is my client I must remember that* she mumbled with tender regrets.

* * *

As Sarah parked beside the carriage house, she grew anxious about cutting off the counter-top and building the wall. The first thing Sarah saw when she entered the kitchen was an envelope Jim left. When she saw it was address to her, things started to run through her mind on what could be written inside. She slowly traced its edges and opened it to find a sweet note thanking Sarah for taking a strong interest in the renovation project. He mentioned how her concern had given a purpose in his life and added excitement to his day. He wrote, how at his age, he had almost given up having an honest true friendship and finding rewarding enjoyment in life. He signed it thank you my friend. Sarah rubbed her forehead and smiled as she said, "You're note is sweet and comforting." Jonathan unexpectedly entered the kitchen, erasing her tender moment.

After measuring, Jonathan and Terry painstakingly popped a chalk line on the Corian kitchen countertop as Jonathan prepared to cut the line. After cleaning the debris, they built the stud wall separating the kitchen from the den. Sarah was excited to see the wall roughed in because it gave her a defining line between the rooms.

By Friday afternoon the crew had diligently completed most of their list. Terry and Jonathan had worked nonstop running electrical wire for the new pot lights, the television viewing area, and for new receptacles in the kitchen. Terry made several trips underneath the house to locate electrical, telephone and satellite feeds and installed the appropriate receptacles. "Jim will appreciate this…I know the cook will," Terry said as he brushed the dirt off his jeans.

Sarah was busy removing debris from the work area with thoughts of Jim and wondering what he must be doing. She saw a shadow cross in front of the kitchen window and realized an unfamiliar face was approaching the door. She immediately went to find a handsome young man reaching for the doorbell. She opened it and said, "Hello."

"Hello, I'm David…Jim's son."

"Please come in."

"I was out in the shop working and saw the trucks here. Dad has spoken often about the plans y'all have made. If it's no problem, I'd like to look."

"Sure, glad you stopped. I'll be glad to show you," Sarah said as she wiped her dirty hands on her jeans and reached out to shake his hand. "I'm Sarah. This is Jonathan and Terry. We can go in the den and I can point out things."

"This new wall area will be the only new construction. The remainder of the project will be refurbishing and redecorating. In this area your dad liked the idea of a double French door with a transom, like the ones going out onto the porch. Plaster will be applied to the wall in the same pattern as the existing walls and then painted your dad's favorite color, a medium shade of green. The bookshelves and trim will get a facelift with a coat of mat polyurethane and the floors will be sanded and varnished." Sarah moved about the room as she pointed to the different areas.

David was intrigued by her explanations of the improvements and was quick to say, "I like the plan. I remember my mom never liked having to clean the kitchen after dinner because some of us were always in here trying to watch television or listen to music."

"Well, this will solve that. It will give a wall for the television/music area and over by the bookshelves and fireplace will be another conversation area with a small sofa and chairs."

"…and a game area?"

"Yes, in that far corner, your dad specified that for the children and his brother's weekends, for card playing gatherings, and puzzles. The new moldings will be made to match the original trim. Any new furnishings will be antiques or fine quality reproductions. Your dad wanted to keep the integrity of the house and I think well of someone who appreciates the historic value of an older home."

"It sounds as though the house is in good hands."

Sarah smiled an exhausted smile as she said, "I hope we please your dad with the new improvements by making it look like the changes have been here for years. In the kitchen, the walls will be painted along with refinishing the floors."

"I'm looking forward to seeing the finished touches. Thank you for showing me around, I don't want to stop you, I'm sure you're trying to get things finished for the week. Can I help you with that bag of trash?"

"Sure, I'll get this two by four."

Sarah was impressed by David and his kind generous nature. As she waved bye to him, she thought, *he has a considerate heart like his dad.*

Before leaving for the day, the den wall was framed, and the electrical wiring was run to most areas. This was only the beginning of the project, but Sarah could already see it taking shape like she had planned. I think Jim will be pleased with the changes.

* * *

David's sister, Helen took a slight detour and stopped by his house for a visit. Her main reason for stopping was to find out what their dad was doing to the house. She wanted to know if David knew how much money was being spent and what was their dad's reason for suddenly wanting the house renovated?

David couldn't answer the questions because he had not talked in depth with his dad. He knew some of the work needed to be done and walling off the kitchen was something his parents had talked about for years until their mom got sick.

"I just can't understand why. I hope he hasn't met someone and is planning to get married. That's our inheritance and not for some young bimbo," Helen said with contempt spewing with every word. "I know things haven't been the best for us since mom died, but I won't stand silently and watch him throw away what's rightly ours."

"Well dad has always been forthcoming so, maybe the construction will give you a reason to stop by and see what's going on, but I'll keep my ears and eyes open."

"When I have time, I'll call you. I'm not sure I want to face him alone after all that's happened."

"You have to forget about that and erase it from your mind. It looks as though the foreman the crew and dad are being considerate of the history of the home."

"Great, let me go. How's your family."

"We're fine just working all the time."

"I know the feeling."

* * *

As soon as Sarah took care of Bob, she walked through the yard and noticed the roses blooming on the far side of the patio. The blooms were deep red, one of her favorite colors. She also admired the pots of colorful impatiens along the retainer wall. She stopped in place and sat in a comfortable chair, as her eyes were drawn to a light blue sky mixed with cerulean with billowing white clouds, with highlighted streaks of yellow, orange, and red clouds that led her to a colorful sunset.

She rubbed her faithful friend's ears as she pulled him close, and confided, "There's something about this sunset that reminds me of Jim…It must be the peacefulness." She made a promise, "I will enjoy more evenings before hurrying inside. The stress of my previous years caused me to forget to stop and enjoy the natural serenity before my eyes."

"It's been a long week for my aging muscles and painful arthritis...I can't resist a glass of wine along with a warm penetrating soak in the bathtub. It's been a long time since I've been so involved with construction. My thigh muscles and lower back pain me." As she slipped into the sultry hot fragrant water and covered herself in bubbles, she found her oasis for deep meditation. The wine also helped her relax as her thoughts drifted to visions of pleasure.

Sarah had lounged in her bath for almost a half hour when her cell phone rang. Her racing thoughts said *I know that's Jim*. Then she let her mind go blank. *I'm letting myself become controlled by my wishes*, but this time it was Jim.

In the hotel gift shop, he was looking at an urn in the color of the sofa and wanted to know if it would work in the room.

"I'm sure it will. We can use it on the shelves or on top of the armoire along with other ceramic accessories. I'm proud of you. You're getting into our project. I mean your project."

"No, it's our project. I couldn't do this without you to encourage and advise me."

"I'm always glad to help," Sarah said.

"It seems my thoughts are on things at home more than on where I am. I really miss you and our project."

"We're working and things are looking great. Jonathan and I have been working late getting things ready for the next day. I look forward to your return, but for now enjoy your trip."

"I'm at the counter now to purchase the vase. Let me take care of this and I'll talk to you later this evening."

Soon the phone rang again, and Sarah expected Jim, but this time it was Mike calling to find out how Sarah was since their dinner. He was in good spirits because he had requested and received a plant transfer to the Atlanta area, to become effective by the end of the month.

Mike was such a caring person who deserved to move up in the company. She thought, *he is an important part of my life, and I will miss him.*

Mike suggested, "Why don't we go out for dinner? I've enjoyed your friendship and would like to spend time with you. It might be a while before I can make it back this way."

"I would like that. I have always valued your friendship and I will miss our occasional dinners out." Sarah explained she was working and could only plan on the spur of the moment.

"Spur of the moment is fine. My evenings are spent packing, so call anytime."

"I will…hope it will be this week. I'm working on a fantastic project and would like to share. Will talk soon."

After a few sips of chardonnay, her body conformed to thoughts other than construction while she soaked for another few minutes. She imagined she was about to bloom and gladly leave behind the Soaps and Wheel of Fortune. She was beginning to laugh, notice sunsets and wish.

She gracefully climbed out of the tub, dressed in her pj's, and went into the den to complete the list of materials for Jonathan to pick up, for installing the sheetrock. After the sheetrock, they would prep the den side of the wall for the plaster crew by attaching wire. After the walls were finished the French doors would be delivered and installed. Sarah felt pleased with their plan.

She soon fell asleep in her chair while watching 'Casablanca' on TCM. She woke in a drowsy state of mind and made her way to the bedroom. She crawled into bed, snuggled under layers of soft covers, and felt warm and relaxed…her cell phone rang. She checked and saw it was Jim.

His first question was "Are you asleep?"

"I'm in bed, but not fully asleep."

"Great, tell me about your evening, did you go out to dinner or something," he said.

"There's not much to tell. My friend Mike called and wants to go out to dinner soon. I ate a bowl of cereal and read a few chapters of a book."

"Is that all?" Jim said with wonder.

"I took a long warm bath and fell asleep in my chair. I just came to bed. I have an exciting life."

"Did you take care of Bob and please don't tire yourself out staying late with Jonathan or with Mike."

"We played around a little, but what are you doing?"

He could hardly answer her question as he thought about her playing around with Bob. "We had an exciting day. I'll have to tell you about it when I get home. The guys are planning to go out tonight, but I'm not sure I want to go. I think I might enjoy lying in bed and imagine what's going on at home. You know I'm not as young as most of the guys on the trip."

"But you're young at heart. Everything is fine here…go and enjoy yourself. We will have plenty to talk about on Monday. Did you get the urn?"

"Yes, they packaged it for next day arrival and sent it out this evening. I wanted you to receive it before I got home."

"I look forward to finding a prominent spot. I'm proud of you."

"It's the first decorative item I've selected on my own in my entire life. I've learned a lot from you. When I saw it, I felt sure it would work, but I wanted to check with you first."

"That's exciting to hear you talk about the urn. It will become a special memory." When Sarah used the words special memory, her mind reflected to what Carrie had always told her *to make special memories as you travel through life*. Sarah realized *she had used the term to describe a memory she was making with Jim*. Her face took on a warm glow that quickly spread to her toes.

"I will be back on Sunday afternoon. If it's ok, I'd love to come by for a while and we can talk about the den."

With a slight hesitation Sarah said, "Call me when you leave Savannah, and we'll see."

That one phrase "call me" was like music to his ear. It made him feel that she wanted to see him at a time other than when they're in the middle of a construction problem. "Good night my dear…I'll talk to you soon," he said.

"Good night to you and go have fun," Sarah said knowing her heart was melting.

As soon as she clicked the phone off, Sarah thought, *how I miss Jim and enjoy talking with him*. The picture of him that popped into her mind was of his smiling face and then she smiled. Pleasant feelings filled her thoughts and she slowly drifted into sleep.

As he clicked off, he said forcibly, "Wow, sounds like a lot has been happening with Sarah while I've been gone. I sure don't want to play nice guy too long and let Mike or Jonathan move in and take her, I wish I were at home, where I should be. And then there's Bob."

* * *

During the weekend, Jim called five times on Saturday, plus one late night call and three times on Sunday morning before his plane left for Savannah. She told him he could come by on his way home, but at seven, she had a meeting. She really didn't...it was just her way of being cautious. It was her innate fear of being alone with him inside of her house that made her feel uneasy. The panic subsided as she thought of the unimaginable story, she had to tell Jim.

Jim stopped by Sarah's, knowing he could stay for only an hour. He didn't want to hold her up from her meeting.

"How was your trip?"

Knowing how much he cared for Sarah, he responded with, "It could have been better."

"Maybe next time..."

"I'm going to count on that," he said with honesty.

"I have some wonderful news for you," she said. "The vase arrived and it's perfect." Her excitement made her glow.

With his exhilaration he was overjoyed to see her excitement, he approached her, placed both hands on her hips, and she almost reached up to his shoulders, but they both withdrew their arms before committing to a hug. They walked into her kitchen.

"Come sit at the kitchen table. Can I get you a cup of coffee or a glass of sweet tea or something?"

Jim was fascinated with her country farmhouse. It was immaculate just as he imagined. The painted kitchen cabinets had a warm aged look, and the green soapstone counter tops were clutter free with only a few tasteful accessories. The painted beaded board backsplash with under cabinet lighting added drama to the French country kitchen.

The walls held original art works which he found out later Sarah had painted...nothing was ostentatious...everything was just elegant and simple. A few antique china serving pieces were used in wrought iron plate holders on the wall between the upper and lower cabinets on either side of the Viking gas range. Oriental patterned china was displayed behind glass door cabinets. The dishes were painted in shades of green and gold with a hint of rust...he recognized all her favorite colors.

He peered into the sitting room as his eyes were led from the kitchen by the beautiful wood floors and striking oriental rugs. He noticed a sofa and several comfortable chairs and a floor to ceiling wall of books. His first thought was, wow, *a woman as intelligent as Sarah probably knows the majority of everything in every book on that wall.*

She interrupted his thought by saying, "I also have a coke and sparkling water."

He jumped as he was jarred into reality. "Water, plain water will be fine and can we tour your house. It's fascinating."

The bedroom was decorated with warm fabric colors of rusty red, brown, and gold. He noticed the calmness of the room as soon as they entered. He wasn't sure what gave him that feeling, maybe the soft colors or the fragrance of a woman, but a sense of warmness came over him. "I like this room," he said with a feeling of comfort. He had often thought of Sarah's home and imagined it would be homey and unpretentious with a mix of antique furnishings...he found that to be true.

"I brought you a little something I also found at the gift shop. I thought it would be something you would appreciate," Jim said as he removed a tissue wrapped gift from his jacket pocket.

"It's perfect. This shade of the wood is exactly right for my office. You must come and look. I love containers and wooden boxes are my favorite."

They went into the office and she removed a piece from atop of a bow front oak chest and replaced it with the wooden box. "Perfect, I can look at it while I work. Thank you."

"Of all the pieces in the shop, I chose the perfect gift for such a special one as you."

Sarah unthinkingly placed her left hand on his back near his shoulder and in her tranquil daze was about to hug him in appreciation of his kindness but stopped and retreated before his arms completely wrapped around her. They both stepped back. She dropped her head, tightened her shoulders, "To change the subject, I discovered something today."

Sarah had some exciting news for him. She had stayed for dinner after church and had made a wonderful discovery while she was talking with her friend Lila who turned out to be a mutual friend with Jim and his deceased wife Ann. Lila talked about how she had worked with them on projects for the community and about Jim's patriotism. She mentioned that Jim had served his country in the Vietnam War. She described him as kind, generous and always with a smile on his face. The descriptive words she used were the same words Sarah had used to characterize his nature. When Sarah heard her friend speak of Jim the same as she…her heart found favor in Jim, and a smile grew across her lips.

Lila also told her about Jim's mother working as manager of a department store on the same street as a store where Sarah had first worked. After hearing more information about her, Sarah remembered that around nineteen sixty-six, when she first married, she had gone into the store many times and talked often with the kindest lady. Her skin was smooth, the color of fresh cream dotted with freckles. Her long straight reddish-brown hair was gathered into a ponytail at her neck, tied with a thin ribbon. Her clothes were simple, always neat, and immaculate. She always greeted Sarah with a smile and soft words. She was kind, generous and lovely. Sarah's heart warmed and almost jumped out of her chest when she realized she had known Jim's mother so long ago. Sarah equated the mother and son's personalities as being much alike.

"I made a discovery today," she said to Jim.

"What kind of discovery?"

"We can go back in the kitchen and sit if that's ok. Today I talked to a lady who is a mutual friend with the two of us and she gave me background information about you."

"Oh no, am I in trouble," he said with a catching smile.

"No, not at all," Sarah said with a warm smile. "It's the sweetest story. Her description of you seems to be right on target with my thoughts of you. She used the same words I would have used," Sarah said with a gentle smile on her face. She reached out and held his wrist as her lower lip quivered for a second.

"So, I'm not in trouble," he said as he took her hand from his wrist and laced his fingers into her fingers.

"No. I just wanted to tell you how special you are. I was talking to my friend Lila about helping with your project. Lila said, 'Oh let me tell you about Jim.' She said you had served a tour of duty in Vietnam and how you are a God-fearing American who loves his country. That's a real compliment as well as reassurance to me to have a friend from your past speak of you so admirably. You have made quite an impression on people. Your character ranks high among those who know you."

He leaned forward, massaged her arm, "Tell me more." His lips parted slightly as his gentle eyes looked upon her captivating expression.

"There was another discovery," she said.

"Is it as good as the last discovery?"

"It's shockingly better."

He stole a kiss from the top of her hand as he tried to sooth her emotions, he said, "Tell me more."

"About forty years ago when I got married and came to live in this area, I needed to find a job soon, because the rent had to be paid. I applied and got a job at a department store and I came to know many of the people who lived and worked in the area. My friend Lila, who was telling me all this managed a clothing store on the same block. She told me about a beautiful lady who was the manager of a store on the same street. I searched my brain and put a face and a memory with the description."

"She was the kindest lady I had ever known and soon befriended me, I loved her, and treasured the moments we spent talking about her family and the hardships she had triumphed over. That beautiful lady was your mother. I knew her and I knew about her son in Vietnam, but I didn't know it was you until I listened to Lila's story. I knew about you forty something years ago." Sarah's voice quivered and her eyes glazed over."

Jim rose from his chair and slowly moved to the island and Sarah followed. He reached out and took her hands as he eased her next to him. He took one hand to his heart and the other to touch away a wayward tear that hung on his cheek as he looked closely at her beautiful dark brown eyes.

Sarah looked at Jim with empathetic questioning as his tears began to form. She touched them away.

"I loved my mother and she loved me as well as her other boys. My mother did have some rough times making ends meet while my Dad was off in the service and eventually met his fate in France. Forty years ago, that would have been in the mid-sixties…I was a misplaced farm boy in Vietnam. My mom wrote to me often and told me about the world back home. Now let me tell you a shocking story that I just realized." He gripped her hands tighter and pulled her closer to him.

"I remember her telling me about a little, brown-eyed girl who came by to visit her at the store. She described her as tiny with dark eyes, short dark brown hair and short skirts to match," he said with a sweet smile. "She described her as shy, kind and talented…with a heart of gold."

Sarah quickly touched away her tears. She lowered her head and concentrated on life forty years ago.

"That person was you. You're my little, brown-eyed girl she loved and adored, and the one I also grew to love through the words in her letters. Each day when I went out to face the enemy, thoughts of you kept me focused and strong. You're the one who kept me sane in such an insane world, and I had a desire to get home and find you, but when I asked my mom, she said you had moved away, and she had no idea where or even your last name. She also told me you were married, but she could see the hope I had for life because of you, so she couldn't tell me anything different. She had to keep the hope alive. Thoughts of you saved me. The way I would describe you today this moment is the same way my mother described you forty years ago. She loved you…I loved you and carried her words in my heart…strong for years, as I looked for the vision, I had of you. It has taken forty years, and today through an unbelievable chain of events, you're beside me," Jim said with deep emotion.

Sarah reached quickly to retrieve a tissue. Tears were streaming down her face. She thought W*hat would the last forty years of my life been like if I had been able to meet this kind man when he returned from Vietnam.* Sarah's thoughts went on hold as she realized she had to handle her feelings.

They reached for each other…Sarah rested her face into the cradle of his neck to contain herself. He wrapped his arms around her, and they lovingly held each other. No words were spoken…no words were needed.

He breathed softly beside her ear as his lips traced its delicate cartilage shell. His arms retraced the strength of her back and held her feather light body as though he were caressing a welcomed gift.

She easily conformed to him and adapted to the structure his body was requesting. The oxygen was depleted from her lungs and her brain was in a daze. Through blurry eyes she saw the image of the man she had yearned for and had often wished could be in her life. This was a dream come true, for she was sure her soulmate had found her.

Jim knew he had found the one he had never forgotten and always wished to be his own.

Her thoughts were saying, *I could hold you forever and never let you go.*

He whispered into her ear, "I love holding you, but I don't want you to be late. I just wanted to see you." Jim exhaled deeply. "And I'm glad I came…I had no idea this would happen." He stroked her hair away from her concerned brown eyes and slipped the back of his hand down her face and they shared a warm gentle un-stolen kiss. "I'm so glad I found my little, brown-eyed girl and I will never let you slip away from me again."

Her thoughts of reality were revitalizing, but she wanted to remain in the dream. "I'm happy, also. This has been an unbelievable discovery. We have been close and didn't know it. I care for you as a special friend."

"I loved you long before I met you." He exhaled against her neck, "I'm not sure what to do next, but I feel I must go…I want to be with you, but I want to search for the letters my mother wrote. I want you to read her feelings of you."

"I would love that. I cared dearly for her. She was a fine lady and I always looked forward to our talks," Sarah said as she unconsciously stroked the soft fabric of his shirt.

"Sarah, I have looked at you on many occasions and thought is this my brown-eyed girl, the one I was searching for. Your eyes, your personality, and that day you said, 'you thought of the ones in Vietnam,' all of that came from my mother's letters. I told myself it couldn't be, I wasn't fortunate enough to have something that outrageously spectacular happen to me, but it did. Bless you, my dear friend," Jim mumbled as he eased her close and gently kissed her parted lips.

"Jim, I really don't have a meeting, I was fearful of being alone with you, but this has turned out to be the best moments. I can't believe how, so long ago, our relationship was beginning and now, how unrelated circumstances have brought us together."

"I will never forget this moment. I want you forever. I really must be going...my emotions are stirring out of control...I must go."

"Will you stay longer...I have warm pound cake and coffee."

"I can't say no to that," Jim said as he smiled.

They laughed and retold bits of the story. They each realized in their own way how this moment has strengthened their care for the other. Jim took her hand, leaned back in his chair, and smiled as he shook his head in disbelief that this truth in their friendship had come forward in a beautiful way. Silently they touched and treasured the moment.

"I'll find the letters, maybe tonight." With uncontrollable excitement Jim embraced Sarah and smiled at the discovery they had made. He insisted she must come early the next morning for coffee, so they could talk.

Sarah reached for him as he turned, *I don't want you to go*. She lowered her head and cried soft tears as the door closed. She found it hard to believe what had just happened. "Our love for each other started a long time ago, and now the kind words he said showed that the care he had for me then is still in his heart. He has touched my heart and soul in an overwhelming way." Tears of need and trust for Jim filled her and she burst forth with sobbing desires.

Tears of anger came next for the loss of years, spent with her selfish heartless husband. Then joy flooded her eyes for the closeness this friendship could bring. She was thankful for the transition her heart was feeling and knew she could see a glimmer of hope for her future.

Chapter 7

Jim called Lucy. "On my way home, I stopped by Sarah's. She knew my mother back in the mid-sixties and the ironic thing is my Mom wrote me letters while I was in Vietnam about a brown-eyed girl and it was Sarah she was talking about, but neither of us knew this until now. I've searched for her for about forty years and now we've miraculously found each other. We must have another supper or something. She keeps talking about some guy named Mike. I need to be with Sarah. I'm almost in tears with excitement, and my heart has been stirred by her sweetness."

"It is your heart?"

"It is. I care for her."

"Let's just plan for Sarah to come to the cay on Friday and you just drop by. I'll ask Carrie and Ben to come over."

"Thank you, cuz for your help."

Lucy called Sarah to invite her to Barefoot Cay for a relaxing weekend. "Carrie and Ben can come for dinner on Friday night and we can teach you to play Pinochle."

Sarah was excited because she enjoyed Lucy and Charlie and of course Carrie and Ben.

On Friday afternoon, Sarah dressed in her favorite jeans, cotton shirt and flip-flops, and headed to the cay with thoughts of a great weekend. She packed a few comfortable clothes along with a bag of snack foods. At the last minute, she threw in a few rib sticking foods because sometimes Lucy didn't like to cook. Often it was up to Sarah and Charlie to prepare the food, and up to Lucy to keep the refreshments flowing.

Sarah arrived around three o'clock and was looking forward to being with her friends. Charlie as always was looking forward to seeing Sarah. He and Lucy had helped to rebuild Sarah's self-confidence through their friendship, but it was her youthfulness that was refreshing to Charlie. He also treasured her soft-spoken ways, and Sarah often sensed his caring friendship.

The cay was a quiet place at the end of a wooded lane on the Savannah River. Charlie and Lucy had relocated there after they retired and wanted to settle into an area near Savannah. Lucy wanted to be near the excitement of the city for cultural events, but in a slow relaxed area that fit her take-it-easy lifestyle. She had family nearby, so they loved the familiar location.

Charlie occasionally enjoyed fishing on the river or a meandering boat ride especially at the changing of the seasons. He was always busy repairing loose ends around the house or helping his neighbors.

After unpacking her favorite river clothing, she went into the kitchen to help with making snacks or supper plans. Lucy had already put a seasoned pork loin into the oven.

"Hello dear, you can mix the raspberry dressing for the salad if you would like. The recipe and ingredients are on the counter next to the frig," Lucy said.

"I love raspberry dressing," as she searched the cabinet for a bowl and whisk.

After checking the loin, Lucy mixed a pitcher of lemonade and added a generous amount of Rum. Charlie popped the top on another Bud and headed outside. After finishing their dinner preparations, the girls took the lemonade and snacks, and meandered to the rocking chairs on the second-floor porch facing a small marsh area next to the untamed Savannah River.

Sarah enjoyed the pleasant fragrance of the springtime air, and the sound of the flowing water. A cool breeze was blowing off the river which circulated the warm air. The trees were swaying gently, and leaves were blowing onto the water and floating away like little sail boats marching in a parade. The scent of Cardinal flowers occasionally drifted through and tickled their noses.

"Look, the hummingbirds are zipping through the wildflowers," Lucy said as she placed the tray of refreshments on the wicker table.

As they enjoyed their refreshing lemonade, they talked about Jim's decorating project. Lucy asked about Sarah's social life in hopes she would mention someone. She spoke of having dinner with an old friend and that's all it seemed to be. Her excitement about Jim and the project was continually on her mind.

With ease Sarah asked, "Will you tell me about Jim's family and the history of the estate. To sit and enjoy the flavorful lemonade, talking about him is the best feeling." Sarah's glowing expression was evident that thinking of Jim created feelings of excitement as she masked a shiver that stimulated her womanly body.

Ben and Charlie were busy on the boat ramp cleaning up after the last storm. They worked and reworked the same troubled area. Maybe the beer and the fact of just being with a friend helped them enjoy the nonproductive time they spent together.

It was six before Carrie arrived. She brought chips and mango salsa tastefully seasoned with cilantro. Within the hour the first pitcher of lemonade was empty, and they eagerly enjoyed the second one, and it wasn't long before they were beginning to feel relaxed. They were laughing at how the guys were acting like Amos and Andy trying to regulate the chains on the boat lift. Lucy, Carrie, and Sarah were enjoying being together.

They heard a vehicle door slam. Lucy looked around and said, "There's Jim."

Sarah looked at Lucy with a surprised look...put her hand to her mouth, but no words came out. Her eyes did the talking and the smile that appeared beneath her fingers were words enough.

Lucy smiled and winked.

Carrie said, "What are you two smiling about."

Lucy and Sarah stood up. Lucy put her arms around her and said, "You're beautiful, I love you. Enjoy yourself."

Carrie stood and they hugged joyously.

The guys looked up and Charlie said, "What are you girls doing all hugging each other. Don't you know you have men down here for that?

"Sometimes we girls just need to hug," Carrie suddenly said.

"I think they've had too much to drink," said Ben.

Charlie commented, "They might be sloshed. We might have to cook our own supper.

Jim let me get you something from the cooler down here, and the girls can do their own thing up there."

"I think I might like what the girls are having. Just kidding, I'll take a bottle of water for now," he said with an admiring laugh and a lingering stare.

Still in a girl's hug, Sarah looked down at Jim and waved. He waved and watched a few seconds longer, and with a beaming smile shook his head and walked over to the guys.

Later, the men came upstairs to check on dinner. Lucy said the pork loin would be ready in about thirty minutes. The salad was made, and the green beans were cooking.

"Yep, I see someone who might need a walk in the garden," Jim said as he reached his hand to Sarah. "Come here to me, my brown-eyed girl."

She took his hand and rose. He slipped his arm around her waist and she quickly circled his nearest shoulder and folded her hands-on top. He pulled her to his side with a tight hug. Sarah felt comfortable and relaxed willingly into his hold.

She looked at him and said, "I think I do need one of your walks."

Jim pulled her to him again.

"You guys go…supper should be ready in about thirty minutes."

He wrapped her tightly at her waist and Sarah held to the stair rail as they made their way down the steep porch steps. As soon as Lucy and Carrie were inside, Carrie said, "Dang, what's going on with Sarah and Jim?"

"Jim has a keen interest in Sarah. He's trying to go slow because of what Sarah has been through, but from the looks of things Sarah is falling for him. Jim has promised he has settled down and ready for a mature relationship."

Carrie mused, "Sarah needs an honest caring companion. I hope Jim understands her…treats her fair and doesn't push her into something."

* * *

Sarah whispered, "I didn't know you would be here tonight. I'm not sure my condition will make a pleasing impression to my dear client-friend."

He was pleased to have Sarah in his arms. "There's and old saying that someone who has had a drink will speak what a sober person thinks. Maybe I can take advantage of this and find out how you really feel about me," He jokingly said as he squeezed her side, and she moved against him.

"I really think you're an inventive gentleman. I sincerely like working on your project and I enjoy all those charming little things you say to me. Oops, I've said too much too fast. I really didn't want you to know how I admire you because you are my client first."

"Do you really mean all that? Did you know I was enjoying being with you," he said as he tugged at her waist?

"Yes, I know, and I enjoy it," she said as she eased her arm around him but stopped to compose herself and remember their working relationship.

Jim spread his hand wide on her mid-section, grasped her undershirt and her top shirt beneath her breast. He held her beside him, as they walked along. "You're the sweetest…you smell so good," he said as he lightly leaned his head against her.

They walked hand in hand along the companion way and turned to catch a glimpse of the setting sun. Jim leaned against the dock railing as he rested his hands on her hips and looked at Sarah with admiring eyes as he wrapped his arms round her in a protective way.

The marsh waters became dark and reflected the setting sun like a tropical mirror. The grasses were swaying as the waters pushed in for high tide. They watched the evening colors fade into a dark blue gray sky, and their mood became melancholy.

"A tropical storm is blowing in, and it will be a stormy night. You're warm, but the breeze is cool out by the water."

The palm and live oak trees began to sway as the wind blew in from a northeastern direction. Small waves lapped under the dock as the tidal waters met winds wanting to push it back down the river. Lightning in the distance brightened the sky and emphasized the outline of the clouds billowing nearby.

"You always take care of me, Jim." She said as he moved her frame more in front of him…took his hand and rested it on her chest underneath her top shirt…he felt her delicate softness.

"I worry about you. It obviously doesn't take much to get you tipsy. I need to be the one who takes care of you…not someone else."

"When I'm with Lucy we laugh and talk, and it happens."

"Lucy can drink a lot and still function. You're small and just a little seems to wipe you out."

"All week I've been looking forward to this afternoon, just to be able to visit, relax and laugh. Lucy and I always talk about you. I was enjoying myself."

"The storm's moving in, but I don't want to let this moment end. Lay your head on my chest. Honestly, tonight I really don't mind your inebriation. It helped me catch you and hold you," he said with a quick laugh as he stroked her hair. "When we're working at the house, you're moving around so fast until I can barely talk to you, and I have never held you like this. I really like the feel of you beside me," Jim whispered against her neck.

Sarah snuggled close and let the tips of her fingers rub the back of his neck. "You're so handsome and have such a sweet sense of humor," she said with a smile. "And warm."

He slipped his hands up and down her lower back as he lightly traced her spine. He moved his hands to her side and felt the curve of her waist as his hands explored her more… occasionally his fingertips stroked the side of her breast as he moved his hands upward. "You're beautiful and your eyes are sparkling."

She moved slightly and resettled. He stroked her again and kissed her forehead, and she moved her hand to the side of his face.

"For safety and other reasons, we might need to walk back to the house."

"Do we have to go?"

"I want to get you some coffee. Hold your head up and let me look at you. You look great, but your eyes are droopy."

"I would like to sleep right here with my head on your chest."

"My dear if we did stay out here much longer and especially let you fall asleep on me…Lucy would hang me from the nearest tree."

"Why?"

"She would say I was taking advantage of you."

"Would you take advantage of me?"

"There was a time in my life when I would take everything I could get and easily take advantage, but you're different. You're special." He smoothed her hair away from her forehead and kissed her. "I want to take care of you because I think you're a kind and generous person. I would like to build a relationship on trust for each other. I want to treat you with respect and let our relationship grow and when the time is right, we will both know," he said as he placed his fingers underneath her chin and lifted her head…he brushed his lips ever so gently against her lips.

"You're sweet," Sarah shivered as her personal haunting memories flashed to destroy her present excitement. She was almost in tears.

They left the dock, walking in a tangled web of hands and arms holding tight to each other. He understood her honest feelings about himself, and she in a clearer frame of mind, heard his honest feelings about her and their relationship. They were each contented in their own way, but unsure about how to proceed.

"If you're not better after dinner, I can drive you home," he said.

"That's thoughtful, but Lucy asked me to spend the weekend."

"I just didn't want you on the road alone. Let me look at you before we go up." He brushed her hair to the side and straightened her shirt as he quickly kissed her forehead as she looked deep into his eyes. He circled her lower back and drew her into himself and they exchanged a passionate kiss. He found her lips to be luscious.

She exhaled as Jim's hand resting on her lower back held her against his frame.

"Now, I might have taken advantage of you a bit on that one," Jim said with a sweet smile.

"…but that was alright with me."

When they walked inside, Carrie said, "Well it's about time."

"Sorry to hold things up."

Sarah went over to Lucy and hugged her, "Thank you." She turned and reached for Carrie.

"There the girls go, hugging again. I'm beginning to worry about them," Charlie said

"Ben said, "I'm not worried."

Jim said with a glowing smile, "I'm definitely not worried."

"Well, if you guys are ok then I'm ok."

With a smile of pleasing admiration, Jim fixed Sarah's coffee with a little milk, and suggested they go out on the porch in the cool air. Before they left, Charlie said a prayer of friendship, and blessed the food.

The guys fixed their plates and Charlie said, "I wish Sarah was in here with us instead of on the porch."

"Oh, Charlie, let Jim take care of her."

"It's just that Sarah is special. I want to make sure she's getting the right kind of care."

* * *

As Jim moved a strand of Sarah's hair behind her ear he said, "You're a special lady, and you deserve to have someone who will say and do nice things for you."

This surprised Sarah because her deceased husband had never been kind to her, and now it shocked her as a man was saying such lovely things. She took his hand and held it over her heart, and he felt the warmth of her heartbeat. They both felt untold passions.

"The coffee's delicious."

"If you're better, we should go inside…you need food in your stomach."

Jim and Sarah quickly fixed their plates and joined their respective groups. The guys were sitting at the island, and the girls sat at the breakfast table near the corner windows. Each group was boisterous as they told stories, but the loudest laugh came from the ladies when Sarah told how Lucy would hang Jim from the nearest tree if he took advantage of her. They laughed so much the guys looked around and Charlie asked, "What's so funny?"

"It's just girl talk" Lucy said.

After dinner, Carrie and Ben soon left for home. Lucy and Sarah cleaned the kitchen while Jim and Charlie talked about the local high school's football team. Sarah and Lucy soon joined them, and the conversation changed to Jim's remodeling project. Sarah was exuberant about the changes and how Jim was actively involved.

Around ten o'clock, Jim prepared to leave. "I need to go home and see what my little decorator did this week while I was away. I want to see if I need to pay her or not," he said as he took Sarah's hand and smiled broadly.

Everybody laughed and Sarah quickly caught the reflective twinkle in his eyes. "Oh Jim, I love your humor. You make me smile." Sarah said as she let her hand slip down his back. She looked at him with a sweet, but disappointing look. She knew he was tired from spending most of the week away from home, but she honestly enjoyed his company and was sad to hear he had to leave.

Charlie told him they were planning to sleep late… maybe work in the yard, and he was welcomed to come back any time tomorrow.

"I would like that. I have things to take care of, but I can come back maybe around two." Jim said as he turned to leave.

"Let me walk you out. I have a bag in my truck I need for tonight. I'll get my keys." Sarah said.

Near the steps, he placed his hands on her trim waist and kissed her ear lobe, as Sarah slowly rested her arms on his firm shoulders. Her lips brushed lightly against his ear and she breathed her warm breath against him.

The delicious vanilla fragrance of her skin and her compliance to his caresses, stimulated by the warm summer breeze and the distant rustle of the river were stirring his ageing masculinity. As he exhaled a long draw of breath Jim said, "Some of my little decorator's fine talents are overwhelming, I really better go," he whispered. As he turned to leave her fingertips brushed his lips, her hand drifted across his chest. With restrained remorse, he looked back as he descended the steps.

Jim brought her bag and keys back up and as he handed each to Sarah, their fingers touched, and their eyes locked into a penetrating stare. "I'll just hand this to you from arms-length. I can't let myself get any closer."

With a sigh and then a meek smile she said, "That might be the safest thing to do."

"I'm sure I'll see you tomorrow. Good night for now," he said as he stretched to lean forward and kissed Sarah on her cheek, but he moved swiftly onto the porch and they intimately hugged good night. Sarah stood in a daze as he descended the steps, watched him drive away…as she whispered his name.

Sarah limply went inside with an exuberant smile on her face. Her body was reeling with aroused excitement as she drifted onto the sofa cushion. Lucy and Charlie saw this as a perfect time to ask questions about Jim. Sarah openly spoke of how he makes her feel, but not in graphic terms. She admired him and melted with thoughts of his touch, but she knew she couldn't let her emotions become unguarded, because of the project and she had a fear of falling for someone before being free from her past.

Lucy advised her to relax and enjoy every moment together. "Remember at our age each moment is special. Don't waste a second of time because everybody deserves a little happiness in their lives."

Charlie advised her to be cautious. He encouraged Sarah to be wise in her decisions and listen to her brain…first…not her heart.

"I appreciate you both. You're right, Jim is a caring person and at this time in my life I cherish being with him in our project, but now more than ever as friends, but I must be cautious. I'm about to fall asleep. My brain is spinning, and my thoughts are rampant. Good night and thank you for this wonderful day."

Sarah wondered off to her bedroom. She snuggled under the warm covers, rested her hand atop her breast, and faded into a restful sleep imagining what a friendship with Jim would be like.

Lucy scolded Charlie for presenting a negative image of Jim to Sarah. "He cares for her and we have to encourage that."

"I feel I need to protect Sarah from him."

"*That's obvious*," Lucy firmly replied.

* * *

The next morning, Sarah woke from the warmth of sleep with a smile on her face. She stretched her arms and peeked through the opening in the curtains and saw the dim light of day outside her bedroom window. She stretched her legs, rolled over on her back, and closed her eyes while thinking pleasant thoughts. Her smile widened as she began to visualize Jim waking up. His muscles must be sore after a week of working. "I hope you are ok, and I do look forward to seeing you this afternoon," she whispered aloud as she drifted back into a peaceful sleep.

Later when she awoke, her room was filled with sunshine. "What time is it?" she said aloud. She grabbed her robe as she looked to see it was past nine. She walked swiftly to the kitchen where Charlie was drinking coffee and reading the newspaper while trying to find information about the storm damage. He had already finished his breakfast, but quickly got up to cook Sarah his favorite, his version of a breakfast Burrito with leftovers from the night before…plus an egg.

"Don't worry about cooking for me. I brought my usual…a bag of old-fashioned oatmeal, raisins and a bottle of Saigon cinnamon."

"Is that what you usually have?"

"Every morning…I've found it to be the most nutritious easiest meal for me to fix. What are our plans for the day?"

"Some planks on the dock need to be repaired. Not a big job, nail a few down and add one or two new ones. I'm going on out…when Lucy gets up, and y'all feel like it come out…I'll have your hammers ready," Charlie said as he patted her on the shoulder.

"See you soon," she said with a smile.

As Charlie left the house, he thought how wonderful it would be to start the day with someone who has a sweet smile and a pleasant disposition like Sarah. He shook his head to clear his thoughts as he picked up the toolbox.

Sarah finished her breakfast, dressed for the day, and straightened her room before going back into the kitchen. Dishes from the night before had to be put away and a few serving platters needed to go in the pantry.

Around ten fifteen, Lucy walked into the kitchen. She looked rested, but not at her best. Sarah hugged her and thanked her for the special evening they had.

As Lucy poured her coffee, she asked, "Did you enjoy being with Jim last night?"

"I really did. We work on the house and I see him almost every day. I have been trying to think of him as a client first and a friend second because of our working agreement, but he is kind to me. Sometimes I just want to cry because he treats me with respect…I've never had that before."

"Don't tell him I told you, but I think he cares a lot for you. Jim has been through some bad times that have caused him to make poor choices in his later life. I think he sees your gentleness as someone pulling him out of his recklessness and back into stability…he needs that. He's a wonderful person, always respectful. Just take your time. I know you're working yourself back to some level of normalcy and he is also. I wish you both the best."

"Thank you. I do need time, but I think I've been smitten," Sarah said with a lovely smile.

"I believe you have and that's fantastic. Let me put on my work clothes and we'll go outside and check on Charlie. Maybe, if you like, we can share the good news with him."

"That sounds great. I know Charlie will be happy for me."

They spotted him on the dock sawing a piece of five-quarter and sure enough, he had a hammer for each of them. "This line of nails has popped up about an eighth of an inch, so start pounding away." It wasn't long before the sun shone bright, the sweat began to pour, and Charlie popped a Bud.

During their break, Lucy got Charlie's attention, "We have good news for you, Sarah's having caring feelings for Jim. Isn't that wonderful, my love."

Instead of Charlie congratulating her, he hung his head and said, "I hope you know what you're getting into."

"I really don't know and I'm unsure of myself because of what I've been through. He is sweet to me. He speaks kind words and I think he even flirts a little. It feels good, but I'm not emotionally ready to move into a relationship. Now we seem to have a wonderful platonic friendship just working on the house."

"It sounds like you have your head on straight. Don't let yourself get swept away."

"I promise. I won't."

Charlie reached out his arm, caught her neck in the bend of his elbow, and pulled her next to him and Sarah felt his overwhelming concern for her. He stepped back and said, "Ok girls, we have work to do."

They worked until lunchtime…then went inside for leftovers. Lucy and Sarah shared a crab cake and green beans. Lucy had a glass of wine with her lunch and Sarah drank water. Charlie made a ham sandwich on rye with a Bud. They were nibbling at their food, while complaining about the extreme heat and in walked Jim. Sarah immediately laid her hand on top of her head to straighten her windblown tangled locks and said in a whisper, "I'm a terrible hot sweaty dirty mess. I'm so embarrassed."

Lucy looked over and whispered, "Just relax you're fine." Then she looked at Jim and said "Come on in, you're just in time for lunch. Hey Charlie, stop eating long enough to get Jim's plate and silverware."

Sarah sat quietly as Jim made his sandwich. She thought she might become invisible if she didn't move. That didn't work because he shifted a stool over to the counter and sat beside her. He looked over and said, "Good afternoon my hardworking little friend." Jim leaned over and kissed her on her salty cheek.

Her heart melted and she felt like the shy sixteen-year-old who had just been kissed by the senior high quarterback.

Lucy's heart quivered and she thought this is the beginning of true love.

Charlie's heart flat lined for a second and he thought, this is disgusting, I hope I don't throw up. If Sarah knew what I knew about him, she wouldn't let him touch her. Charlie used his old poker face to hide his feelings.

They worked all afternoon and Charlie found numerous jobs for Jim. Occasionally Sarah took him a glass of water or just gave a sweet look from her gorgeous dark brown eyes as she passed his way. Late in the afternoon, Sarah sat down beside Lucy on the sandy riverbank.

As Jim made the rounds with the weed-eater he wondered what they were talking about. When Charlie saw their hand motions and smiling faces glancing at Jim, he knew.

Sarah got up to go into the kitchen, and her path crossed with Jim. "I found the letters," he whispered.

"Great. I'm anxious to read them."

"The letters are so personal…I would like for us to be in a private place."

She looked deep into his eyes and read his heart. She laid her hand on top of his and the vibration of the weed-eater frightened her, and she jerked it away, but quickly placed it back on top of his hand and said, "I completely understand. I would like that also."

"There might be things I need to explain or some of the things she wrote might rekindle some old emotions. I would enjoy being alone with you."

"Will after work on Monday work? We can have quiet time and enjoy every word."

"That sounds best. I would like for this to be our secret."

For him, having a secret with Sarah was creating a deeper level to their relationship that demonstrated how much he trusted her with his most personal feelings. Her heart quivered at the thought of sharing an intimate part of his life.

"By the way, you look great this morning dressed in your handsome beach clothes with your tanned arms. I can tell you've been working outside all week, or were you just fooling me and spent your week at some Caribbean resort," Sarah said with her cute smiling face as she twisted her body close to Jim as she walked away. She couldn't help but try her hand at flirting.

But she immediately regretted her actions, and as she made her way into the house she whispered, "I'm the one so determined to remain business like, and not let my feelings fester while I struggle to reconcile my past. That was a foolish thing to say," she mumbled with disgust in herself.

"Wow, her eyes are beautiful," he said in a low voice.

Lucy walked past and said, "Yes, they are beautiful and so is she."

"How well I know."

Sarah wrapped the potatoes and placed them in the hot oven. She put the steaks into a zip-lock bag, poured in some Worcestershire Sauce and laid the bag aside on the counter. She washed and cut up two heads of broccoli and placed it in a pot with about two inches of water. She searched the refrigerator and found everything needed for making a Caesar salad and stored the items on a refrigerator shelf. Everything was organized so it wouldn't take long to finish dinner. Sarah hurriedly walked out the back-kitchen door and ran square into Jim.

Her spontaneous reaction to their closeness caused her to reach forward and touch his chest, but her brain told her to stop. *I have gone too far too fast. He is my client even though we have had some sweet moments lately...I must watch myself.* As he stepped closer, she thought, *how handsome he looks all sweaty from working, and I love his manly fragrance.*

"I wanted to check on you, give you a hug and get a glass of water."

Through controlled excitement she said, "I'm glad you came...I'll fix your water"

"My hug will be sweaty."

"I like sweaty hugs," Sarah said as she felt a warm glow.

"Come here to me. I'm glad to be with my little decorating friend," he said as he rubbed his hands up and down her back and rubbed his mustached face against her cheek in a jovial manner. As his hands came to rest on her lower back, Sarah arched herself back playfully in response to his tickling mustache.

"Just friends, you're still my client." she said in response to his outrageously lavished hug.

"Yes, just friends...the den is turning into something beautiful and I can only thank you. When I saw it last night, I cried out for you, I wanted to call and thank you, but I decided to wait until today. I'm glad I found my browned-eyed girl," Jim said with control as he reached for her hand.

She dropped her head and took one step back, then returned to his open arms and he pulled her small body against his warm manly frame. Sarah weakened as his arms tightened his hold and she became comfortable. Then her body became rigid and her back arched and she backed away.

Sarah thought, *I admire this captivating man and my heart is saying its right, but my brain won't let me trust his sweetness. My past has scarred me deeply.* She moved her hands up and down his upper arms...looked at his chest...then his eyes with an uneasy stare as her eyes became glassy.

"I know what you're thinking...I'm your client ...water, I need a cup of water. Meet me at the banana trees...I want your help with clipping."

"Thanks for understanding, I'll see you there." With a glowing smile Sarah's hand drifted across his chest as she turned to leave.

Jim felt her warm fingertips as they crossed his heart, and he whispered, "I will never grow tired of waiting for you, I hope soon you realize I honestly love you." He rubbed his forehead as he breathed deeply.

They enjoyed working together while trimming the banana trees, and Charlie noticed how they teased each other. "Sarah seems happy with Jim, so maybe things are better than what I thought, but I can't stop caring for her welfare," he whispered.

The exhausted work crew went inside to finish dinner. They enjoyed reliving the day's work by telling how they ran over the clematis vine with the lawnmower, and almost fell off the ladder while trying to hang onto a swaying banana leaf. They were looking forward to a restful evening.

After dinner, Jim and Sarah went for a walk up the wooded lane from the cay. They soon learned the art of walking silently, bodies brushing against each other and feeling a thousand unspoken words. They were not only feeling words of respect and encouragement for each other, but also words of compassion.

"I must leave soon and wanted to say our goodbyes away from the house," as he held her closer.

"I have honestly enjoyed being with my client who is becoming a dear friend. I can't explain why I feel this way, but being with you is so comforting," Sarah faithfully said.

He reached his hand out to her, "My dear Sarah, it's not easy to find words sweet enough to tell you what you mean to me. You're truly an unforgettable lady."

They moved into a strong embrace and Sarah kissed him on the neck. They looked into each other's eyes…smiled a knowing smile, and he couldn't help but steal a kiss which Sarah truly wanted.

Jim soon prepared to leave the cay and Sarah was saddened, but Lucy and Charlie assured her, there would be other times they would spend together.

Sarah went to bed with a smile on her face because the weekend had been the best. She thought about the letters and was looking forward to being alone with Jim while reading them. She felt, *having our secret will be a binding factor of trust in our relationship, a sign that he trusts me.* Sarah remembered *the closeness I had with his mother and imagined the sweet words she must have written to him.* She pulled her arms close and thought of Jim.

* * *

Sarah arrived at home about six o'clock in the afternoon and around eight-thirty Jim called. He was excited because he had finished his pricing for one of the St. Mary's jobs, and would present his bid Monday morning. He was ecstatic about the thoughts of possibly starting a new project on the coast, and Sarah was also thrilled for him because he was always eager to work and strived to do his best to help his customers.

"Tomorrow morning I'll be up by six and ready by seven. Come when you can, I need to leave by nine. I have something for you."

Chapter 8

Sarah arrived at Jim's house earlier than usual. She used her key to let herself inside and immediately started the coffee brewing. She was lost in her thoughts while putting a few plates and flatware into the dishwasher. She turned quickly and to her surprise saw Jim casually leaning beside the island watching her work. She smiled and said, "Good morning."

"Good morning to you, Sunshine."

"That brightens my day," she said with a smile.

"I want to brighten your days," Jim said seriously as he walked closer.

"I quietly tapped on the door and no one came, I let myself inside…hope you don't mind."

"That's what I would want you to do. Feel free to make yourself at home," he whispered.

The beeper sounded on the coffee pot. "While we drink our coffee, I can answer your questions about our construction plans for today."

"I really don't have any definitive questions. I needed to be with you early this morning and have coffee," Jim said. Sarah was standing at the counter, and he moved behind her and lightly touched her side as he softly kissed her neck.

"That's sweet," she whispered

Jim lightly stroked her arms as he gently said, "If you like, we can sit on the porch near the magnolia tree."

"That's perfect, the blooms smell delicious. I've opened the door several times this past week to let the aromatic fragrance into the house. Do you have a special cup? I know you like sugar and cream, but I'm not sure how much," Sarah said with interest.

"This cup will be fine, and I'll add the other. You drink yours with a little milk," he said.

Yes, I try to think I'm getting calcium from the milk and holding on to the flavor of the coffee by not adding sugar."

With a pleasing smile he said, "Also, no sugar helps you keep your slim hips." As Jim opened a loaf of wheat bread he said, "You look as though your conscience of your weight. I guess I need to back off to only one spoon of sugar. Would you like a piece of cheese toast for breakfast?"

"I'm fine. I had a bowl of oatmeal at home," Sarah said as she watched him.

"The electrical wires for switches, receptacles and phone lines are routed, so we will finish the sheetrock for the plasterer. But first I must talk to Jonathan about painting the walls and refinishing the floors. When Terry arrives, he will work on sheetrock, and I'll be their runner today," Sarah said with confidence.

"Let me refill your coffee before we go outside."

They stepped into the warm mid-summer air and became aware of the fragrant magnolia blossoms. Each was drawn to the comfortable sofa close to the tree as they sat in silence and absorbed the sounds and fragrances of the morning. In a simultaneous manner, each said, "You know something it's wonderful being here with you."

Jim reached for a bag at the end of the sofa and handed it to Sarah. "You're always admiring that faded denim work shirt I wear, so I thought you would like to have it as your work shirt."

"Yes, Jim I would…This is perfect. I love it. Your gift is personal and to me special."

Jim's shoulders dropped as a feeling of contentment came over him…he kissed her hand…held it as they swayed with thought and conversation as they finished the last swallows of coffee. When they heard Jonathan's diesel truck drive into the yard, they looked at each other and knew their peaceful moment had ended. "I have enjoyed our morning together and look forward to reading the letters this afternoon.

"The day has had a wonderful beginning." Are you working close by today?" Sarah said as they gathered their dishes.

"About three miles from the cay, we're installing a boat lift, but first I have to deliver my bid for the coast project. I hope to be here by four. Have a great day," he said as they gently hugged.

Jonathan rang the doorbell and Sarah looked at Jim and said, "Our day has begun. Let me open the door, his hands might be full of boxes of nails or a bucket of plaster.

"Come in Jonathan. Let me help you," Sarah said as she grabbed the nails and a Lowes bag of something.

Jim took two other Lowes bags and said, "Good morning Jonathan."

"Good morning and thank you for your help," Jonathan said with a smile.

"Sarah, I'm leaving now. We all have a lot to do today."

"Yes, we do," Sarah said as she turned, and saw Jim's folder. She hurried after him and he smiled with appreciation as he saw her coming.

Jonathan in passing said, "Morning Sarah, he seems to be a nice fellow."

"He is…very thoughtful."

"Before we get to work, I needed to ask you about the floors. Jim would like to have the floors refinished and possibly left natural with a mat coat of urethane applied. What are your thoughts?"

"I know a guy in Dublin who will come in and do it all. The mat urethane is more durable and the easiest to maintain."

"At Jim's age, the urethane will be the best because we older folks appreciate something with low maintenance."

"Ah Sarah, you're not old."

"But I often feel that way, my child," Sarah said as an arthritis pain stiffened her finger.

"Well, you look great and you're so active. I hope I have your energy and excitement for life when I'm your age," his reply was spoken like a placated response as though he thought he would feel young forever.

With a *you will see* smile Sarah said, "When you're young it's common to think mid-sixties is old age and you see it as being decrepit, but you'll see, you'll have energy and excitement, but at a slower pace."

"I'll give Jake a call and arrange a time to come look. I've always found his pricing to be reasonable, but the main thing is he's good. We should be ready in three weeks?"

"I hear Terry driving in, can you guide him through any last bit of electrical and then start the sheetrock. Also, would you and Terry consider painting the two rooms? Think about it…I'll be your gofer today…call on me," Sarah said.

"No problem, we'll get it done." Jonathan said with a smile as he searched for Jake's number.

After some discussion, they accepted the job and Sarah gave them the paint chips. The wall color for the den is a medium shade of Irish Coastal Green and the kitchen will be painted a medium shade of Ecru. Depending on how the floors look after sanding a polyurethane will be used and if needed stained a warm umber. "I'll work with you also," Sarah said

After installing the pot lights in the ceiling, the electrical was finished. By the end of the day, they were finished with the sheetrock. Jonathan and Terry left about four o'clock after loading the construction scraps.

* * *

Jim arrived before five and greeted Sarah with a smile and a quick kiss on the cheek. "These are for you, a few wild roses I found growing by the boathouse at the job site."

"Thank you. That's so sweet and thoughtful. Let me find something to put them in." Sarah took the flowers as she looked for small vase or a tiny canning jar. *What a sweet fragrance,* she thought, *as she remembered the pungent sweet aroma of the aging gardenia bush in her grandmother's yard.* "I've been looking forward to this afternoon. I'm excited to read the letters, to find out what your mother said to you."

"I thought I might look at everything you and the carpenters finished today, maybe go out for dinner, then catch a movie…" Jim said with a mischievous smile that accentuated his face, along with a glassy twinkle in his eyes.

"You're just teasing. Please don't make me wait any longer," Sarah said as a broad smile filled her face.

"I won't," he smiled sweetly and touched her side. "Your eyes are fascinating, and I feel entranced by their dark color."

"Your words touch my heart. I almost forgot, David and Helen stopped by this afternoon."

"David called and told me he liked the improvements. What about Helen?"

"I actually missed them…Jonathan and I had gone to my house searching for sheetrock blades and a few electrical items." Sarah said.

"I've already told them briefly about the renovations and David was complimentary, Mary Beth was somewhat agreeable, and Helen was suspicious. I invited them to come by, but I wish they had let me know…I would have been here."

"I'm sure, after this unannounced visit, they'll let you know when they can stop again." Jim was a bit upset with the children for dropping-in, so Sarah hoped her response would comfort him.

"I'll call and set up a time. Then we'll arrange for you to explain your decorating plans. I've got to use kid gloves with Helen. She gets upset with me easily. Now, let's get our minds back on the letters."

There was no place to sit in the den, so Jim suggested they go to the summerhouse. The summerhouse was a raised open pavilion his grandmother had built at the end of a lush rectangular lawn shaded by a canopy of enormous old pecan trees. "She eventually had a boxwood hedge planted which became the courtyard. The men played croquet there almost every Sunday afternoon in the summer. Their wives would sit under the shaded pavilion enjoying lemonade and tea cakes, while they watched," Jim said humbly as Sarah was charmed by his story, and imagined the men dressed in white, impressing their ladies.

Jim made a pitcher of Country-Time lemonade, opened a box of ginger snaps, and arranged a handful on a Blue Willow plate. He placed everything on an ornate silver tray along with the stack of letters.

As they walked, Jim told her about the piano recitals and summer concerts his grandmother held in the courtyard for the community. "She would have at least fifty white wooden folding chairs set up on the lawn and folks would come dressed in their best Sunday clothes… and by the way, my grandmother's name was Sara, without the *h*. In the back area beyond the courtyard, the older boys, who could slip away, quietly played flag football. A few girls were always there to cheer us on."

Sarah was mesmerized by Jim and clung to the visual images his words were creating of his life in the late forties and fifties. The way he told his stories was enchanting to Sarah.

"I have the letters in chronological order." On the wicker settee, Jim placed the stack tied by a now frayed red ribbon with a Happy Valentine heart tied into the bow. He poured the lemonade and they settled on the sofa and read the one dated early nineteen sixty-six.

Before they got to the place where Sarah came into the picture, they read his mother's description of the hard time she had working and raising her family without a husband, and her regret of the lack of time she had to spend with her boys. Jim gained a new perspective of her. He knew how she suffered, but now forty something years later, he felt the pain she had endured.

As he dropped his head, Sarah cradled his face with her hand, and leaned beside him. She looked into his sad eyes, "Your heart is made of gold."

"No, it's not. I was remembering what an inconsiderate jerk I was. I knew my mom had a hard time, but only now do I feel the degree of her pain and hardships."

"It's only natural to try to avoid pain you can't fix. You were far away in such a high-stress war zone. You couldn't eliminate her conditions, and you did what you could. You were the one she trusted, and you listened to her pain. She depended on you as a sounding board. Sometimes a good listener is the best relief in troubled times, and you helped her. Someday, I would like for you to share your experience in Vietnam, also tell me about your dad."

"You're sweet. I feel as though I could tell you anything, and you would understand and be encouraging. As far as the war, most of what you saw on television was the way it was, but I suppose it was the emotional side of the war you seldom had a glimpse of…that was the hardest to handle, but I will tell you as much as you want to hear."

With a trembling voice Sarah said, "I appreciate your comments and your trust."

At that moment, Jim came across the letter he was searching for.

They both leaned against the sofa cushions and Sarah wrapped her arms in his for warmth and comfort during this soul-stirring time. She leaned her head close to hear each word clearly and see the words his mother had written. Jim read aloud:

My dearest Jim,

Today is a beautiful day. The sun is bright, the vegetable garden is producing, and the flowers are blooming. I wish with all my heart you could be here and not there. I have something interesting to tell you. There is a beautiful, but shy young girl who comes into the store quite often. She works nearby, so I get to visit with her several times a week. I've told her about you being in Vietnam. She knows the danger you're in and she is concerned about your welfare. Every time she comes in, she asks about you. She is so sweet and has lovely dark brown eyes. I know you would like her, too. Please know there are folks here who love you and think about you all the time. Thank you for the money you sent. I used it for the farm loan payment.

With Love Your Mom

"That was the first time you were mentioned in one of her letters. I remember the vision I had of you, an image of the beautiful girl back home who was thinking of me."

Sarah turned, and nested her face into the curve of his neck, as his arms circled her, and she nestled affectionately upon his chest. Her hand touched the side of his face and wiped away the beginnings of a tear. She could feel his words filling her heart.

He held her tightly, and thought of the, *what ifs of his life. What if he had had this wonderful person to come home and care for after the war? What if he had had a life with someone so warm and giving?* Jim imagined, *would I have messed it up and been the same jerk I was? I can't think of my past, I have her now and I'll take care of her.* "I've found my little, brown-eyed girl. Our personal secret makes me love and adore you," he said as his hug gave no sign of relenting.

"Our secrets are a special adhesive that binds and holds me to you." Sarah clung to her emotions as a way of controlling her heart but was longing to cry out to Jim.

As she breathed the sweet pureness of the moment, her thoughts also wandered from past to present. *When I was in my mid-twenties, I thought moving away from my family would be easy but adjusting to a marriage and a new family had turned out to be extremely difficult. During those afternoon breaks, Jim's mother listened to my fretting, and gave an experienced mother's advice. As I got to know this sweet older lady, I found myself laughing and enjoying conversations about her raising a family and the lean times after her husband died. She had the boys to raise, educate and mentor, and a farm to manage during trying times in our country. Jim's mother also shared her stoic sorrow about the baby girl born a month after her husband's death, who mysteriously died a week after she was born. We shared the painful times as well as many occasions that brought us joy, but I could never express to her completely the mental abuse I was suffering and the depth of the struggle I was enduring.*

The truth of Sarah's existence in the arms of Jim brought her to a crashing halt, as she realized her emotional growth was because of the secure feeling she had with Jim. While holding each other in an enduring embrace in complete silence, each knew this was a feeling of honest togetherness, but they were afraid to let the other know their true feelings. Sarah exhaled, and she felt the safety and security of his arms.

His voice quivered as he said, "You're the one who helped me survive and then I lost you. I'm afraid to let you go because I'm afraid of losing you again. I so desperately want to be with you, talk with you and care for you. You're the link between me, my mother and my survival not only through Vietnam, but thoughts of the brown-eyed girl have been with me since the first time my mother mentioned you."

"It seems like a miraculous intervention that all this is happening. I'm in shock and amazement. We were so far apart and now we are here together. I don't want to leave you because I want to talk more and get to know everything about you," she loosened her grip. His arms embraced her more and she exhaled and settled against his chest. In this highly emotional setting, she knew if she stayed much longer other needs might prevail, and that couldn't happen, not now. She had to be sure of her feelings, and not let herself go, but foremost she had to think of the project.

With a pensive look of caring in his eyes Jim said, "I care for you and you have a place in my heart."

"I cherish the man you are. Your mom and I had a wonderful relationship. She talked to me and I listened. She told me a lot about her sons and those thoughts gave me peace during some rough years." Sarah stroked the softness of his shirt as her intimate feelings flowed. "I was close to you, but only in an image in my thoughts. I was so far from you…I couldn't see you or touch you. I loved my vision of you and cared long before I knew you. I have to go my emotions are getting the best of me."

"If you're going to cry, I want to be holding you. I don't want you driving or home alone feeling emotional, whether they are joyful tears or painful tears, I want to wipe them away and comfort you."

"This moment is important to us. It might be difficult to talk about it now, but I think sometime soon we will share more of our feelings."

"I feel the same way, and I thank you for stirring my emotions in such a lovely way," she said as she parted from his chest and looked into his eyes.

He stole a kiss, and she stole one back. Slowly he reached out his hand and took hers. He glanced at her fingers. "We have secrets. Our thoughts seem to be in sync. My thoughts are of only you, my dear. There won't be any kind of rush in our friendship because I'm respectful of your wishes, but anytime you need me, I'm here for you. I look forward to tomorrow morning, we can have coffee…and I'm the one who should be thanking you."

Sarah drove home in an emotional daze, as her thoughts tried to sort her feelings while she honestly spoke aloud, "I know my concern for Jim is true, even though I feel I have to contain my feelings. I enjoy being with him and love the feeling of comfort he gives me. I know my troubled past causes me to show ambivalent feelings at times, but tonight the emotional bonding created by the letters has filled my heart with deep compassion for Jim. In my heart I see him as more than a client friend, but as a dear potential loving companion created by his honesty of life which fosters hope."

As soon as Sarah got home, she decided to send Jim an email explaining the plaster finish work and having someone from Dublin to refinish the floors. After the excitement of reading his mother's letters, she had forgotten to mention construction plans. She thought how close his mother's letters had made her feel toward Jim, and without hesitation signed *Your Friend, Sarah* as she closed her message.

Jim called Sarah early the next morning to tell her his plans had changed, and he needed to talk with a customer about adding a covered boathouse. They talked about her questions in the email, and he agreed with her plan. Near the end of their conversation, he said, "I noticed how you signed *Your Friend, Sarah*. I like being *your friend*."

"I thought after sharing the letters, you meant more to me than a client. I feel you're my dear friend. I hope I didn't assume too much."

"No, not at all, I agree with you. I think our relationship has developed into a caring friendship…which means a lot to me. I will always be here for you, so please let me know if I can help you." Jim was excited about the growth in their relationship because that was what he was wanting.

* * *

Several areas of the den were nearing completion and Sarah was anxiously trying to decide on the last items needed to finish the decorating part of the job. She called Jim to ask if they could meet that evening, but he was going out with the guys for their monthly dinner, so Sarah agreed to come early the next morning for coffee.

Jim had the coffee ready when Sarah arrived. She needed to ask him about a price range for rugs in the den, a few paintings and some smalls needed for the kitchen area. He didn't have much time to talk, but he was enthusiastic, and gave Sarah full authority to buy whatever she thought would work. "Maybe we can have another shopping trip."

"If we do, I need to work up a detailed list of things. A shopping trip to Savannah sounds great and there's a Persian rug dealer who carries a great selection."

"Do you think we can plan a trip to Paris to shop?" he said with a mischievous look.

Sarah looked to him and smiled that lovely thin smile, "I've never been to Paris, possibly one day, but for sure…not now."

"That sounds as though I might have a chance one day…I'll just keep trying." he said with a smile and a little boy's devilish grin, as he reached his arm out and his fingers slipped along her wrist and forearm. His touch tingled against her skin and as he reached the palm of her hand, she twisted her fingers around his and held him as she looked into his dancing eyes.

* * *

During the next several weeks, Jonathan, Terry and Sarah finished most of the construction work and made a detailed list of items needed to finish the project.

During this time Sarah thought of having an afternoon free to have dinner with Mike before his transfer to Atlanta. She casually mentioned that she needed an afternoon off because Mike wanted to be with her.

A rushing heat flushed Jim's face, and it turned red after hearing this. He thought of someone other than himself being with Sarah, and he was upset with himself with thoughts of playing the *Mr. Good Guy* role too long.

With his frustrations under control he asked, "This guy Mike, exactly who is he and what does he mean to you?"

"For many years I've known Mike. He knew my husband's personality at work, and from the first time I met him, he always looked or spoke to me in a concerned way. I thought of him as my silent protector. When my husband was in the hospital after his accident, he called and visited with me often. He gave *me* respect, consideration, and encouragement. There has never been any romantic thoughts or involvement. He has always been a true friend, and that's what he means to me."

Jim in his fury said, "I can't stand the idea of you being with someone else."

"Jim, I'm sorry, but I had a life before…separate from the life I have working with you on the house. I treasure our time together, but Mike is my friend and we're doing nothing wrong."

"I'm sorry," Jim said as he rubbed his forehead and walked toward Sarah. "You're such a wonderful young lady…I know you have a life, other than before this, but I selfishly don't want to share you with anyone. I thought Mike might mean more, and I was afraid. You mean so much to me and it frightened me to think that in some way, I'm losing you."

"Mike requested a company transfer to the plant near Atlanta. He will be leaving in a week and we just wanted to visit one last time. We're meeting at Brown's and I'm sure he wouldn't mind if you came with me."

"No, I couldn't do that. It's just I enjoy being with you and honestly care for you. It hurts to think you would be sharing your sweet personality with someone else."

"Mike is an acquaintance and I wanted to let you know about our meeting because I didn't want you to hear about it and think something different from what it was. I told you because you are important to me."

"Thank you for your honesty. Now we need to finish our shopping list and decide if it's Paris or Savannah. I'm holding out for Paris." Jim said with fondness, as he thought of Mike with Sarah.

It was decided on a Thursday shopping spree to find rugs, other pieces of furniture, lighting, and accessories in Savannah. Jim and Sarah were looking forward to spending the day together looking for the final items.

Jim left early for Sarah's house, he had two small iron scrolls he had heated and bent into coat hooks. He welded each onto an ornate piece of iron work he had found in his shop.

Sarah was always touched by his unexpected surprises. She was especially warmed by this gift because she had mentioned that she needed hangers.

"You're so thoughtful. I need these in my mud room."

* * *

On the way to the downtown Furniture Mart, they passed Telfair Square on West Presidents Street. Sarah was amazed by all the beautiful blooming hydrangeas and day lilies. The park was filled with people enjoying the warm sunny day. As they approached downtown, the sidewalks were crowded with college students dressed in skimpy clothing, showing appreciation of the warmth of the sun. It was refreshing to see the young folks eating at sidewalk cafés and strolling as innocent lovers on this warm afternoon. She thought of her youth and became lost in a dream.

Jim asked, "The Garman said we should turn here. I thought we had to go straight to reach Bull Street," Jim exclaimed.

His voice awakened her from her dream, and she had to ask him again what he said. By that time Jim had turned, and they were fortunately heading in the right direction.

"I'm sorry I didn't hear your question. I was looking at these young kids while thinking my age now and remembering my youth. Thinking of their life when they become my age and hoping they're treasuring every moment and appreciating what they have instead of finding fault with life. I hope they won't be naive, careless and unprepared for their future."

"I hope they value their education and become hard working dedicated providers who become a strong example for their family," Jim said with thoughts of his upbringing.

After searching through the Mart, they found the perfect pair of Persian rugs in a light mossy green background that blended with the wall color, and small clusters of reddish flowers that matched the sofa. The traditional rugs were a forgiving blend of colors that would work well in the television, fireplace, and walkthrough areas. Sarah found some other unique accent pieces to use on the antique English chest. They searched diligently and found the library chest and two small antique tables to fit beside the settee.

The order was scheduled for delivery two weeks from the day of purchase. *This will be the last of the major shopping trips needed to furnish the den. With previous clients, I looked forward to the final shopping excursion, but this one was different, it meant an end to the warm feeling of seeing his smiling face after a day of decorating, to his sweet construction notes and to his touch.*

Before leaving the store, they decided to search for a lamp to go beside Jim's chair. The Mart manager recommended a lighting gallery about five miles out on Abercorn Street. While riding out, they passed Grant Park and decided to stop for an enjoyable walk on this lovely spring day.

The park's grounds were glowing with an abundance of flowers and palm trees. The fragrant smell of lavender was in the air along with an occasional whiff of fried seafood from a nearby restaurant. Jim politely touched her waist or arm often to direct her or whatever reason he though was appropriate. Sarah noticed she on occasion had reached for his elbow as they crossed a street or walked over rough cobblestone pavement. It was all gentle and welcomed.

Sarah was wearing a teal green cotton sweater over a matching draping shell and off-white slacks, but the heat of the afternoon sun caused her to remove the sweater. Her delicate figure was evident to Jim, as they strolled among lovers sitting on benches or sweethearts lying on blankets in a sun induced gaze twirling dandelion blooms… with dreams of love. He wanted to touch Sarah in a more caring way but feared it would add stress on our work outing.

Suddenly, he grabbed her hand, to escort her around two running children and held it tightly before suddenly pulling her toward him and reaching for her waist as she reached and took hold of his shoulder to brace herself. Sarah and Jim laughed as the children yelled, "Excuse me" and ran off to their parents.

Their bodies continued into a rhythmic whirl and in a split second they were wrapped in a romantic grasp. Sarah rested against his chest. Then backed away while continuing out of the whirl, the rotation changed from closeness, to a tight hand hold, as she looked at Jim. Eyes caught in a gaze can often say more than words. Her dark eyes were strong, but soft…Jim's eyes were set and wanting.

The appreciation of the moment was captured by their look. He pulled her back to him and their faces were only a few inches away. He wanted to kiss her lips. He felt her hand resting on his shoulder, as he slipped his hand over the smooth shape of her neck and shoulders.

As her anxiety eased, she widened her fingers to conform to the shape of his body. She gently laid her head against his chest and exhaled as they enjoyed the warmth of the sun.

Sarah turned and they looked deep into each other's eyes as bridled desires coupled with lingering hesitation overtook their thoughts. He kissed her forehead as he stroked her fragrant warm hair and held her delicate body a minute longer. He took her hand and with hearts pounding, they quietly meandered from the park. With strong emotions stirring in their relationship, they continued the journey out Abercorn Street.

At the lighting gallery, they found a lamp that was perfect for Jim, and a pair of iron lamps to use on the English chest. After completing these purchases, they made their way to downtown for a quiet dinner on River Street.

After dinner, they meandered hand in hand by the river and later strolled in and out of a few shops looking for a souvenir for Jim's grandson, his namesake. He found a Savannah Gnats Tee-shirt and baseball cap.

For Sarah, Jim spotted a silk shawl with roses the same color as the den sofa. He insisted she should have it, so he draped it around her shoulders and with a warm smile illuminating their faces, he tugged her in his direction.

In his eyes he saw a lovely lady he wanted to wrap his arms around and hold forever. His hands gracefully lay on her shoulders as his fingertips trace its outline through the soft silken covering.

She reached forward and gently touched him at his side.

As he gazed into her eyes, he imagined *cradling the side of her face in his hand, drawing her to him and covering her with sweet kisses.* His eyes danced downward to her lips and back to her eyes. A warm heat rushed over her as he gently eased her compliant frame close to him and he whispered in her ear, "The shawl is beautiful against your face. You must have it."

The cashier was complimentary of Sarah because she had watched the loving encounter the shawl had created. The lady could see the love each had for the other. "You must wear this, my dear, I think it's magical. In fact, I think I'll purchase one for myself." She clipped off the tag, skillfully draped it around Sarah's shoulders and tied a simple loop at the side. Jim paid for the scarf and arm in arm with a glow on their faces left the store. He stole a quick kiss, but this stolen kiss was not stolen, it was one she wanted.

They meandered in the crowd nearer the river, but as they entered the tree draped quite area, he encapsulated Sarah into his arms, and she welcomed the secure feeling. "You know, I don't think I've ever been to Savannah just for enjoyment like we've had. I come here for business and my mind is just on one thing, trying to finish the job and on to another. I've certainly enjoyed our day."

"It has been wonderful. Usually shopping for items is frustrating, but today has been the best. What did you enjoy most?" she said.

"I enjoyed the park and our little twirl when the children ran between us. I enjoyed being close to you, and buying the scarf created a warm feeling." Jim said with a smile. "If you would like, I would like to do this again soon."

"I would like that," she said as they laced their fingers.

"You know being with you and this might sound odd, but it's like being with a real person. You're talented, charming, witty and so much more. You are so special to me and you have done so much to bring out the best in me," Jim said.

With silent tears welling in her eyes, Sarah quickly looked at Jim…then dropped her head. She had no idea she had such a valued meaning. They held each other as they meandered to his vehicle. "The shawl looks beautiful on you," and a sweet "thank you" were the only words softly spoken.

They arrived at Sarah's house at about ten o'clock. Jim walked her to the door, and she invited him inside. Without closing the door, she expressed how much she enjoyed the day and how she looked forward to having coffee with him the next morning.

Jim placed his hands on her waist, and said, "I look forward to you being there. I enjoyed our shopping trip even though it wasn't Paris, but who knows maybe one day."

She lightly touched his forearms and forbid herself from moving higher on his arm, for fear of reaching his shoulders and then gently holding the nap of his neck. Sarah felt refreshed.

He kissed her gently and clasped her bottom lip before slowly backing away. Sarah felt the smoothness of his lips and her insides quivered as she savored his wet kiss. Her eyes glazed and she froze in mid-air. Before she knew what was happening, he was almost out the door.

She slowly managed to say, "Good night."

"Have sweet dreams, my dear."

"I know I will," Sarah said as she locked the door, and ambled to her bedroom in a dreamy state of mind.

The seed of tender affection had been firmly planted after they shared the secret contents of his mother's letters, Sarah could feel the warmth of her heart growing for Jim. She removed the scarf and laid it on the table beside her bed. "I want this to be the first thing I see when I open my eyes in the morning." Sarah smiled broadly as she replayed their day…as she lay in her warm bed and drifted into sleep with a smile on her face and her arms pulled to her breast.

Chapter 9

"Guys, we have a few weeks before the furniture is scheduled to arrive. It will take steady work to get the renovations completed in time. We should be able to finish painting the walls and trim this week, then start the bookcases."

"I think we can get it on time," Jonathan said.

Jonathan and Terry prepared to paint the kitchen. It took two days of concentrated effort, along with Sarah painting the trim. To complete the kitchen construction, Sarah added the switch plate covers, new brass doorknobs and replaced a bulb in the stove hood.

As she cleaned the last of the construction dust from the kitchen, Sarah was imagining accessories as the icing on the cake. As she removed a paint can from the counter, she found a note from Jim tucked neatly under the edge. He commented on her extensive dedication to the project and how much he appreciated all she and the crew were doing. 'Your help means more to me than you know. Have a blessed day.' She repeated the phrase,' You mean more to me than you know.' It's my fears from my past keeping me from moving forward,"

Sarah said as she tucked the note into her pocket and tears glazed her eyes.

Sarah had cleaned the den in preparation for Jonathan and Terry to paint and was amazed as it change from a dark dungeon into a warm green retreat. The characteristics of the new plaster blended perfectly into the old as the paint merged the two…it looked as though the new wall had been there for years. Sarah took a deep breath and exhaled with a feeling of satisfaction. The second coat would go on the following day, leaving a few places for her to touch up.

* * *

Jim had called his children and arranged to meet at five, so Sarah and the guys cleaned the area making it easier for Jim to show his children around. Helen called her brother and sister to question them as to what this meeting was about. Neither David nor Mary Beth could tell her anything to satisfy her probing thoughts because all they knew was their dad invited them to come. David suggested she just take it easy and have a wait and see attitude, but Helen was sure something was going on in that house.

David was agreeable with everything his dad had told them and seldom questioned his plans. He understood the need for the renovations and improvements. Mary Beth agreed, but with reluctance went along with Helen who asked pointed questions and looked at Mary Beth for agreement.

"I'm getting older and realized I needed to update a few areas. I'd like for you all to observe the improvements," Jim spoke with humility.

Helen thought is he dying and wants to get the place in shape. Maybe I should lighten up. I'll just call David later and question him about this. I'm sure when I return, I'll look at dad more closely.

* * *

Jake the floor refinisher came a week later, and Sarah and Jonathan discussed the job with him. He was to refinish the foyer, den, and kitchen floors by sanding, possibly staining, and applying a polyurethane finish. After listening to his recommendations, timeframe and cost Sarah said, "Let me make quick call to the homeowner."

Sarah returned to the den, looked at Jonathan and shook her head yes as Jonathan agreed. Jake asked, "Will it be alright to start working this afternoon."

The crew covered the completed bookshelves and enclosed the stairwell with plastic to minimize dust from collecting on the newly painted surfaces. The sanding process was a meticulous endeavor, so Jonathan and Terry spent time outside cleaning their equipment and the work area. Sarah dusted Jim's heirloom pieces they had stored in the living room and Terry made a quick trip to pick-up several pieces from a local upholsterer. As she worked, Sarah thought of Jim, he was on a junket.

After three days of sanding and a day of cleaning, Jake returned, and the decision was made to apply polyurethane to the beautiful, aged wood grain. After two days of drying the second coat of polyurethane was applied. At the end of the day, Jake painted his way out of the kitchen door, as Sarah locked up and hung a wet paint sign on the doorknob.

Sarah was beginning to feel job relief. The renovation part was finished, and the result was beautiful. Sarah had a new appreciation for Jonathan and Terry as beginning builders and would recommend them highly. She knew Jim was pleased and that was foremost to her.

As she drove home, she realized how exhausted she was, but looked forward to calling Jim to share the good news. As soon as she walked inside, removed her boots, poured a glass of wine, and sat down in her recliner and pushed speed dial for Jim.

He had gone to his room early after a fruitless attempt at Blackjack. He had slumped wearily into a masculine leather chair and covered himself with a thickly woven Irish Shetland wool blanket. As he anticipated her call, he visualized Sarah, and as soon as the phone rang, without looking at the name he immediately said, "Hello Dear." In a flash he thought; what if this isn't Sarah? He felt much better when he heard her voice and realized his quiet room had put him into a tranquil state of mind. He straightened himself in the chair, as Sarah described the outstanding job Jake had done with the floors.

He loved her excitement and drew strength that nourished his heart. His feelings of husbandry for her were dedicated to supplying the smallest of needs to this lovely lady. His excitement grew and they talked for thirty minutes or longer about the house, the workers, and his trip. Saying good night took longer than usual. He missed her and wouldn't have left home except he needed to be out of the house for a few days. He couldn't wait to get back and Sarah was looking forward to his return.

Soon after Jim arrived at the airport, he called to let Sarah know where he was and to ask about having the children over for a tour. Sarah thought because of their progress Thursday would be perfect. All three children were quick to say they would be there about threeish. The floors would be finished, and Sarah and her crew would be working in the den. Jim saw this as a chance for the children to also meet Sarah.

* * *

Sarah was busy on the ladder wiping the bookshelves and Jonathan and Terry were carrying boxes of books and accessories into the den and placing each on a blanket beside the shelves. Sarah heard the kitchen door open and thought it might be Jim, but instead heard a sweet voice say, "Hello."

Sarah climbed down from the ladder and went to greet the voice. She was delighted to see a beautiful young lady with dark eyes and brown hair. Sarah extended her hand and said, "Hello, I'm Sarah."

"…a friend of my dad's?" she asked.

"I'm working on the renovation and decorating part of the project."

"Hello, I'm Mary Beth. I'm just astonished to find a woman working in construction. Decorating I understand…please forgive me of my blundering. It's nice to meet you."

"It's nice to meet you, also. Your dad said his children would be coming by today. Well, what do you think?"

"The house really needed freshening, so I'm glad to see the changes. I'm excited that it looks as though it's the original construction," Mary Beth said.

"Your dad specified that, and we appreciated his respect for the original architecture. Come in and let me show you the bookshelves."

"I think it looks beautiful. I wish my mother could see this."

"With all the packing, clearing, and preparation, I've gained an appreciation for your mother. She must have been an excellent cook."

"She was and she taught us to cook. She just died long before her time," Mary Beth said with a trimmer in her voice while staring through glassy eyes.

Sarah instinctively reached over and hugged her, and whispered, "Bless you sweet child."

Unknown to them, Jim and Helen walked into the room. Jim saw them in a deep hug and felt emotional by their show of affection. He wanted to go and embrace both girls.

Helen saw the same thing and thought, what's going on here. Who is that hugging my sister? She suddenly pierced the room's quietness and said, "Who are you?"

Sarah and Mary Beth turned in their direction. With astonishment, Jim looked at Helen and said, "This is Sarah the contractor/decorator for the project, and Sarah this is my daughter Helen."

"It's nice to meet you," Sarah said as she swiftly made her way across the room. Her outreached hand met a limp handshake. Sarah thought, *the sisters are different…Mary Beth has a heart like her dad.*

"Jim, I'll be in the living room helping the guys unpack things."

As Jim reached for her arm he said, "Wait a second, I hear David coming in the back door. David, we're in the den."

With an outreached hand, Sarah found a firm handshake. "Hello David, nice to see you again."

"It's nice to see you, also. It's changed since last week. Wow dad, I know you must be pleased."

A look of admiration came over Jim's face as he laid his hand on Sarah's shoulder. "I am, but the credit goes to this lady and her crew. They love the old architecture of the house and have a respect for the place. I'm glad they're doing the renovations…and decorating," Jim said with a smile as he turned to face Sarah and was warmed by the thoughts of her encouragement as he was purchasing the vase for the den.

David and Mary Beth saw the way he reached out to Sarah and the sparkle in his eyes as he spoke. They could see his appreciation for her, and Helen noticed how Sarah raised her arm in the direction of her dad's waist, but let it fall. Helen only saw uncertainty and reason for doubt.

"Thank you, Jim, it has been a pleasure working here," she said as her eyes sparkled, and her smile was warm. "I'll leave you, but if you have questions, I'll be in the next room. It was nice meeting you all," Sarah said as she looked into the eyes of each of his children.

The children responded simultaneously, even though Helen was barely audible. Jim winked at Sarah and she responded with a slight smile. Helen thought, *it's her*, while David and Mary Beth were sincerely hoping it was Sarah.

Chapter 10

Early the following week the furniture order had arrived from the Furniture Mart. Jonathan, Terry, and Sarah worked franticly storing the furnishings in the living room as the men brought in the pieces. The rugs would be the first things to place in the room then the sofas and chairs. Next the armoire and the English chest were placed. They wanted to have the main pieces of furniture set before Jim came home from work, so he would see the beginnings of an attractive room as soon as he entered the house.

Jim checked in with Sarah several times, and at lunchtime, he surprised the crew with deli sandwiches, cokes, and cake. He said, "Y'all are having way too much fun, and I want to do my part."

The room was coming together, and Jim was pleased with everything. He especially liked the oil painting of the lambs over the English chest. He was a country boy at heart and thought the subject matter was perfect.

As he studied the painting, his mind traveled back in time to when he was young, and his father died. He was too young to realize the hardships the family would have and the financial struggles they would endure. As soon as he was old enough to walk the cotton rows, his mother had him carrying water to the pickers. He looked forward, he thought, to getting taller and older, so he could start picking cotton and make a little money. In hard times that day came sooner than he thought but the money was limited.

Year after year he faced summers in the tobacco patch and cotton fields, and the fall stacking peanuts. His dream of adventure with cleaner work and decent pay weighed heavy on his mind, but he was the last of the children and he felt he had to stay on the farm and physically support his mother.

During his senior year of high school, he made plans for college with no knowledge of how to pay for his dream. He was beginning to set his future course because he had always wanted more than the farm could provide. Jim saw college as his way out.

As the war in Vietnam intensified, Uncle Sam requested he serve in the military. Proudly wanting to serve his country, he put his education on hold. Months before he was discharged, he received his acceptance to the college of his choice in his home state.

He worked a night shift at a local laundry ironing clothes to pay his way and was able to send money home to help with the monthly farm loan payment. His brothers also sent money and with her frugal living their mom was able to keep the farm afloat. When the loan was paid, he along with his brothers advised her to apply for a manager's job in a local 5 & dime store in town and rent out the farmland. That advice was good news to her, because she needed a less strenuous job, but had regrets about renting the farm. She objected to the two oldest sons replacing her old farm truck with a shiny used Chevrolet, but they knew for her safety it had to be done.

The boys assured her, all those years they spent on the farm had taught them how to work, save and manage. Skills she had taught them by her example. Not only did she teach them to be good businessmen, but taught them to be kind to others, generous to the less fortunate and to love graciously with a forgiving heart. The brothers never forgot their mother and their humble beginnings.

Jim saw the country painting as a perfect symbolic reminder of his young days on the farm, and in turn, now had the financial ability to purchase an original oil painting by a noted artist. In many ways his life was coming full circle, and he felt in his heart this was an exhilarating time in his life with an opportunity to share it in a kind and loving way with someone special. It was comforting to Jim to entrust his heart-felt feelings to Sarah and her humble caring nature.

He dropped his head and rubbed the center of his forehead, "Jim, do you like what you see?" Sarah said, as she motioned around the room.

In a thoughtful frame of mind, he said, "I absolutely love what I see." With outstretched arms he moved from in front of the painting and put his arms around Sarah and softly said, "Thank you."

She caught the glassy glint in his eyes as he turned, and she knew where his thoughts had been. Her frame relaxed as he came nearer, and her hands traced along his strong workman shoulders. She felt she knew his heart.

When his snuggling chair was placed, he sat and watched comfortably as the delivery guys brought in the garnet red sofa. It was a more suitable match in the room than it appeared in the showroom. It looked gorgeous next to the new custom plaid drapes Katie had made.

Sarah went over and sat on the end of the sofa nearest to Jim. "Well, what do you think?"

"It's more beautiful than I imagined. I had a difficult time visualizing how the things we bought would come together. I remember the day you had a faraway look in your eyes, and you said 'perfect.' I didn't know then what you were seeing, but now I know."

Sarah smiled and felt his sincere compliment, as she thought he really likes what we're doing. With a catch in her throat, she reached over and rubbed his hand to affirm his statement.

The television was brought in and placed in the armoire. While Jonathan worked on its installation, Sarah gathered the color coordinated ceramic pieces to accessorize the top. She wanted to place the deep red urn Jim had purchased in a prominent position to the left top side of the armoire in front of a large decorative plate, accented by other coordinating containers.

Jonathan connected the cables to the satellite and the picture was perfect after making a few phone calls to the satellite technician. Jim's phone rang and he stepped outside to talk, so Sarah took this opportunity to add the ceramic pieces.

When Jim returned to the den, he saw the arrangement and was instantly excited. He was especially pleased to see something he had purchased placed in such a prominent spot. In amazement he put his arm around Sarah, as his voice became choked-up. "Granddad would have been pleased," he said.

They walked through the rooms arm in arm inspecting each piece of furniture. Sarah said, "Accessories will be added to the bookshelves as soon as we open each box, we packed twelve weeks ago, and that will almost complete the room."

"Then we can move on to another room?" He quickly said with a smile as he squeezed her waist and then gave Sarah a bear hug that completely caught her off guard. His exuberance surprised her...

She gently smiled and shook her head in agreement. "I suppose, if you want me around."

"*I want* you around. Why don't we go out for dinner and celebrate? I can't just let you go home. I want to let you know how much I appreciate you. We can go to Emmaline's or Paul's."

Sarah dropped her head, and her reluctance began to show.

"Emmaline's… it's quiet and private." He took her hands and looked into her eyes. "We can go just like we are…I know we've been working all day, but that's what makes this moment special."

With a sad look on her face and a flashback to her solitary life shaped by her past…glassy eyes developed. She looked away and said, "It's not easy to resist your invitation. I feel the excitement as well, but I haven't been out celebrating with anyone since long before my husband's death. I would feel awkward."

While holding her upper arm, Jim lifted her chin and held the side of her face as he said, "Tonight we can celebrate the excitement of the two us working together. That's all, and in turn we will begin to work on the other."

"That's sweet. I know I must get on with my life, so thank you for helping me gradually move out of my cocoon. If you're sure it's ok to be dressed like this…I'll go because I'm also proud of what we've accomplished." With slight reluctance she said, "Give me a moment to freshen."

When she returned to the den, he took her hand, "You're beautiful, work clothes and all."

"And you're a natural prevaricator," she said with a twinkle in her eye.

"I hope that's good."

"Tonight, it's good," Sarah said with that tiny smile he loved.

Emmaline's was a rustic, dimly lit BBQ restaurant suited to their workday look. Sarah was excited about celebrating with Jim on their almost completed project. When she saw the crowd of people inside a heated quiver struck her body, she closed her eyes thinking, *I am going to faint. I have an urgent thought of saying, I can't go through with this, but I'm too embarrassed to say it.* She held every prop she could find to support her weakened frame as they were seated.

Sarah had also not anticipated seeing her deceased husband's acquaintances. During the evening many of his friends talked with Sarah and gave her words of encouragement…demonstrating how little they knew about him and his narcissistic personality. Their comments upset her emotionally because she was trying to move beyond that part of her life.

Jim noticed the change in her expression and was unsure what to do except reassure her of the hurdle she was crossing as she stood strong in front of these people. He touched her hand and told her, "You will be stronger after this."

Also, Sarah felt it necessary to apologize and explain her reason for being out with someone. "Jim is my client and we're here to celebrate a job almost finished," she often said.

It was a painful evening mixed with ambivalent feelings sparked by Sarah's past and her venture into a new future. They soon realized they preferred the quiet comforts of the summerhouse. The chance to celebrate didn't happen, so they collected their meals in to-go boxes and decided to go out another time… maybe to a distant city for now.

Once inside the truck he gently massaged the palm of her hand and laced his fingers with Sarah's, "This was a difficult evening more than a celebration. The transition is not easy, but until you're comfortable, I will always do what I can to help you through, no matter what… because I care for you."

"And I appreciate you. I could see the man you are during our short dinner. Thank you for the time we shared, and I'm sorry for the emotional part of the evening," she humbly said.

"All evening, I wanted to see your smile and laugh at the fun we've had, but the location just wasn't right. Sometime soon, we'll have a real celebration, I promise."

"I accept and look forward to your invitation, my friend."

On arriving at Jim's, he excitedly said, "I'm glad I'm not just a client anymore and I'm looking forward to a hug every time you leave, my friend."

Sarah laughed and they grasped on to each other and rocked back and forth as the solemnness of the evening turned into joyous laughter. With a glad feeling they kissed with intimate passion and Jim commented, "There was something different about the feeling of that kiss."

"I felt it also." *I wondered if it could be the feeling of love,* Sarah thought.

During her drive home, the emotions took over. She cried out and beat on the steering wheel as she became frustrated about her feelings weighted by her past, while wanting to see hope for the future. "I'm tired of my past haunting my present. My heart is fighting to control my head. My head is giving into my heart. I know I want to believe in myself, venture onto a new path and break out into a new world." With her newfound courage she felt confident, but within a few hours her decision was challenged by her struggle with thoughts of self-doubt which caused her to tremble.

Later that evening, Jim called Sarah. She was lying in bed reading through sleepy eyes. Their conversation was sweet and caring. "I would really like to see you this weekend. Maybe we could go shopping or meet at the river with Lucy and Charlie."

Sarah and her girlfriends had already planned a girl's weekend retreat, but she thought *how nice it would be to spend time with Jim instead, but maybe I owe it to Jim to break away from him, because I can't seem to shed my past…I'm doing him an injustice.* Their conversation ended with a weak good night from Sarah because she couldn't share with him her true thoughts.

The girls had plans to go to an exclusive outlet mall near Forsyth for a weekend of shopping and relaxation. They were staying at the Ritz-Charlton on a lake near Greenville. They had already scheduled facials and a French carriage ride through the historic district.

Before she could talk to Carrie, Jim called early the next morning, "I really wanted to ask if we could go to Savannah for the afternoon on Saturday."

She quickly took the less intimidating way out. "I've already promised my friends I would go shopping with them. We have our hotel reservations, and they also need me to drive my suburban. I'd really love to be with you, but I've made plans," she said with aching reluctance.

"I have to go out of town next week for work and would like to spend time together before I leave. This was the first time I've asked you out for an evening that wasn't work related. Are you afraid to go out with me as a friend instead of as a client?"

"I can't answer that."

"You have to answer in order to move on with your life." *Our life*, he thought. "You must answer. I want you to go with me…please tell me why you can't. Is there someone else? Is it Mike? Are you going away with your girlfriends in hopes there will be someone else? Please tell me where I stand in your life." Jim was stressed and he recognized it in his voice. He made himself calm down because he couldn't let his questions bring stress into their friendship…especially at this time when he thought their relationship was going so well.

In her calm sweet voice, she said, "There is no one and I have no desire to go looking for anyone. I suppose I find safety with my girlfriends. I have anxiety about us going out. It's not you…it's me…my problems…it's my past that at times torments my future."

Sarah had come to understand a future relationship with Jim was possible, but she knew that relationship couldn't go forward if her baggage was still in her thoughts. She knew if she let herself go any further, she needed to relinquish her past, forgive, and forget, and take one small step into the unknown. It was a step she was having difficulty taking because of her fears of not yet trusting her life. *I fell in love before with someone I thought was a caring man, so I question Jim because he is so caring…is he real, or will he turn into a fake like Glenn,* Sarah thought.

"Jim, I need to walk away…you deserve better. I can't get past the struggles of my marriage. The flashbacks are controlling me." Sarah said as silent tears filled her eyes.

"I can't just let you go…you're a part of my life. I've enjoyed the things we've done together…our project, the things you've taught me, the way we talk to each other. We've laughed, cried and shared secrets. You must keep me in your life, you mean so much to me.

"Jim, I care for you and all the things we've shared…I love you with all my heart. I feel it's so unfair to you to care for you with these flashbacks that cause me to feel uncertain."

"Sarah, I love you and you have a place in my heart. I can't walk away…please let me help you…I will be patient like you taught me, I will wait for you, but please let me have a part of your life…please don't walk away." Jim said with heartfelt honesty and trembled as he spoke because he recognized the seriousness of each word.

"My dear, I understand what you're saying. Maybe if we can take it slow for a while then I will have time and space to work through my thoughts."

"If your plans change, then hopefully we could go to Savannah, just for the afternoon. We had fun when we were shopping for the house. I know...we can shop for a wool blanket for my cuddling chair," he said with mischievous excitement.

Sarah laughed and said, "You're so clever. I'll let you know soon."

"Please think it over and reconsider going. Just remember, I'm always here for you."

Jim wanted Sarah to answer quickly, but she hesitated. He mumbled aloud, "Something might be going on. What could that mean? I know she left early one afternoon, and Jonathan said she had dinner plans...could it be Mike or Bob. I can't question her again about that. If I don't find out something soon, then this will be a restless morning."

Later that morning Sarah called Carrie, "Sarah you have to move on and know the past is over. Jim is not like the person you were married to before. I've noticed how much he cares for you. He truly adores you."

"I honestly want to go with him, but I'm just afraid to venture out. We have been alone in a working environment, and he is extremely kind. I care for him, but I'm afraid to let myself show my true feelings for fear of getting hurt. If I go forward without feeling comfortable with my past, then it would be an injustice to Jim and an untruthful time for me. I don't know how to determine when I'm ready to move on."

"Going out with Jim is not the same as venturing into the unknown. If you are unsure about your feelings, then let me tell you what I see in him. I've noticed how he extends his hand to you...he looks at you and always recognizes your needs before you mention anything. I've watched him and I can see in his eyes how much he cares. He smiles every time you come near. He politely opens your car door. He does kind things for people even when no one is looking.

You've known him for a year now and if he was going to act or speak in a hurtful way, then I think he would have already, but he hasn't been angry, only kind and generous."

"You're right. I've never had anyone treat me so kindly, and sometimes I find it hard to believe. With Glenn, soon after the vows were said, he started treating me like a door mat. That fear is still there, but I can honestly say, I haven't seen or heard one degrading word or action toward me or to anyone or about anyone for that matter."

"I think you have your answer."

"Yes, I do. You can drive my vehicle…I'll give you money for the room…and please buy me something pretty. I might need something because it's time for stepping out," Sarah said with a timid playful laugh.

Sarah immediately called Jim. "Are you still interested in going to Savannah this Saturday?"

"Yes, but only with you."

"I talked to Carrie and she said go with Jim. We can all go shopping another weekend, so a friend of Lucy's is going in my place."

"I'm glad to hear that. We will talk again about what time we need to leave. I'm looking forward to our afternoon."

* * *

Helen had told David the news about seeing Sarah at Brown's with a gentleman. "They seemed to be old friends, judging by the way they laughed and talked. It could have been more than friends the way he hugged Sarah as she left."

David was in shock when he heard this, and silently took it upon himself to help his dad in his relationship with Sarah. Assuming his dad was going to Savannah with Sarah, David had insisted his dad use his sports car instead of the work truck. He helped him buy a spiffy outfit and have his mustache professionally trimmed. David also exchanged Jim's Old Spice or his British Sterling cologne.

Jim arrived at Sarah's at twelve-thirty on Saturday afternoon. She was dressed and ready when he arrived. She was wearing white pants with an aqua, cream, and white paisley print semi-sheer top over an aqua camisole. She carried a small matching Kate Spade bag.

"You look fantastic, as always," he said as he handed her a rose from his garden and leaned forward to kiss her cheek.

"Thank you let me put this in water," as she looked down with an embarrassed expression, sparked by the insecurity on this first date. *My outfit is a little bright for me and makes me feel self-conscious. My attempts at stepping out haven't been easy and wearing something even a little provocative is out of my comfort zone*, Sarah thought.

"The rose is in water...so I'm ready if you are."

"Wow, a new sporty car."

"It belongs to David...he insisted I borrow it. I told him about taking a lady out this afternoon. He said this was special and I needed to drive something decent and not the old work truck."

"It's nice, but your truck does have special memories from our shopping trips. I wouldn't have objected."

With a smile on his face he said, "Let me open the door for you on this special occasion my dear. You will have to forgive my blunders. All of this is new."

"It's new to me, so please excuse my nervousness," Sarah said with faltering courage.

"We'll take care of each other and laugh at our mistakes. Is that a deal?"

"...of course." Sarah smiled and settled into the cool leather seats knowing she was in good hands.

After they drove away from the house, Sarah asked Jim if he told his son everything about their plans.

"I only told a little, just that I was going out with a special lady. I know you're shy, so I didn't give him a name. Then he quickly started to give me advice about what to wear, what to drive and what to say and do. It sounded as though he wanted me to impress my special friend. I think he has hopes of marrying me off to someone, maybe anyone, so I'll ease up on him at work, and spend more time around the house," Jim said with a laugh.

Sarah responded with a nervous smile, "It really sounds like he cares about his dad."

"He does, and of course I do the same for him and his family. You haven't really gotten to know David yet. His wife has a great personality, and Abby and little Jim, my grandchildren, are special."

"I'm sure you enjoy being a Grampa."

"Grampa is my name; how did you know?"

"I just took a wild guess. You look like a sweet caring man who should be called Grampa."

"Well, I try to be," Jim humbly said.

They slipped into a lull for conversation, but after a while Jim said, "Last Tuesday, I went to Brunswick to look at a job, and was so impressed with the location. Harry O'Malley and his wife have a beautiful place on a deep brackish river. It's an enormous compound with a beautiful northern seaport style home with a sloping lawn with flawless landscaping. They want a ramp and a large floating dock to accommodate a yacht. I wish you could see their place."

"It sounds like a home I would like to see."

"The manicured lawn slopes to a seawall that holds back a fairly swift river. He has a pier over a marsh about eighty-five feet with a pavilion and wants to come off the side of the pavilion with an aluminum ramp leading down to the floating dock."

"That sounds extremely nice."

"He wants the best of everything, so the price will be quite high, but it's what he wants. I hope everything goes smoothly."

"Jim, I know it will. You've had plenty of experience in marine building…everything will be top notch."

"Maybe before the job is completed, you can come down and take a look."

"I would like that."

* * *

They had tickets to the three o'clock show at the Old Lucas Theater located in the heart of the historic district. Sarah enjoyed the ride through the city squares and admired the beautifully restored homes and businesses. The noise of the cobble stone streets was distracting, but the charm of the architecture and the oak tree moss shaded streets were warmly captivating.

The performance was a lighthearted comedy routine, with Broadway style musical renditions before and after each comedian. When they started to play and sing the Johnny Mercer tune 'Moon River', Jim held her hand securely. At the conclusion of the song, he brought her hand to his heart, kissed her fingers, which she wound around his hand. Sarah looked at him and felt sure he could see her chest rise as her heart pounded deep inside.

She leaned close and whispered, "I love that song. As a young teenager I remember, almost every morning while getting ready for school, listening to *Moon River* play on my transistor radio. Sometimes

I would dance around my bedroom and of course sing along. It's a song with special memories of innocent naïve daydreams."

"It was a favorite of mine. I was an older teenager with an interest in music. I imagined myself singing that song to all the girls."

"…and I'm sure you did," she said quietly as she glanced at Jim with a playful smile.

"Well maybe a few," he whispered.

The comedians were hilarious, but the music was romantic and often they looked at each other with penetrating eye contact. He was handsome in his light-yellow Ralph Lauren shirt and cream-colored Docker pants. His workman's hands were strong, and it was evident in his touch. Occasionally when something was especially funny, he reached over and patted her arm. Both had become contented with being together, and it showed by the way they enjoyed the evening.

Jim was patiently guarding his feelings for Sarah. He wanted to say more and hold her hand continuously. He couldn't overreact and come on strong, but it was obvious to him that she was enjoying being in his company. He took a long breath and rested back against his seat as he dreamed about the future he would like to have with Sarah.

Sarah noticed his complacency as he gently stroked her fingers. She didn't say a word but enjoyed the serene silence of the moment.

After the performance, they drove to River Street in search of a place for dinner. The street was crowded with tourists looking for the perfect souvenir or searching for the best place for the entire family to stand for a snapshot.

"Would you like an elegant meal or something light?"

"Honestly, I don't eat many elegant dinners especially this late in the evening, so you choose according to how you feel. No matter where you stop, I'll find something to satisfy my hunger."

"You aren't hard to please when it comes to food. That must be how you stay so slim."

"I love good food, so I can always find a delicious treat."

"What about the *Chart House*? I can park here if that's ok."

The restaurant was quiet and intimate which gave them a chance to talk about the performance and enjoy the evening in a more gratifying way. Jim laughed at her impersonation of one of the comedians, as he laid his hand on the table palm side up beside Sarah's, he expanded his fingers, and without hesitation Sarah placed her hand atop his, as Sarah looked at their twined fingers, then softly at Jim. In his thoughts he wanted to reach over and hold the side of her face and gently kiss her lips as the romantic mood of the moment touched him to the quick.

After dinner they strolled casually in the moonlight beside the river as a dinner cruise steamboat loaded their festive guest. With a romantic feeling for Sarah, he put his arm around her shoulders as she gently circled his waist.

In the distance they heard a saxophone playing a melancholy rendition of a Billie Holliday song. The sounds of the saxophone drifted through the waterfront park and the trees filtered the distant somber notes into a muffled sound like a siren moaning for her companion. Nearby a street artist was drawing a young lady with flowers in her hair. The rippling sound of water came from a freighter guided quietly by tugboats up the river.

Jim said, "What did you enjoy most about the day?"

"I think I enjoyed the performance of 'Moon River' when you took my hand, but dinner was peaceful and contented. I loved watching your eyes sparkle in the candlelight, and your laughter."

As she said "laughter," he rolled her around to face him and his hands circled her back. They were face to face and each with untold desires was almost petrified at the thought of what to do next. He caught a moment of hesitation in her face as she realized she was in a decision-making position. He was holding back but desired her tenderness. He wanted to hold her intimately but knew he must give her time to make the next move.

With her feelings of hesitation, she stroked the back of his neck and looked deep into his eyes. Her mind began to rationalize the moment. "We're deeply involved with your project, and I feel I can't jeopardize its progress by a more involved relationship with you my dear friend. I might be using the 'client relationship' as my reasoning for holding back."

With honesty, Sarah continued to speak. "Also, to be honest with you, I fear the baggage of my past might still be lingering inside of me. I fear befriending you would be unfair if my past is unsettled. An intimate romantic encounter is a beautiful joining of souls and I wouldn't want anything to bring injury to that special moment. I fear the emotional aftereffects of being intimate while weighted with my past." With tears tracking down her cheeks she said, "Please understand…grant me your patience, knowing how I care for you."

Now at this crossroad she was afraid to trust her feelings. *In my heart, I know I want to be affectionate with Jim, but that could be setting my-self up for pain, if things went wrong. I do not want to be hurt anymore. I'm not sure I can handle remembering painful flashbacks with more emotional loss.* Sarah whispered, "I have been complacent for such a long time and now I'm afraid to let go, but my heart is telling me it is time." *I know if I touch him, I will be on the path to a deeper relationship.* As her eyes focused on his shirt button, searching for the answer she said, "I know how safe and secure I feel in your presence, how I trust you…I've felt that way for some time now."

Sarah thought about her married life and said, "I walked on eggshells in my husband's presence. My days were tense and controlled by him. Now I look upon my life with the prospect of hope. I treasure the thought of being in my older years feeling thankful." She moved closer to Jim and kissed his neck just below his ear lobe. She let go of her past, realizing, *my time with Jim has given my life a new direction, and I have become trusting of our relationship.* She exhaled and her frame became completely relaxed into his arms.

With the back of his fingertips, he stroked her cheek and looked deeply into her mesmerizing dark eyes. Thoughts of marriage and an intimate relationship were soaring in his heart.

With wanting hearts, they experienced a warm passionate kiss. His lips were open, smooth, and grasping. He was so gentle. His arms were holding her, and Sarah could feel his compassion.

Sarah's journey fueled by faith and hope, gave her a rewarding feeling of contentment. She felt a twinge of ambivalence that would always be there, but in her head and heart, she was ready for her commitment to Jim. Emotionally she was not completely healed, but felt he understood, so for now, she would be watchful of her heart.

With prudence lurking, she knew, *a happy beginning wouldn't always equal a happy ending. What I must remember is life doesn't promise perfection. My earnest desire is for my next intimate feelings to be shared only with a matched pair partner. I feel Jim is my soul mate. In my ideal desire for security, I want to look at the beginning, and know it will give the perfect conclusion, the Happy Ever After Syndrome, but I understand there are no guaranties in life.* She had to decide as she felt the back of his hand drift slowly down the side of her face and his fingertips trace the curve of her upper lip and the fullness of her lower. The tips of his fingers lightly moved down her neck and his hand circled her there and his forearm rested lightly against her heaving breast.

Unexpectedly a flash back to her marriage made her shudder as she remembered, *how something as simple as having to cook a meal in front of Glenn brought on trembling stress because of his criticism. Often, I saw my life as inadequate, felt like such a failure and often sat in his presence in a rigid manner. It is the fear of losing sight of hope, once more, that causes me to hold back my feelings.* She knew she couldn't survive a recurrence of her past.

Deep inside my heart, I honestly see Jim as different, and Carrie has always said Jim was a caring man, unlike Glenn. Jim treats me with dignity and respect, which Glenn never did. Jim is gentle and causes me to smile each time I think of him.

I will believe in our future and give my heart freely. I feel I've surpassed the alternative of giving up and being content with exploring my desires in the claw foot tub.

They kissed with passion and a carnal feeling swept through their bodies. Sarah pulled back, looked down, laying her head on his chest, as his arms held her tenderly. She eased closer…they kissed with warm romantic passion and her decision was made as she rested her lips against his warm skin.

He inhaled a long draw of her perfumed neck and slowly breathed his warm breath beside her ear and a magical charge rushed over her.

She weakened into a cloudy daze as his lips traced her neck and she expressed a delicate moan. He kissed away the goose bumps, as Sarah exhaled and relaxed. His hands moved to caress her. Feelings were happening and each with strength of character knew it was time to withdraw from their embrace.

They released and in a knowing way, without saying a word… walked slowly to the car for the long ride home.

* * *

The following day after lunch Helen eagerly called David to find out how their dad's trip to Savannah had gone. David mentioned their dad's evening was spent with Sarah and spoke of his positive enjoyment.

"You must not have told him about me seeing Sarah having dinner with a man. I don't think everything would have been positive if he had known. I told you some woman was playing him along in hopes of getting something. He's always been a sucker for a skirt...and that's been going on since mom died. Maybe I should tell him," Helen said in a shrill tone of revenge.

"Sarah seems to be a nice lady...let's hope it was an innocent dinner. She and dad seem to get along well, but I will check on this."

"If you're going to mention it to him, then I won't say anything, but if you're not let me know, soon. I'll say something because we can't let someone slip in and take what's ours. Let me know what he says. Thanks, talk later."

Chapter 11

Carrie called to tell Sarah about the shopping trip, but she was more interested in Sarah and her evening with Jim. "Good morning sleepy head."

"Good morning to you Carrie."

"Now tell me all about your evening with Jim."

"It was wonderful. We went to Savannah to the Comedy Club at the Lucas Theater, but it was also a musical performance. The young folks sang lovely romantic songs that soothed the warm summer night. He held my hand while they sang, and often looked deep into my eyes. When they sang "Moon River" he took my hand and held it to his heart. We talked afterwards and discovered it's a favorite song for both of us.

"That sounds sweet," Carrie whispered.

"We had dinner in a romantic restaurant on River Street. After sharing a dessert, we walked by the river and he had his arm around me or was holding my hand the entire time. We kissed with sweet passion."

"Enough, I'm becoming passionate."

"I've never in my life been treated so kindly. I'm growing excited just thinking about our evening. I feel cautiously in love, I'm convinced of his generous nature and I appreciate his charm and respect. I can see hope," Sarah voiced with tender affection.

"I believe soon you will be saying you are truly in love... how exciting."

"I feel you're right, but at this time, he seems to have an understanding, that I need a bit of patience, not because of him, but because of me. Now tell me about the shopping trip."

"Darling, it was nothing like yours. Maybe we can all go back, that is if you have time. I did find you a lovely blue flowery lounging pajama set and a gorgeous sterling silver necklace. I thought you might have a need for something special."

"Thanks for looking after me in such a special way," Sarah said with a feeling of appreciation for Carrie's thoughtfulness.

Both girls continued to chat. We must visit, I want to see the glow in your face.

* * *

On Sunday afternoon, Sarah went to Jim's to take three pictures she had framed and to pick up several flower arrangements that needed to be reworked. That afternoon was unusually warm, so she casually dressed in Army green cropped pants and a sleeveless cotton blouse.

On instructions from Lucy, Jim had a bottle of Riesling cooling in the refrigerator along with a plate of cheese and grapes. The crackers were sitting in a container on the island along with two crystal wine glasses.

"Wow, I'm impressed," Sarah said with a delighted look.

He smiled, hugged her and she kissed him softly on the lips. "I wanted to do something special this afternoon since I'm going away for a week. Would you like a glass of wine? It's not Lucy's famous merlot… it's a sweeter wine." he said after their brief embrace.

"Yes, I would like a glass."

While Jim opened the wine, Sarah placed the cheese plate on the counter beside the crackers. She placed two small dessert plates beside several colorful cocktail napkins which she displayed. The napkins were imprinted with *every moment is special!!!* She read the inscription with a smile and said to herself, *this has Lucy written all over it.*

"You know your way around the kitchen," Jim said as he poured the wine.

"Part of it's just a woman's intuition and being here and watching you for the past several months. While you're at the O'Malley's, I have things to work on in the kitchen, I plan to clear everything away and accessorize with your personal items."

"Here's to us," Jim said as they raised their glasses.

"Yes, I agree. Here's to us."

With an inquisitive look Jim said, "Do you really agree? Do you feel there **is** an us?"

"I'm fond of you, and you have been patient with me and my nervousness. I would like for there to be an us in this client/decorator/friend relationship."

"I want that also," he said as he placed his hand gently on her arm, while searching her dark brown eyes. "As we walk through the rooms, tell me what you're considering."

"I've almost finished the den, so the kitchen is next. I'll clean and choose accessories from items you have, so it shouldn't take long to finish. Now the breakfast room needs two buffet lamps, the picture exchanged for a mirror I saw in the hall closet...also the dishes in the hutch need to be rearranged and a few decorative items added...items you already have."

"I'm glad you found things here. I like using the old pieces."

"I like that also and if you know of other hidden treasures, let me know," Sarah said as they meandered into the entrance hall.

"The entrance has an inviting look since the floors have been redone and the walls are freshly painted. It's bright with light from the transom and sidelights around the front door. To go with the traditional, but somewhat eclectic look of your interior, I bought several needle point pillows for the lovely antique English settee and the antique console table will be enhanced by a gorgeous ornate gold leaf mirror I found in the attic."

"Let me interrupt for a second, what does the word eclectic mean?"

"In your case, it means in this room you have furniture from different time periods and sources. The bench is English, the table has French legs, and the hall tree has an early custom look. Possibly your grandfather had it built for this wall. It's a collection selectively picked from different periods of time or locations and tastefully placed into the room. That's a good thing to have a collected look."

He was mystified by the way she described the room and used her delicate hands to emphasize her colorful words. "I'm glad to hear that it's a good thing because all of these pieces have been in here for as long as I can remember. One day soon I'll have to tell you the history of each piece of furniture."

"I would like that. As a house ages and owners travel, they buy pieces they loved. The home becomes personal instead of a period showcase house. Your home is filled with items your family appreciated and through generations have continued to relish their aesthetic value."

"I never knew how to appreciate what's here until you started helping me and explained the history and arrangement of the furniture and accessories. You're amazing."

Sarah responded with an appreciative smile and said, "I have new lamp shades stored in the bedroom and the rug is at the cleaners. Today I will take home the flower arrangement you said you cleaned with the air compressor and add new greenery for a fresh look. The lighting highlights the historic architectural details and enhances your brass and crystal chandelier. Your grand flowing staircase gives a dramatic charming welcome to your home. Soon the foyer will be finished."

"When you're working, think of what you would like as if this were your home. I trust your decorating skills. We're ready for a refill," he said as they meandered into the kitchen.

"Tell me about you're work site for next week."

He placed her glass on the counter next to his. "Remember the O'Malley's in Brunswick who wanted the floating dock for his yacht. He agreed on our price, we start on Monday. We have a good bit to do, so we thought instead of spending time traveling we would just stay nearby."

"It's also safer to stay. I'm sure traveling after a long day's work could be dangerous."

"Maybe by staying we can work early or late and finish sooner, hopefully in two weeks."

"Where's your work area located?"

"The house is on the Satilla River in a community called Dover Bluff. It's the next exit off the interstate after Brunswick."

"Yes, I remember, the one with the gorgeous Cape Cod styled home, you mentioned."

"That's right. We built the floating dock in sections in the shop here and it's loaded on two trailers along with our other tools and welding equipment. We have a guy lined up to put in the pilings for the dock, and the aluminum ramp will be purchased from a local supplier in Darien."

"Sounds as though you have been busy preparing."

"We've put work and thought into this. Please think of us…that it all goes smoothly."

"I love the coastal area, it's beautiful, but I can see the dangers of working on the water," Sarah said as she gently massaged his hand."

He tenderly wrapped his arms around her, and they silently held each other while thinking of their time apart.

Slowly she started to talk as if mainly trying to change the subject away from the dangers of his work. "I like Brunswick and Jekyll Island. There's a great outdoor grill at the end of the pier in front of the Old Jekyll Hotel. It has the best low country boil, oysters on the half shell, and the coldest Ultras. It's a picturesque place to dine, or just sit and watch the sun set, or the shrimp boats coming in for the day."

"You make it sound like a laid-back romantic place, almost like a coastal picture postcard. Fresh fried or boiled shrimp are my favorite."

"Yes, their shrimp are fresh and delicious. They usually have an entertainer on the dock who sings James Taylor or Jimmy Buffett type music."

"Maybe while I'm down there I'll have a chance to check it out."

"Not without me in tow," Sarah said as she laughed and laid her hands on his chest.

"Please plan to come down and visit me at work. We'll take some time off and go out to the island. I shouldn't pressure you like that, but I would like to go there with you."

"Maybe, after our projects are finished."

"You introduced me to the fun side of Savannah, now I'm ready to try the Brunswick area." He leaned in and kissed her, and she languished in his touch.

He gently placed his hands on her waist, "You're important to me and a special part of my life. I think about you all the time, probably more than I should. You certainly have a special place in my heart." The more he spoke the more intense his eyes became, and his fingers massaged her sides instead of merely holding her there.

The touch of his hand sent feelings radiating through her body. Sarah reached out and softly placed her arms around his shoulders and slowly eased closer. He held her as he spoke softly, "I'll definitely miss seeing you. We plan to return Friday afternoon and go back Sunday," he said as he slowly moved his arms around her with feelings of affection.

"I'll miss you also. Especially your sweet construction notes, and our time together each morning. I always look forward to seeing your smiling face," Sarah said with dazed emotions.

"Would you like to stay here at the house and piddle around, work on the things you've told me about?" He whispered against her skin as he caressed the side of her face.

As her vision tunneled and her breathing quickened, "I would get lost in this house all by myself. I was planning to take home several things to work on."

"You have the backdoor key, so if you think of something, then please come over and make yourself at home, also feel free to call me anytime whether you have a question or not." He moved his hand slightly lower and cradled the side of her face. He eased away the collar of her blouse and kissed the curves and hollows of her shoulder.

"Your home is beautiful, and I've developed such a fondness for it, but I'll work at home unless something changes," she whispered with thoughts of missing him.

Jim held her waist tighter and twisted her slowly and said with a smile, "Do you think an old ghost might come out and frighten you?"

"OH, I hadn't thought of that. It's knowing I'm alone that would bother me."

"So, it's my presence that gives you comfort," he said with proudness.

"Umm yes, I think that's it," as she leaned back and smiled.

Jim grinned and hugged Sarah and began to talk as he looked into her gorgeous brown eyes. "When we first met, I saw sadness and loneliness in your eyes." he said as he began to finger her hair. "You had a shyness about you that was akin to a frightened animal. I wanted to hold you and tell you everything was alright. I felt you needed to be comforted and cared for…blanketed with a feeling of security."

His grasp tightened and she gave to him. "I was afraid to touch you, for fear I would frighten you away and I knew I didn't want to do that. I've noticed how you've changed and feel confident with our relationship. I'll be away for a week, and I want you to know, I will miss you."

"Sarah, I've fallen in love with you. I see the real you. You're filled with warmth that glows in your smile. Your heart is filled with kindness, and your thoughtfulness has changed me for the better. You're a woman in every way radiating with genuine love, compassion, comfort and beauty. You're so caring and easy for me to want to love. Sarah, I will do anything for you, and as the old saying goes, I can't *unring* the bell…you have my heart."

"My darling Jim, you know my feelings. You know me. I've come a long way, and it has been with your patience and compassion." In a gentle voice, with her caring heart pounding she said, "I can't *unring* the bell either…I'm not even considering it."

As Jim held Sarah, there was a saddened feeling of missing her and the emptiness of being alone that created a warmth invigorated by his touch.

She felt the vibration of his cell phone and jumped when it intruded into their serene tranquil world. It violently vibrated again as his lips moved against her cheeks. They both yielded to its command as he exhaled a tearful primal moan.

"It's my son. He's on his way here to pack-up the equipment. He should be here in a few minutes," Jim said in an exhausted tone.

With a long draw of breath and a slow exhale she slowly said, "I also need to load a few things," as she exhaled a heavy breath.

"We will, but I need one minute longer," he said in a mumble of wet kisses on her neck.

"I will look forward to seeing you as soon as you return…I will miss you. Please be careful and know I'll be thinking of you and the crew." She said with a stammering voice and a dazed look in her eyes knowing that sorrowful tears were building.

"I'll call you when we leave on Friday…and while I'm home, I'd like for us to spend time together," Jim said as he looked deep into her dark eyes. They hugged in silence knowing their emotions.

They loaded the dust laden flower arrangements and a box of assorted things. She also took a picture frame with gold leaf missing from each corner, and several books with frayed bindings. With a smile on her face, she said, "This will give me plenty to do while you're away. Now, let me go. I'm sure you have things you need to get done."

"Please take this wine and cheese with you and remember me as you enjoy it."

"I will remember you my dear friend, I will call, but I don't want to bother you," she said with an intriguing look on her face.

"You never bother me, in fact it's comforting to know someone cares enough about my welfare to sweetly call," Jim said as he reached for Sarah.

They smiled and limply held each other with a gentle embrace and tried to soothe away the aroused desires. A need for companionship in a caring relationship filled with love was foremost on their minds. True love was brewing and flowing one to the other, and the thought of the seven days of separation was heavy in their consciousness. This had become an eye-opening awareness of their care for each other.

Feelings of being apart are churning deep inside of me, "I know you have to go away, but the reality of you leaving is causing such emotional distress...I must recapture my emotions because I'm about to cry with missing you. My emotions are acting selfish and immature or is it the feeling of caring that has saddened my heart." *I will contain myself before over reacting.* As Sarah looked into his eyes, she stroked the side of his face and said, "I miss you already."

"I will see you soon, I love you. And when I get back, we will have a long face to face talk," he said as his hand slipped from behind her neck.

"I always leave you wanting to talk to you longer and spend more time together. I love you. Take care of yourself and the crew."

His emotions were at a high and he could hardly bear the thought of leaving her. With his index finger, he traced the contour of her face as though recording it to memory. He slowly traced and retraced the curve of her lips. She felt the excitement of his touch.

Their eyes were locked into a penetrating gaze. A strong bond was building, but each retained a respectful restraint for the other.

They hugged and kissed with gentle passion. "It's not easy to let go." She soon left and he watched with sadness as she slowly drove away.

On the way home, Sarah had an empty feeling inside her chest. Sweet tears filled her eyes as she thought *how much I care for Jim. He has a hold on my heart. He's calming and sweet, and how nice it would be to share my life with someone so caring.* Instantly she began to smile, as she thought *of their tomorrows.* Her shoulders relaxed as she thought of him.

She talked aloud straight from her heart as though she had reached a new milestone. "In my heart, at this time, I'm living the life I have always wanted to live. I'm being true to myself and I feel a sense of freedom. I feel hope surging because of my struggles. For a long time, I lived the life others required me to live. I remember the pain. I can see the difference between how I felt then and how I feel now, I like the one I have become," Sarah said with confidence.

"Jim has been sharing his time with me and treats me with dignity. He shares his special homegrown roses and leaves sweet notes, not because it's a need, but because he cares. I've always been able to smell the fragrance of his presence even when he wasn't there. He brings me a feeling of peace and contentment…it's comforting."

Chapter 12

Jim and David along with a small convoy of trucks left early Monday morning for their five-hour trip to the coast. It was their first job working in this area and working with a marine barge contractor whom Jim had talked with only twice. The unknowns made them feel apprehensive.

Jim's thoughts turned to Sarah knowing she would be fast asleep at this time of morning. When they passed the road that led to Sarah's house, he unconsciously looked. He thought about yesterday afternoon and how he enjoyed her warm…

"Look out there's a deer on the right-side edge of the woods. She's running this way," David yelled with excitement.

"That was a close one. Call Rex and Bo to see if they're ok. We don't need to start our work week with an accident. The sound of the horn scared her off."

"Everybody's ok."

Jim thought *gee I like thinking about Sarah, but maybe I'll have to wait until I'm safe in my room tonight before I let my thoughts wonder.*

"Dad, I have something to tell you, it's about Sarah."

"…about Sarah?" Jim said with a bit of surprise.

"Well dad, I think the world of her, and I think she has helped you in so many ways. Helen told me she saw her having dinner with a man. It breaks my heart to think of this."

"Yes, son Helen was right. His name is Mike and he's an old acquaintance of Sarah's who is being transferred to a plant outside of Atlanta."

"Are you sure it's an old friend…Helen watched him hug Sarah and said it didn't appear as a casual hug from a friend."

"David, she told me about their plans for that dinner, and I know she has known this guy for many years. She told me earlier that Mike knew the temperament of her husband and had offered his support if she ever needed a way out. I don't think it was anything more than that, but I will certainly ask a few discrete questions. Thanks for telling me this."

"You and Sarah seem to get along so well. I don't want to think something suspicious is going on."

"Well, I hesitate to mention this, but she sometimes mentions another fellow's name. I'm feeling worried and confused. When we were together yesterday afternoon, there didn't seem to be any problem. I thought she was talking to me with honesty. I can't worry about this now…we have a job to do…I'll wait until I get home."

"If what Sarah told you is true, then she was innocently meeting her friend. Helen has a suspicious nature toward Sarah and could have embellished the story a little. I admire Sarah…can't see her doing anything to betray the relationship y'all have. It could just be Helen." David spoke encouraging words to his dad in hopes of soothing his wounded ego.

"Honestly, David, I think I'm in love with Sarah."

"Good for you dad…I think you should think in that direction."

* * *

The crew parked in the service area of the compound and evaluated the workspace. A concrete boat ramp would serve as the launch sight for the dock sections. One by one the six sections would be transported to the river by a front-end loader. Ropes would be attached to the crane on the barge which would float each unit out into the river and into position.

Jim looked over the work area as the first floating section was aligned six feet out the side of the existing pavilion. Knowing the dangers, he had insisted the men working with this unsteady section, secured only by ropes, wear life jackets. He was concerned for the workers but knew as soon as the pilings were installed it would be anchored. He had thought about the tides, weather, and river currents, so Jim was sure to have a life vest and raincoat for each man, but the men complained about wearing the heavy vest.

The crane driver began the tedious job of slipping the first piling into the opening of the dock section. David and Bo assisted him to determine when the piling was plumb. At that point, the crane driver attached a hydraulic driver to the top of the post and started the meticulous job of driving the pilings into the river bottom.

The tide was rising, and the river was growing swifter, so when the first section was secure the captain and crane driver left for the landing in their dinghy. "This had been a productive afternoon," Jim said and was anxious to get to the room so he could call Sarah.

"Hello Sarah, the construction is going smoothly. Harry, the homeowner, is super nice and seems to be a hands-on guy. What have you been doing today?" he said with excitement.

"As soon as I woke, I started missing you. Everything I worked on had memories, so my day has been a little melancholy."

"You sound a little sad," Jim said with understanding.

"I think I am, tell me about your location."

"It's beautiful…almost like a Caribbean resort. You would enjoy the beautiful yard and flowers, and the house is extraordinary."

"I would love to see it."

"My Dear, almost every turn I make I see something beautiful… today's sunset was colorful, and I thought of you. Just continue to remember how much I care, and it won't be long until Friday. Darling, I need to go. The boys are ready for supper. I'll give you a good night call when we get back. Love you."

* * *

Sarah woke early and after her coffee and oatmeal, she took the floral arrangement apart and washed each stem. As she worked, she vividly thought of Jim. She imagined his smiling face and wondered how his day was going. As the afternoon dragged on into evening, Sarah was feeling sad as she missed him.

The crane driver was late that morning and Jim was frustrated. By lunch time the second section was attached to the first and secured by three pilings. At the end of the day the third section was secured, and the perimeter supports were added along the first two sections. The day had been extremely hot and physical exhaustion had overtaken them. They were eager to call it a day as they cleared the site.

Jim's phone rang, "Jim, this is Mark, I wanted to know if we could meet tonight and talk about the aluminum ramp."

"Sounds good…where would you like to meet?"

"There's a place on the water on Jekyll with local seafood. It's a good place to introduce you to the coast life. I'm not far from your motel, so I can come by and pick you all up around six."

"We'll be in the lobby."

* * *

After dinner Jim could hardly wait to get back to the room and call Sarah. From the description she had given him, he knew they had eaten at her favorite place on the island. As soon as she answered he said with an excited voice, "Guess where I went to eat tonight?"

"The pier, I bet."

"Yes, and it's just as dramatic as you described. Another contractor on our job treated us with dinner out. As soon as we parked, I knew the rustic dockside restaurant was your special place…I thought of you."

"Isn't the food and atmosphere just superb and so laid back."

"It was, but I wished you could have been beside me. Soon, I promise, we'll go there."

Sarah could feel the tiredness in his voice, so she quickly told him about her day spent completing a few things. They sluggishly expressed their concern for each other. "Darling," she said. "You sound tired, please rest and have a good night. I love you."

* * *

Jim was excited to see the early morning sunshine and clear skies. He just knew this great beginning would result in a productive day. With contained optimism he watched the crew as they prepared to launch the next dock section. At mid-afternoon, their productive day came to an end as a cigarette boat came past at top speed. The endless roll of waves created a domino effect at the work site…

"Sarah, this is David, I sorry to tell you this, but we've had an accident here. A boat made a large wake that snapped the anchor ropes on the barge that shifted the entire dock. Dad fell into the river…we can't find him."

"Oh no, that can't be…not now…no," Sarah cried.

Through sorrow David said, "Lucy and Charlie are coming over to be with you. The Coast Guard is here, and we are all looking. He is wearing a life jacket and that's good…if he wasn't hurt in the fall. I will let you know as we search. Sarah, my dad loves you and he told me about how thoughts of you kept him alive while he was in Vietnam. I'm sure he's thinking of you now, as he also knows your thoughts. Our family loves you, and we need you…please stay strong and take care of yourself."

"Your news is shocking, but I'll be strong for Jim and you all. If I can go and help you, I will. I'll be praying."

"I love you Sarah…stay there for now and I'll contact you often."

Sarah walked to the kitchen and said aloud in a sad mumble," I won't have Jim to talk to tonight about arranging the flowers he used the air compressor on, or the bookends and paintings that will look good on his bookshelves." Sarah wilted as she thought of her dear missing friend, and how she could only reach out to him in her thoughts. Sarah thought of Jim's daughters. When Lucy arrives, "I'll get her to help me reach out to them." Sarah's knees were trembling. "The doorbell."

As soon as Sarah saw Lucy, she broke down and Lucy understood why, and they cried. "I can barely stand the thoughts of Jim being lost, alone, in danger and could be hurt."

"I know how deeply you care. We wanted to be with you and comfort each other. Come in here, we need to sit down."

Sarah's phone rang, "Its Mary Beth…I have to be strong. Hello my dear."

"Sarah, I would like to be with you…is it ok to come over?"

"Yes, my dear, come on…be careful."

"Mary Beth will need our comfort. I'll go make a pot of coffee," Sarah said as she slowly walked into the kitchen.

Charlie said, "If they don't find Jim this afternoon, we can go there tomorrow, if you would like."

"I would like that…we can decide tonight after David's calls," Sarah said with trembling hands as she pill-rolled her tissue.

The foursome in somber disbelief snacked and cried as they thought of Jim. Mary Beth mentioned that she didn't want to be alone and could she spend the night with Sarah.

David called at eight. "The search parties didn't find dad and will be going out tomorrow at daybreak. On his life vest is a whistle and a blinking light. A plane is going out tonight searching for that light."

"That sounds encouraging. Lucy and Charlie are here also Mary Beth…we have been talking with Helen. Your family, is there something we can do for them?"

"Thank you they are alright and I'm glad Mary Beth is there. I appreciate Helen calling. I'll call you tomorrow morning as soon as I know something. I will go out searching and the crew will clean up our job sight."

"Thank you for everything, take care and be safe…love you," Sarah said as she heard him whimper."

Lucy held Sarah's hand, "It's almost bedtime and with Mary Beth with you, if you feel alright, we will leave. Call me after David's call.

"Mary Beth is in the shower, but I'll find out her plans and maybe we can go to Brunswick day after tomorrow. I appreciate your coming over, I don't think I could have made it without your help."

"The shower felt good. Sarah what do you think?"

"Darling, I think your dad is a strong, courageous. intelligent man. I believe he will do all he possibly can to survive and be found. I have confidence in him that he will come back to us."

"Thank you, I needed to hear you sound so assured. I also think dad is strong minded and I'll continue to believe in him…and in you."

"You're welcome my dear."

* * *

David's night had been a restless one. He awoke finding himself wet with sweat as he relived the accident. His muscles were sore after waking several times in a tense drawn fashion with thoughts of the shifting crane and snapping cables…and seeing his dad fall into the turbulent water. He quivered and said with questioning optimism, "Please let this be a better day. Help us find dad."

"Mary Beth, the plane didn't find your dad. The Coast Guard went out this morning. David will call us as soon as he learns something," Sarah said as she reached out to Mary Beth and they hugged and she mumbled, "Something good will happen soon."

"David said Harry had given them the option to close down the work in progress, but the crew will continue working because his dad would want it that way. David is going out on a search boat. If they don't have good news today, I would like to go there just to be close by. Lucy and Charlie want to go tomorrow."

* * *

The barge captain and crane operator arrived on time and added the last piling to the fourth section. After lunch, the fifth section was floated into position and the process of securing it to the fourth section was flawless. Tomorrow if all continued to go well, they would secure the sixth and final section. Completing that dangerous part of the job would be a relief to the crew.

"Hello Sarah. They didn't find him this morning. The Coast Guard is asking for our safety records and the number of life vest we have in use. I'm getting nervous. I'm wondering if they're trying to find us or the barge Captain liable for the accident. Sarah I'm so exhausted from fear and worry. The stress of knowing dad is lost in the water is upsetting, and now I have a fear of a legal accusation."

"I'm sure you are stressed. Lucy, Charlie, Mary Beth, and I want to come down. We want to be close to where this happened and support you and the crew. We can be there this afternoon by six. We must think of Jim and hope no legal problems arise."

"That sounds great. Be careful and I'll appreciate the comfort of family. I'll call you at lunch with an up-date…and Sarah thank you."

"Hello Sarah. They found a shirt with a pen and pencil in the pocket…I know it's his. There are several torn places, so he might be injured. They will concentrate on land and water in that area. I'm on my way there now. The last section of the dock was secured this morning and the crew will leave for home. They will reload the trailers and come back on Sunday afternoon. I'm going to stay, so please come. We have rooms and I'll text you the address."

"That's good news. We will leave soon. I talked to Helen…she would like to go, but with children and the business, she feels she needs to stay here. Is there anything we can bring you?"

"I can't think of anything. Be careful and I look forward to seeing you."

* * *

David rushed to the door when he heard Lucy outside in the hallway. The excitement of seeing a familiar face at such a stressful time created a need to hug each one. Sarah was last, and when their eyes met, he had to choke back his feelings. He grabbed her with a zealous hug. "It's good to see you all. This means so much to me."

"I knew you didn't need to be here alone…we also wanted to be near with our thoughts of Jim," Sarah whispered almost in tears when she said Jim's name.

"We know you're going through a lot. We just couldn't stay away any longer," Charlie said.

"We haven't heard anything this afternoon, but the search leader said he would call around six. I went out yesterday to the place where they found the shirt. We searched the wooded area and found a piece of paper that could have been a piece of his drafting paper. For several hours we searched thinking he might have wondered from that area, possibly looking for food. I found another piece of paper and the search leader is there looking for a paper trail."

"That sounds encouraging. I hope he will have good news for us," Mary Beth whispered.

"I left a bottle of water and crackers in case he comes back that way. Harry said he would take us out tomorrow morning."

Sarah spoke first, "I would like to go…I have this feeling inside that the strength of our thoughts and our presence will pull him from where he is back to us. We came prepared to search."

"That sounds great. We can go next door for dinner and return here to wait for the call."

When David's phone rang, he instinctively looked at Sarah. "Hello this is David." The search leader talked for a while, David said,

"Four members of my dad's family are here and would like to go to the search area around nine o'clock tomorrow morning. Alright, thank you."

He said, "They found more pieces of paper, so it's definitely a trail from dad. Also, they found clam shells in an arrow pointing north, and where someone had attempted to build a fire. Tonight, a helicopter with a heat sensory camera will fly over the search area.

* * *

The group was excited with the good news and with going to the area where Jim seems to have spent some time. Sarah took a bag of hats, snacks, and other needed items. In addition, she packed a separate bag for Jim. She included a red plastic poncho, a cap, water, high energy snacks, a flashlight, matches and a first aid kit with a tube of Neosporin. She felt if Jim returned to that location, her care bag would show her faith and optimism in him.

When they arrived at the construction site, Harry was waiting in the Boston Whaler. David pointed out the new dock area as they floated by. With an assortment of flash backs and imaginings they quietly headed out for the south side of the Satilla River. As they cruised along, Sarah couldn't help but visually search the swamp grass that softened the edges of the ominous river.

Sarah often observed David…she could see the stress in his face, and Mary Beth had a look of being lost. She thought, *I'll reach out to Helen when we get home. I'm heartbroken missing Jim…I see it's important to comfort his children.*

The group felt devastated as they loaded their overnight bags the next afternoon. Their searching had turned up no results. It was difficult for David to say goodbye and upsetting for the group as they drove away.

About two hours from home, Charlie suggested they stop for dinner. He was starving and Mary Beth and Lucy were ready for a pit stop. They ordered soup and salad, and hurriedly left the table for the restroom. "Sarah I'm glad we have a few minutes alone because I wanted to mention something. From the first time we met, I've admired you. I was infatuated with your caring nature and felt protective of you, particularly in your relationship with Jim."

"Oh."

"Yes, I've known Jim for quite some time, so I know his ways. I thought you were getting into something where you would get hurt. Lately I've seen him mellow and I've seen how happy you are." With damp eyes he said, "I want you to be happy, so I'm giving you and Jim my blessings. For your sake, I'm hoping he will be found soon and come home to you."

* * *

David slowly dragged his feet off the side of the bed and stretched a mile. He ambled to the coffee pot, showered, and made himself ready for the day. He felt confident with the feeling of this being the day.

The search leader told him the plane had pinpointed a location and they had gone out before day searching. David called Sarah with the news. He hurriedly followed the team into the wooded area to the pinpointed location and fanned out to search. They discovered Jim's trail was leading in a circle south in the direction of where the shirt was found.

"Sarah, good news, we're on his trail. It's leading to the place where you left the care kit. Let's hope he's there now. I will call as soon as we know something."

"Thank you, I'll call Helen. Mary Beth is here. David I'm excited. Be careful."

After several hours David called, "Sarah, I've spotted him with the binoculars across the marsh. We should get to him in maybe an hour. He's back where he started. It looks as though he's asleep with the poncho you left covering him. I hope he is alright…just lying down resting. I'm walking through a swampy area. I'll call you back."

"Mary Beth, more good news, David has spotted Jim, and should be with him in maybe an hour. He'll call back. Helen you're here. I'm so thankful and beside myself with excitement."

Mary Beth was joyfully crying and hugged Helen, as Sarah wrapped her arms around both the girls."

"Sarah, put your phone on speaker…I hear him snoring…what a beautiful sound. I'm touching him now. He looks good considering… thank goodness, his eyes are wide open like being in shock. Dad, we found you. Dad it's good to see you."

"Son," Jim said as he cried out and reached for David. "I'm glad to see you, I'm so tired…hungry. Can we go home?"

"Yes, dad the doctor needs to check you…lie still for now…and soon we can go."

"I found this bag and Sarah's sweet note…It saved my life…I love her."

"Here dad, she's on the phone, talk to Sarah."

"You will never know how your care bag gave me hope…I love you and will see you soon."

"Jim, I love you and was praying you would find it. I'm looking forward to seeing you, my darling. Helen and Mary Beth are here… speak to them. I love you." As Sarah handed Helen the phone her trembling knees almost buckled. She silently trembled with emotion and with a thankful heart.

After Mary Beth spoke to her dad, David said, "The doctor and the rescue boat are here…I'll call you back soon. Also, he said for me to be sure to get the care bag Sarah left because it saved my life," David managed to say as everything became emotionally heavy.

The girls sat in silence as the relief of the past few days brought on a mixture of feelings. Mary Beth smiled and laughed with optimism while Helen openly cried after seeing and feeling the stress her family had been under. Helen had purposely worked long hours and spent extended time with her children, in an attempt, to appear strong, even though she wanted the motherly comfort Mary Beth was feeling from Sarah.

Sarah moved to sit between them and put her arm around each one. She comforted them as she said, "I'm not sure when Jim will come home, but we need to ask if he would like a home coming family dinner or a small gathering of his friends. We'll talk to David and he can let us know how your dad is feeling and what would be best. I have chicken salad ready for our lunch."

In the late evening after Jim was examined, David took him to their motel room. He had several cuts and a bruised shoulder, needed rest, but first wanted a shrimp dinner. Jim was anxious to be in the room for rest but wanted to call Sarah.

"Sarah," Jim said with a weak voice.

"Yes, my love."

"This is the second time that thoughts of you have kept me alive. You are my angel. I love you with all my heart. I'm looking forward to seeing you soon," Jim's voice trembled.

"I want to see you. Please rest knowing you're safe and loved," Sarah said in a whisper as she struggled to control her voice.

With a weak whisper Jim said, "Sarah, I wish you were here…I want to hold you…you make me feel at ease…I need you."

When David arrived at the job site, he gave Sarah a call, "Sarah, Dad wants to see the dock. He feels bad about appearing weak and not being on the job. He plans to rest today, but tomorrow morning wants to watch the guy's work. I'll carefully observe him. We are near finishing, so we will stay at least until Friday. I'll call and let you know our plans. Also, Dads phone landed on the dock when he fell, so I'm sure he will be letting you know how he's feeling. Sarah you have been a blessing and have given all of us strength. Thank you."

"Yes, he just called, and it was wonderful to hear his voice. David, I wish I could be there with him," she said in a whisper.

"I wish you were here, also. I feel he would love that."

* * *

Harry and Mark greeted Jim with an enthusiastic welcome back. They watched as the crane lifted the aluminum ramp, Bo centered it within the railing opening, and installed ten-inch bolts into the flange that mounted the ramp into the pavilion's flooring frame. When the last bolts were secure and seeing the ramp resting squarely on the floating dock below caused the men to drop their shoulders and exhale a deep breath of relief.

David called Sarah, "We plan to leave tomorrow morning coming home. Dad is doing well this morning and I'll take him back to the motel after lunch, while we finish the last details."

"David, do you think Jim would want a coming home family dinner or a friends-drop-in."

"He is tired, and I really think for now, you're the one he really wants and needs to see."

"That sounds so sweet and I know in my heart, I'm looking forward to seeing him," Sarah spoke with emotion.

* * *

Jim spent the afternoon resting, but in between his naps he checked in with Sarah. Sarah it's hard for me to find the words sweet enough to express how special you are. I honestly love you," Jim said with deep sincerity mixed with emotions.

"My darling, you mean more to me than you can imagine. I want to love and care for you through hard times like this and through the good times. I want you to know I'm supporting you in all that you are, my love," Sarah said with reassuring fortitude.

After their conversation ended, Jim broke down as he thought, *I will be home soon. My heart is lonely and filled with a need to have Sarah's comforting arms holding me during this release of emotions. I have never in my life had anyone care in the way I feel Sarah cares for me.* In a muffled tone he whispered aloud, "Sarah, I love you with all my heart. I love you just the way you are and as soon as I get home, I'll tell you how I feel and what my intentions are and have been all along."

* * *

The next morning Jim was feeling better and enjoyed seeing the finished floating dock. He was proud of his crew's work during the time he was lost. "This has been a good lesson for me. I thought I had to be hands-on with every project, but now I can see that great things can happen with me not around. I just need to trust other people to manage things," Jim said to David as a trembling smile filled his face.

Jim sat under the pavilion and called Sarah as the crew looked over the work area and loaded their equipment. His voice quivered when he described his sunburned face. "I was weak and the thought of being lost and alone haunted me, I thought what if I pass out somewhere in this marsh and slowly give up, but when I found your note, I felt new life inside of me." As he talked uncontrollable tears flowed and Jim felt embarrassment for weeping, but also found contentment in knowing Sarah was a tenderhearted soul who would not see weakness in his stressful release.

"I want to comfort you, my love. Soon you will be home."

"Harry is pleased with the dock and knows it will work for his family. He said, 'you're a man of your word, and your crew worked on faith, I appreciated that.'"

The stressful work along with the emotional exhaustion had taken its toll on the crew. With a feeling of welcomed relief, they *all* loaded in their trucks for the long ride home.

"Sarah, we're leaving for home and should get there about six o'clock. I'll call you as soon as I take care of a few things for the crew."

"Glad you're on the way and I look forward to your call. Lucy asked if we could go down to the cay when you get home. Would you like to meet there tomorrow morning after you rest and get your energy restored?"

"As soon as I see you, I'll have my energy back."

"Come to the cay and we'll relax all day on the boat in the inlet or in the hammock by the river."

"That sounds nice to me. I have so much to tell you," he said as thoughts of being with Sarah caused him to shudder.

Chapter 13

Late Friday afternoon, Sarah went to Lucy and Charlie's place at the landing. She unpacked her clothes and thought of Jim. She felt of her soft comfortable things, worn jeans, flip flops, a cotton under-shirt, and top shirts. "My clothes are casual, but it's what Jim likes."

The next morning, Sarah was outside piddling in the flower bed, when she heard Jim's old diesel work truck rounding the last curve before pulling into the driveway. As she walked his way her emotions surged as she thought of seeing Jim, and tears began welling up in her eyes.

"…come here to me," he said when he saw her swiftly walking from the far corner of the yard. His eyes admired her as she came.

Her pace quickened to a brisk run, and with opened arms and without hesitation, she entered his embrace. They held each other with loving feelings for several minutes as they remembered the stressful weeks apart.

Sarah cried as she drew his fragrance inside of her and whispered against his neck, "My love, it is so good to feel you beside me…I love you."

"I've missed you as well…every day. I missed stealing kisses from you. I missed the fragrance of your skin and our quick little touches," he said as he kissed her neck, and readjusted his hold in hopes she could catch her breath.

Words mumbled from her mouth as tears flowed down her face. "I longed for your smile, your laughter and all those wonderful stolen kisses I let you take from me."

"You've been letting me take those kisses." Jim exclaimed as he snuggled against her with his lips loving the warm feel of her skin. He held her close beside himself.

"I've willingly let you take as many as you wanted and wanting to give more. My heart is so warm for you. The accident and your time away created a deeper sense of aloneness and a need to be near you. You're filled with loving compassion…I adore you. Oh Jim, I love you."

"I'm glad to hear you say that. I love you with all my heart. I want to hold you and touch you," he said. His hands drew her close, while his hands massaged and traced her body. His lips were wet, and his kisses were filled with passion.

They whispered loving phrases, and Sarah could feel his wishes growing strong. As they gained control of their emotions, they slowed to a soft tenderness. They looked into each other's eyes and saw affirmation, trust, and love.

"I wish…" she said with a long pause.

"I know…I'm wishing also." They each took an arm full of groceries and hurried up-stairs.

"Where are Lucy and Charlie?"

"They went into town for food and then on to Alice and Fred's house for an afternoon visit," Sarah said as they deposited the grocery bags onto the counter.

"Then we have the house all to ourselves." Jim said as he quickly grabbed Sarah from behind and wrapped his arms around her stomach and pulled her back beside him with gentle eagerness. He kissed and nuzzled her neck as his hand opened wide against the front of her stomach and eased up to rest under her breast.

"Lucy said they should be back around six."

As they turned to each other, a small bag of apples popped open and scattered across the floor. With her raging body she pressed him against the refrigerator and spread her wet kisses over his face and neck. "I'm glad to be holding you. I was afraid…you're here now."

"I'm here and we're alone." Jim whispered.

"Yes…all alone, for once."

They quickly picked up the apples and put the cold items in the refrigerator and he immediately removed her top shirt as they looked at each other with wanting eyes. He could see her maturity protruding against the under shirt, and it made a distinct visual impression that swept over him like lightening.

He gently placed his hands high on each side of her waist and let his fingertips rest in the trench of her spine and eased her one step closer. As he touched her delicate frame, he felt warm smooth skin he had never touched before, and it stimulated his senses.

"I love your hands touching me…you excite the woman inside. It makes me tingle all over. I'm small, but you make me feel so special," she passionately said.

"You're perfect…your skin is warm and smooth. Oh my, I want to be with you."

"…come to my room."

"Yes, I would love that…if you're sure," He said as he breathed heavily.

"I'm sure. I've missed you. I want to be close to you."

They kissed with loving passion and were fixed in a trance for each other. She totally loved and cared for Jim as strongly as a wife loves her husband. The tension filled weeks she stressed over had opened her eyes to Jim's ability to survive on thoughts of his family and Sarah.

"I planned our first time together like a bride plans a wedding. I had the location picked, my clothing planned and words ready, but this is so wonderfully spontaneous. My body is tingling for your touch. I've cared for you for so long," Sarah mumbled between passionate kisses.

"I also dreamed of the perfect romantic location, but I've missed you so. My heart wants to be next to you."

"Here's my room."

He touched and admired her body through the cotton under shirt as she unbuttoned his shirt and admired his gorgeous graying chest hairs.

Her lips were teasing his masculine chest, as he moved his pulsing body against her hand as she fumbled with the last button. Her arms slipped around him, as she became entranced by the muscular grooves of his back.

His thoughts were of tender affection, as passion stirred his manly desires and her lightly covered breast, warmed him all over. He tenderly took hold of her and brought her to his waiting mouth. He kissed with wet roving lips and she moved against him in response to his passion.

She reached down to remove her undershirt. He watched with desiring eyes as she slowly raised her shirt. His hands slowly traced her body as the rising shirt cleared her waist. As it traveled up her mid-section, his hands grasped her extended rib cage. And then just below her breasts, she stopped and looked into his wanting eyes. His hands were beginning to move under the shirt as she leaned forward to raise it again. When the shirt began to expose more of her body, Sarah expressed loudly with excitement and panic, "That's a car door slamming."

"It can't be, not now. Look out the window, who is it?" he cried.

"It's Lucy and Charlie."

In a rage of intimate passion, she rubbed against him as she kissed her way up his chest. They looked at each other with aching sorrow as she began looking for his shirt as Jim tried to straighten her undershirt.

Sarah quickly buttoned her shirt and fastened her jeans while Jim put on his shirt and she hurriedly tried to button the buttons. "Something's wrong, the buttons aren't fitting, you have your shirt on wrong-side-out. Hurry take it off. Now I can get it started, but my hands are trembling."

She breathed heavy and laid her head firm against his chest. She wrapped her arms around his lower back and felt the warmth and strength of his body.

"This is torture…time is running out. We've got to pull ourselves together. I'll go into the bathroom and can you handle things out there?"

Sarah brushed her hair, dabbed on coral lipstick, and ran into the den. She checked her face…straightened her clothing. She hurried to the counter and tore opened the case of cold Cokes Jim had brought. Poured her a small glass and sat the can on the end of the counter as though Jim had been sitting there for a while. She ripped open a bag of chips and sat down on a kitchen stool as she gulped a swallow…took a deep breath to relax.

Jim came out of the bathroom looking rosy faced, but cool. His clothes were orderly as though nothing had taken place. He took a long gulp of coke and looked at Sarah, "Your hair should be red, because you are a stirring young lady, almost too much for this old man."

Sarah smiled at him and touched his mid-section as he leaned over and planted a soft kiss on her lips. He calmly sat on the kitchen stool behind her.

"Hello guys. Hello Jim, it's so good to see you my dear. Darling we were so worried about you, but this one, Sarah, she broke down a few times in private, but she was strong for your children. She took care of every situation with courage. You would be proud of her for her strength and support she gave. I think her compassion for you has made your family stronger."

"I know you're right. At first, I saw her caring way as rescuing me, and then I saw Sarah's nurturing ways influencing my children and our relationship. She has a place in my heart. I thank you and Charlie for your help in kindling our friendship," Jim said with gladness.

"We're all glad you're here," Sarah mumbled with trembling lips. "Can I make your lemonade?"

"Sure can. Let me change into my jeans."

While Sarah mixed the raspberry lemonade, Jim stood close behind her. "You're so caring and gentle. I love you so much." he whispered as he struggled to hold himself in check.

"There are things I want to say to you. Thoughts fueled by passion but based on the love and care I have for you. I know if much more is said, I might fall apart."

He whispered. "Maybe we'll have a chance to walk out to the dock. We need to talk."

Sarah looked up at him, "We will."

Lucy changed and returned to the kitchen. She took a few snack items from the refrigerator and spotted an apple on the floor under the edge of the cabinet. As she picked it up, she said "I wonder where this came from."

Sarah smiled and without hesitation poured Lucy a glass of lemonade. Lucy finished it to her liking, sat at the counter and enjoyed a small plate of mango salsa and tortilla chips.

Lucy noticed Sarah twirled a few olives on her plate while Jim seemed to be mesmerized by a bottle cap as he looked up at Sarah as though thinking of something. "You guys look exhausted, like you've had the rug pulled out from under your feet."

"I'm sorry, I guess I'm a little exhausted," Sarah said.

Jim looked deep into Sarah's eyes and mumbled, "I think my thoughts are on something besides food. Sarah, I think I need for you to take me for a walk out to the dock. Cousin Lucy, will you forgive us if we go outside."

"Oh no my darlings, enjoy yourselves. I need to marinade the steaks and get the potatoes wrapped. Do you want your drinks?

"No, I really don't think I need that."

"Neither do I," Jim said.

Lucy watched them as Jim held her hand and they walked down the steps. They put their arms around each other as they meandered to the dock. Lucy thought their quietness after being apart during such a horrific event had created a heartwarming sign of seriousness. Lucy quivered and thought, Charlie hurry on up here.

Charlie was visiting with the neighbor and in mid-sentence he noticed how Sarah and Jim seemed to drift in the direction of the dock. He noticed how Jim's hand rested gently on her shoulder and Sarah circled his waist. Her head was turned as though he was whispering something in her direction. As his eyes followed them for a while, he thought, *their demeanor seems different. Sarah just looked up into his eyes. Something is different.*

"It's beautiful out here. I love the sound of the water rushing past the dock."

In a quiet manner Jim said, "It is peaceful and that's what I need right now. I wanted to get you out of there. I need to be alone with you." He kissed her hand and held it tight against his chest. He palmed her head into his hands and held it next to his, "My darling Sarah you're so warm, snug against my chest...let me wrap my arms around you."

"Would you rather sit inside the boat?" Sarah whispered.

As Jim stroked her hair he said, "Yes, I would like that. When I was lost and would lie down at night, I would think of you. I feel so connected to you because of our past, and the sweet affection we have for each other. You make this old man feel worthy and energetic again."

Sarah took his hand and held it against her heart in a symbolic suggestion of having him deep inside her chest. "From our first meeting I was a nervous wreck who was struggling to find my way. You have been patient with me, and I appreciate that. Because now when I'm with you, I feel cared for and comfortable. I have a feeling of being needed and that gives me a secure feeling...a feeling of hope."

Jim looked intently into her eyes. "I want you to feel secure...I care for you and love being with you. I'm not a young man, but I feel our relationship is growing as two mature individuals can grow a relationship."

"I love being with you the ages we are now. I wouldn't want it any other way," Sarah said with honesty.

"You're the most considerate little lady. You see the best no matter what's going on with us. You're so patient and understanding." He pulled her into his frame and kissed her with gentle warm passion. "When I was lost and it was cold at night, I cried for you."

"My love, I cried out for you, I missed your...," Sarah's voice quivered as she whispered against his neck. She became choked as tears flowed. Words became unimportant, with feeling his warm body against her and his arms holding in a loving embrace. "My darling, I was afraid, but my love, you were found."

"I'm glad I'm here, but especially glad I'm here with you. I wanted to mention something. Since this happened, I'm going to make some changes in the business, and let David take on more," Jim said with confidence.

"I like that. It will be good for you and for David."

"We need to go back to the O'Malley's next week for about three days to finish our punch list, but this time I'm going to ask David to take the crew and finish the project."

Sarah looked at Jim. "I think that's a wise thing to do…it will give you more time to recover, us more morning time together, and not to mention, more of your sweet notes you write," as her thin tender smile warmed his heart.

"…more time to have coffee on the porch." He smiled, laughed a little and pulled her against himself. "What am I going to do with you?" he held her face and gently kissed and nudged her lips in a teasing loving way.

"Just love me," Sarah said with a feeling of intimate passion.

After some time, Sarah nudged Jim and said, "My love, I hear Lucy calling us for dinner. She made a homemade French Coconut Pie but being here with you is much better than any dessert, but we need to go before she sends the search hounds," Sarah said with a wilting smile.

He held her close and whispered in her ear, "You're the one I think about, the only one I care for. You have a place deep in my heart."

"That's comforting." She looked into his eyes and said, "I love you, all of you and only you."

He smiled as he lifted her to her tip toes. "I wish we could stay longer, but we better go."

Chapter 14

"Lucy, we need to have another dinner party. I would like to ask Sarah out, so it will be official that we're starting a relationship."

"I was thinking of having a little get-together Friday night."

"...friends and my immediate family."

"Hello Sarah, Lucy is planning a casual dinner on Friday, would you like to go, I can pick you up about four-thirty."

"This Friday we'll be working extremely hard. We have furniture to place, pictures to hang and who knows what else. I'm not sure I'll be good company."

"If you're tired that'll just give me a chance to take care of you. I'll walk you to the truck…open your door. I'll help you up the front steps…fix your plate and do whatever I can for you to have the best evening ever. Besides, you'll be working on my house…I'll give you the afternoon off…with pay."

With a hardy laugh she said, "You're convincing. Will this be like a date?"

"I'd like to think of it as our first time out with friends and family. I want to arrive with my lovely lady by my side. I know we talked about finishing our project before we let our friendship blossom, but I feel I can't wait any longer. I want to share special times with you and enjoy your company."

"You know I will go with you."

"Lucy is making a casserole, salad and dessert. Bring sweet tea if you feel you must bring something. I'll pick you up at four-thirtyish. Don't wear white because I might come in my work truck."

"I will be fresh, dressed in brown and smelling like a rose."

"That's my girl. I love roses. Remember the saying…*just one rose*."

"I remember and…"

* * *

Sarah and the guys staged the room with Jim's original antique furnishings. Coordinating pillows were added to the English settee, and above the settee, they hung portraits of Jim's great grandparents. An ornate carved mirror was hung above the French credenza which gave it a stunning look.

Sarah had refreshed the silk flower arrangement and placed it on the credenza along with an antiqued gold memory box, and an heirloom Chinese figurine found in the attic. A new shade for the polished brass lamp added a fresh look to the French chest.

The now cleaned antique hand hooked rug was placed and the entrance was settled. Sarah took a deep breath as she locked the back door and thought another room ninety-five percent finished.

* * *

Jim left his house with a lighthearted lift in his step, as he whistled a pleasing tune. He was looking forward to their evening with friends and his children.

When Sarah answered her door, Jim said, "My dear your carriage has arrived and awaits you on the grassy lawn, because it's dripping power steering fluid." Then he stole a quick kiss as Sarah laughed at his charming sense of humor.

"Your subtle humor catches me off guard, but I love your lightheartedness. I'm ready for your carriage, my dear," Sarah said with a warm smile.

"I know you said this would be a tiring day, but you look radiant. Your dress looks great and the turquoise color of your sweater accents your beautiful dark brown eyes. You're lovely."

"You have a way of making me smile, even though I ache and feel sore."

He put his arm around her waist and said, "Just lean on me…I'll support you. Let me open the door to the carriage…do you want me to lift you inside. Ah, look at that girl hop in like a twenty-year-old."

"If laughter is the cure for tiredness, then I will be fine in a few," she said as Jim leaned over and gently kissed her lips.

As he cranked the truck, she said, "You make me feel so special and I thank you for that." Sarah leaned in his direction and he kissed her again.

"You do smell like a rose." He moved his arm around her waist and pulled her closer in his direction. "I'd like another whiff of my sweet rose."

Ben, Carrie, and Jim's children had already arrived and were excited to see Sarah and Jim walk into the house. Everyone hugged, laughed, and talked as the second glass of wine took away Sarah's aching muscles and replaced it with a lighthearted easiness that beamed as a lovely radiant woman became filled with joy and happiness.

Jim was proud of Sarah and mentioned, "Lucy, Sarah has been tirelessly working on the house…you need to come over."

Helen quickly turned and stared at him as he praised Sarah. Helen's unresolved jealousy flared as her dad spoke. It was difficult to hear him praise a woman. Realistically she knew Sarah was a treasure to their family, but deep inside the irritation was there.

Sarah reached out and touched her warm hand to Helen's arm and smiled as she brought her back to a pleasant reality.

As Jim looked at Sarah with admiring eyes, he thought *how perceptive.* He saw how she calmed the storm with her look and touch. *She is sensitive to feelings of others and knows how to respond. She does the same with me,* he thought.

Soon after the last guest left, Jim and Sarah helped Lucy gather stray cups and place plates in the dishwasher. During their quiet time, they both expressed to Lucy and Charlie how wonderful the evening had been and how much they appreciated their friendship and support.

As they walked to his truck, Jim felt a warm feeling of love for Sarah as he remembered watching this vivacious woman as friends gravitated to her out of a fascination for her intellect and irresistible charm. The feeling saturated his body, and Jim felt exhilarated.

When they arrived at Sarah's house, they sat in his quiet truck and talked. They enjoyed the peacefulness of looking at the full moon and reminiscing about the evening.

Something was weighing heavy on Sarah's mind and she impulsively said, "When we met, I was depressed and wounded by the way my life had been, but you came to me with love. A love I was frightened of because I was afraid to let go and reach out. Since that time, I've seen the man you are. I grew to love your heart, then your intellect and the way you talk and create, and now, I find myself in love with all of you. I've given my heart to only you because I trust and respect you. I'm just that kind of person."

"Come to me, you stole my heart without even trying. I knew about your life, and I've watched you become comfortable with me. We discovered our connection through my mother and finding my brown-eyed girl, my thoughts have been only of you. We will be fine."

"I wanted to mention something, the O'Malley's are having a gathering of friends next Friday to christen the new yacht with a lawn picnic and a cruise down the river. They have invited me and the crew as their special guests. They insisted you come…I would like for you to be my special guest. We would stay just for the afternoon…leave here about 7a.m. and get home around eight-thirty that night."

"That sounds nice, I would love to go."

"We'll need to carry hats, sunglasses, sunscreen and other things needed on the water."

"I'm looking forward to seeing their home and the dock, you and the fellows built."

Jim spoke softly as he held her close. "I'll gladly show you the dock, for which we're pleased with constructing. We'll be going on our own," Jim said as he thought about being alone with Sarah. He stole several delicious kisses. "As soon as I know more, I'll let you know."

With a contented heart, she laid against his chest while he quietly stroked her hair and occasionally massaged her back.

"I enjoyed the evening," Sarah said as a yawn caught her in mid-sentence.

As Sarah yawned more often, Jim said, "It's time to get you into bed."

"Not yet, this was a lovely first date and a perfect evening. Sorry to fall asleep, it's not you. It's just I'm a tired worn-out old woman… can we sit here longer," Sarah said as she restfully collapsed into his waiting arms.

"Of course, we can…you're not worn out and you're not old… you're just the sweetest always," he whispered as he nestled her into a warm embrace as his hands stroked her face. His thoughts were of this lovely woman. He enjoyed holding her as they talked. "You feel wonderful…snug in my arms." After a while, Jim carefully assisted Sarah out of the driver's side and safely into the house.

* * *

Jim was working all week at the Landings on a boat shelter for his friend. The trips to the work site were longer than usual and his workdays were tiring, but he wanted to help his friend. He couldn't make it back until after Sarah left for the day and that caused him to miss her even more. As he worked, he was aching inside remembering the mornings they spent having coffee and the contented feeling he enjoyed while being with her. His heartache for Sarah was evident by his constant reminiscing of her sweetness.

As Sarah embellished the kitchen, she felt melancholy as she imagined the stories behind each countertop memento she washed. Her heart became heavy as she realized how a tragic loss, or a series of wayward mistakes can change the direction of a family. She changed her thoughts *to believing a family tragedy can be transform into a beautiful thing.* She thought *about herself and Jim and was thinking maybe this was the beautiful results of our stressful previous lives.* "Wow, the sun is peaking through the clouds," Sarah said as she felt warm.

"It's lonely to enter the quiet house and leave in the afternoon and not see your smiling face. I'm looking forward to spending the day with Jim as we travel to the O'Malley's," Sarah whispered as her mood lifted with sweet thoughts of Jim.

After leaving the work site early, Jim called Sarah and asked about her evening plans.

Sarah said, "I'll visit with Bob for a while…enjoy a long soaking bath…maybe eat a little something…go to bed and probably finish reading this Italian novel."

"Italian novel…? That sounds like it could get your blood flowing."

"Well, this one certainly will."

"Maybe you can bring it over sometime and read to me on my new sofa."

"I'm not real sure I could read to you from this book. It's a real girl's book."

"Well maybe you could tell me a little about what you've read."

With a warm smile on her face and a quick laugh, "Ha, ha," she said. "You are so cute and funny. Just think again." His personality was quick and constantly teasing. He was a real charmer and Sarah adored him.

"Well, I just keep trying. Enjoy your bath and that book. Don't forget to make a few notes."

"Just for you I will." she said with a broad smile and a laugh.

Later that afternoon, Sarah was washing a few decorative platters and vases, when she heard the garage door open. She felt sure it had to be Jim even though he wasn't expected. As the back door closed, she recognized the sound of his shuffle and the hum in his voice. Sarah smiled and felt warm inside.

She stood waiting for his touch. Without saying a word, he walked to her and placed his hands tenderly on her waist and moved close to her. She arched her back, stretched her neck up to him and he kissed her there. He breathed heavy on her neck as he reached to nibble her ear lobe. His fingers expanded in response to her movement as he covered a large portion of her chest and held her close.

His lips were wet against her neck.

The back door opened. "That's David. I love you," he whispered.

He kissed her once more and straightened her shirt. He lightly patted her shoulder and moved beside the counter. "By the way, would you like to go to that deserted island, far away."

She breathed deeply and smiled then shook her head in a yes fashion. "It would be nice to have time alone."

"That day will come, I promise. I canceled my appointment and came home to get things ready for our men's get together tonight, that I had forgotten about until about fifteen minutes ago when David called. It's our turn to host the gathering. We need to provide the salad, bread, tea, and baked potatoes for about twelve guys. The fellows will bring their own steaks"

"How can I help?"

"We do have to make tea," Jim said. "David is bringing everything inside."

"I'll put the tea on."

Sarah dried her hands and went over to shake David's hand. With an apprehensive smile on her face, she said, "So good to see you again. Your smile is like your Dad's," she said as she continued to hold his hand.

"That's a compliment. It's great seeing you, and I really like the changes you've made in the house."

"Thank you," Sarah said as she placed a glass pot of water on the burner. She cleared the sink as Jim and David washed the baking potatoes.

As the tea was steeping, she asked, "Do you have silverware, plates, napkins and cups at the pond house?"

Jim turned to David with a questioning look on his face.

David said, "I think so, but I'll grab more when I go by my house."

"I'll set the oven temperature." Sarah first checked the oven to see if it was empty. "Oh my, a pizza box is in here." She set the temperature at four hundred.

"That box has been in there for days."

An assembly line was formed with David buttering the potatoes, Jim salt and peppering, and Sarah wrapping. David placed the potatoes one by one on the oven rack and Sarah filled a shallow roasting pan with water. David placed it on the rack below the potatoes while Jim set the timer.

"The water will add moisture during the cooking process."

"We can start the salad next." The lettuce was cored, washed, and set aside. "David just for you we will chop more tomatoes and less onions," she said, as she took three small serving bowls from the cabinet and they began to cut-up the tomatoes, peppers, and onions.

"How did you know I like tomatoes and don't like onions."

"I have my ways," she said with a smile as she found a large aluminum bowl, and the guys broke the lettuce into bite sized pieces. Sarah gathered the salad dressings and placed it along with tongs at the end of the island. She made the tea and started the second making.

"Now, I'll gather everything you need for the rolls. Bake at three hundred-fifty degrees for twenty minutes. If you guys need to go get ready, I'll finish up here."

"I do have to shower. Jim placed his hand tenderly on her back as he kissed her cheek, "Thanks Sarah for your help. We couldn't have done this without you. Don't leave before I get through. I need to talk to you about some changes in the entrance hall."

"I'll finish this and wait for you."

Jim made a mad dash to his bedroom. He searched his closet for a pair of freshly ironed jeans and his new blue shirt. With his hectic work schedule, he had gotten behind with the laundry.

"David do you have a small cooler to transport the potatoes. The cooler will keep the potatoes warm until you're ready to serve. I'll bag everything and place it here on the counter."

"I'll bring a cooler from home, and if you can, stay and watch us load." David placed his arm around Sarah's shoulders and said, "I'm sorry we rushed in and interrupted your plans, but thanks for your help."

"I'll stay," she calmly said. "It was a pleasant interruption. Anytime I can help you and your family, let me know. Your mom's cook books have helped me know a lot about you all."

He spontaneously reached out to Sarah and hugged her. "Thank you, my mom was a good cook. I also wanted to thank you for helping my dad. Since you have been here, he seems to be a different person. Before you came, he was always up tight like a down-hill skier racing on the edge of his skis. He seems to be calmer, and it has helped with our relationship."

"I have enjoyed working with your dad. He talks a lot about his family. He praises you for your maturity and work ethics."

"He does?"

"Yes, he's proud of you."

"Thanks for telling me, and thanks for everything. I better run," he said as he patted her shoulder.

While straightening the kitchen she thought about how perceptive David was to have noticed the positive change in his dad. She was glad they had a chance to talk, because it made her feel as though her presence was important in the lives of Jim and his family.

About fifteen minutes later, Jim walked into the kitchen. His presence brought a warm smile to Sarah as she said, "You look handsome."

With a boyish grin he said, "Does this shirt match these jeans?"

"Perfectly, you smell good too," she said as she straightened a little tuck in his collar. His summer cotton shirt was perfectly ironed and neatly tucked inside his pants. His jeans were slightly worn and looked soft and comfortable. He had the appearance of a dapper gentleman with a pleasing expression on his face with all intentions of attracting this beautiful lady standing before him.

"I'm glad I had a chance to be with David. He's a nice young man, much like his dad," she said as she rested her hand on his arm...then lightly touched his shoulder. Also, thank you for the sweet note you left this morning...I enjoyed the strawberries for lunch."

"David's a good young man, and I'm glad you enjoyed the strawberries. A customer gave me those...please take some home. I think having a bowl of strawberries and cream while taking a bath in your claw foot tub would be a good thing," Jim said as he reached out his hand and drew her close.

Sarah easily went to him. "It does sound like a good thing. The imaginative side of your brain is working," she said as she sniffed his Canoe scented neck. "Be sure to tell David often how good he is at his job. I can tell he's trying to grow and mature like his dad."

"I hope not completely like me. Maybe he will learn from my mistakes."

Sarah smiled as she said. "Talk openly with him. He needs you."

"Did he say something? How do you know all this?" Jim said as he looked into her eyes.

"It's just a perception."

"Your perceptions are usually right on target, so I'll take your advice," Jim said.

"We have seventeen minutes before the buzzer goes off."

"Great, seventeen treasured minutes alone with you in the peace and quiet of the kitchen." He put his arm around her and pulled her close to his side. "I wanted to ask you something." They stood silently for a while and enjoyed each other. "I miss having someone to help me like you did today. My wife would help me some, even though she always resented getting things ready for the guy's night out. When we were wrapping the potatoes, I had the most heartwarming feeling. I wanted to put my arms around you when you would make a joke, or we laughed at one of our little mix-ups. Did you enjoy giving up your afternoon and being with us?"

"I did enjoy it. I've missed you so much this week and to have a chance to do something special for you was a positive thing and to help David, made it even more special. Today working in the kitchen has had an emotional effect on me. I really needed to be with you."

Sarah dropped her head. "While working, I found a box of your wife's handwritten recipes. I thumbed through the stack and found notes about which one was best and what she would change if she cooked it again. One recipe called for black olives and she had written in the margin *we don't like black olives!* The most heartbreaking of all was an old grocery list with special request from the children. Mary Beth always wanted chocolate chip cookies. I cried when I read the list and thought about how this family was torn apart by their mother's untimely death." *A letter I found addressed from his oldest daughter to her mother, seemed too personal to even hold, so I placed it neatly back into the recipe box. Possibly Helen would like to have this keepsake,* she kindly thought.

During her silence, he eased more in front of her and wrapped her securely in his arms. Her chest jumped three times in rapid succession, she squeezed her nose and held her breath to stop herself from crying. He kissed her forehead as he recognized her emotions and whispered, "I love you."

She couldn't speak for fear of tears flowing down her face. Finally, she said, "It has been an emotional day. The kitchen is command central for the woman of the house. I found so many things that belonged to your wife." They wrapped each other into a cocoon and stood silently for a long while.

"Your heart is tender, you see everything in a special way," Jim said as he moved her hair from her eyes and tucked it behind her ear. "Are you really ready to go away with me to that far away island?"

"I'm ready."

Jim exhaled and said, "I think I hear David."

They kissed warm, wet, and gently as the oven beeper sounded its alarm. Sarah turned to probe a couple of potatoes with a knife to test for doneness. "They're ready."

"I know I will never forget my past and my wife. Over time I have come to appreciate the care she gave our children. I want to build new and lasting memories like the fun we had today and the fantastic memories you and I have made while working together on the house. I don't want to forget my past, even though sometimes it brings a sadness that looms over me. I would like to constantly build new memories."

She rubbed his back and kissed him in affirmation of his profound statement. His fingers gently touched the side of her breast as he ran his fingers up and down her side. Sarah moved into his path and he hesitated. He pulled her strongly against his excited frame with far reaching desires and she accepted him. Their breathing grew strong, as their feelings remained, and their thoughts came under control because David would soon come in the back door.

Sarah stacked the baked potatoes in the cooler while Jim and David loaded the sacks, the tea, and steaks from the refrigerator. Sarah made a final check, and as they said their farewells, she reminded them to turn the oven on for the rolls. "Have a wonderful evening and I'll see you tomorrow," she said.

"Thank you dear for everything. Have a good night," Jim said as he kissed her cheek, and David hugged Sarah.

Her drive home was filled with tears and smiles along with hopeful wishes for an uncertain future for which she was willing to commit. She felt honestly in love with Jim. She loved his ways, his heart, and the sweet gentleness in which he treated her. She arrived home to find playful Bob waiting at the garage. She reached down to hug him and then sat on the steps and let him lick the tears from her face as she noticed the sun sinking low in the sky. She and Bob enjoyed a walk around the yard as Sarah watched the rosy red sunset accented with billowing white clouds change into the gray dimness of evening.

Sarah went inside with a feeling of being alone and missing someone she adored. She rechecked the beach bag with final preparation for their trip to the O'Malley's. She moped around the kitchen, nibbled on Ritz Crackers smeared with a dab of cream cheese. She took out a wine glass, filled it with a Chardonnay and headed for the bedroom.

She prepared her bath, as she drank a swallow of wine. Her undressing was almost rhythmic as she imagined removing her clothing in front of her lover. She nervously clenched her shirt and thought *no*, as she felt a response to her excitement. She took another swallow of wine and thought of being with Jim. Her movements were soft and gentle as she removed her shirt, and her body swayed. She took another swallow of wine and removed her remaining clothing and slipped into the warm bubbly water. She relaxed completely and her thoughts began to drift as the lavender fragrance engulfed her wellbeing.

"Now is the time for a new start," she whispered. "I've never before felt so contented and cared for. This secure feeling is the best I've ever had, and I miss all of him when we're not together." Sarah rinsed the warm water over her body.

Sarah's heart softened as she forgave her husband of all his marriage wrecking philandering ways. She cleared her heart of all his wrong doings. She saw how his ways had made her strong and now she was living and loving with a giving heart. Because of him, she had the vision to see and appreciate Jim for the truthful honest man he is. With a feeling of a renewed, clean person, Sarah symbolically rinsed her body, dried off and dressed in her favorite silk gown. She retrieved her book from the den, settled in bed and began to read the final few chapters of the Italian novel.

* * *

David and Jim's friends slowly arrive at the pond house. David had the oven hot and the grill heating. "You know dad I don't think we could have gotten everything together if it had not been for Sarah."

"She does know how to organize and think through everything, almost nothing is forgotten," Jim said with confidence.

"I've been around her several times, I got to know her more when you were lost, but today she talked to me like we had known each other for years. She seems so honest, humble, and so perceptive. It appears she has figured us both out. You know dad, I really like her."

Jim looked at David with an astonished expression on his face. "Son, I absolutely know I like her, too." Jim thought, *David has observed some of the same qualities in Sarah that are obvious to me. This is not a dream. She is real. Her mannerisms and feelings for people are genuine and not a show for anyone.*

Jim could barely concentrate on the evening for thinking about Sarah and her Italian book and her soaking bath, and most of all her warmth. Several of the guys commented on Jim's smiling facial expressions and his lack of interest in them. One of his close friends guessed the meaning of the change and often winked at Jim as the others teased him.

After about twenty minutes with the guys, Jim became anxious… he had to leave the room. He went out to help his son finish grilling the steaks. The air was filled with the aroma of searing meat, but as the wind blew, he felt sure he smelled the fragrance of Sarah or was it the sweet fragrance of his rose garden. *It's a vivid reminder of the roses I shared with her. He noticed the sun going down over the pond and the distant sky filling with clouds white as snow. The poplar trees behind the pond were reaching above the pines, forming a glowing yellow arched tree line that illuminated against the darkening sky. This sunset reminds me of Sarah.* To bring his thoughts back to the work at hand, Jim said, "I put the rolls in the oven for Tim to look after, sat the food out, and I had to get outside for a while."

"I think Sarah must be on your mind."

"How did you know?"

"I can see it in your eyes, the look on your face and the drop in your shoulders. Since you started the project, I've noticed a difference in you. Your eyes are brighter…you laugh and smile more. All in all, you're a heck of a lot easier to get along with," David said as he put a bear hug around his dad.

"Sounds like you've noticed a change in me because of Sarah and it's a good change," Jim said with a smile.

"I wasn't a hundred percent sure what was causing the change until I started observing you and Sarah. I could see it today when we were working in the kitchen and I could really see it in both of you when you said *good night* to her. The change has been a good thing. You need to take care of this soon because I can see it's heavy on your mind."

"You know son, I think you're right, I will. Thanks for your advice," Jim said as he turned to leave.

"I'll clean up here…now go and do the right thing."

Jim made a quick look back to say, "What is the right thing?" *Maybe I need to ask you for more advice*, Jim thought as he started to descend the back steps.

"Hey dad, do you have protection?"

"Ah son, I'm not even thinking of that, at my age, that's usually not a real problem."

"You should, just in case."

Jim waved his hand as he cleared the last step and jumped into his truck. As soon as he drove away from the pond house, he automatically pushed speed dial for Sarah.

"I just left the guys. I couldn't concentrate on the game for thinking about you. I just really needed to hear your voice. Talk to me… what are you doing…what are you thinking? Please talk to me. I need to see you, tonight, now, if possible."

"Jim, I can't help but think of you."

"Just please keep talking."

"Now I'm in bed reading the Italian novel I told you about. I'm wearing a cream-colored silk gown. My bedroom is cool, so I'm covered with a sheet and a light spread."

"Cream colored? I imagined red. What is the book about?"

"It's about two unintentional lovers. She is broken on the inside, but strong and regimented on the outside. He is a confident Italian Hollywood actor, who pursues her as a challenge to his ego, and she with reluctance gives into him, but only on her terms."

"And what are her terms?"

"Their intimate relations will be just for fun and enjoyment, and there will be no emotional attachments. They agree to the terms and start to play the game."

"Is that all the plot?"

"No, near the end of the book each one starts to find admiring qualities about the other. They don't share this, but an intimate caring romance is brewing between them."

"That sounds good."

"They become more compassionate…their rendezvouses are more intense."

"I like the word *intense*."

"They speak of things like *the room smells of love when we're together* and *the sweet fragrance of lavender drifts through our bedroom*. Their feelings and words are very sensual. They talk about *the warm gentle breezes that flow through the open farmhouse windows*."

"That sounds exciting. I love sensual."

"The word *sensual* has a delicious sound. I have another chapter to read, so I don't know how it ends. I'll let you know and maybe I can read some passages to you someday."

"Do you think you could read to me now?"

"…over the phone?"

"No, I'm at your door."

"You're kidding me. If you're here, ring the doorbell." With excitement brewing, Sarah threw the covers back and raced toward the door because she wanted him to be there.

"I'm not kidding. The light must be out. I can't find the button, where is it?"

Her heart was pounding harder, and the excitement was growing. The doorbell rang, and she knew he was there. With a few quick motions, she unlocked the door for him to enter, then locked it as his opened hands came to rest on the delicate sides of her body.

Jim immediately wrapped his arms around her small frame and without hesitation she circled his strong shoulders. Sarah noticed his eyes sparkling in the dim light of the nightlight. His manly fragrance brought an air of contentment and his quietness with an intense look sent chills racing down her backbone, into her lower stomach, and she softened to his touch.

"I love you."

"And I love you."

Restrained desires intensified with excitement, which was evident in both. In the quietness of the moment his hands began to roam her back with tender gentle movements, slowly slipping down her sides and in passing, his thumbs stroked the sides of her breast. He reached her lower back and massaged her gently as he encouraged her to ease closer to him and rest against his body.

As she leaned in, she felt her breast resting snug against his chest, and found herself to be deeply moved. She held firm against him and tugged at his shoulders.

He moved his hand tenderly over the silk gown, as he kissed her warm luscious lips. He felt the warm smoothness of her womanly feelings heightened.

As a flourish of heat came over him, he eased her delicate frame securely into his longing. "I want to be with you, I love you so much, I want all of you," he whispered into her ear.

The strength of his body caused her to relax and yield to his grasp with no resistance. "I love the feeling of you next to me," Sarah whispered.

He moved his hands up and placed his palms on each side of her face, and in the dim light he looked into her dark brown desiring eyes, knowing they were anxiously wanting to surrender all.

She took his hand and they walked hurriedly to a bedroom, other than her own, in the far reaches of the house. They entered the room and she quickly took the tapestry throw and decorative pillows from the bed and turned back the covers.

Jim sat on the end of the bed and Sarah perched on his thigh and rubbed him. As he slipped both straps off her shoulders, her gown fell to her waist. He was admiring her structure with his fingertips and tasting the sweet fragrance of her skin. Their heated passion became unchecked and their sensual loving desires took control.

Sarah finished unbuttoning his shirt and gently tossed it over a near-by chair. She ran her fingers through the hairs of his chest as she rubbed against his masculine upper trunk.

While keeping his eyes locked on Sarah, took her hand and as she began to rise, her gown puddled on the floor, which he gathered and laid with his clothing. Sarah moved to the bedside and slipped in under the silky Egyptian cotton sheets and he reclined beside her and admired her loveliness as he stroked her smooth stomach and gently undulating hips.

He kissed her softly as his hands studied the curves of her body. His mouth found her, and accepted her offerings, as his hand continued to massage her yielding movements.

She watched him, touched him and her carnal knowledge from many years before returned and it all became wonderfully natural. She brought her shoulder up to offer him more.

It had been a long time since someone had honestly wanted him unconditionally. It had also been a long time since he had wanted to be close to someone in a devoted way. He marveled in the excitement of her movements and the tender opportunity of loving someone so dear to him.

This was their first time alone, and neither one wanted to rush the moment, but their craving desires and care for each other were wanting more. He gasped as he found her lusciousness and became eager as the scent of her excitement warmed his desires.

"My love, what a feeling…" he moaned.

"Oh my, what a wonderful, exhilarated feeling this has been. I'm excited from my head to my toes and pleasantly exhausted," Sarah said as she vigorously kissed the man she adored.

He pulled her nearer. He loved her and he knew it to be true. He held her and as he felt soulful passion brewing in his veins.

Sarah cared deeply for Jim and knew in her heart this was the most beautiful moment of her life. She wondered how she could control her raging emotions as they entered this new level of their relationship.

She felt warm and secure as though she could stay near to him forever, but her head began to clear, and reality was coming into focus. She knew it was late, and tomorrow they were leaving early to go to the O'Malley's, but she really didn't want the night to end.

"It's almost eleven thirty and I need to go, but I sure don't want to leave you. All the feelings I have saved in my heart just seemed to weigh heavy in my chest. I've wanted to be with you from the beginning, but I knew I couldn't push you. The time we shared this afternoon, and tonight when we were talking, it just seemed right to come to you, so I came to your door. I hope I didn't offend you in any way," Jim said with reservations.

"No, my love, you never displease me. I've always been intrigued by you, and I've enjoyed your advances and your sweet flirtation. Often, I wanted to give in, but I was afraid of what you might think of me and what I might think of myself. I'm glad you came, but your right, tomorrow will be a long day. Gee, I love tomorrows."

* * *

When Jim got home from Sarah's, he took his time looking at what Sarah had done and was completely amazed at how beautiful his home was. The pillows were placed on the sofa with a throw draped across a corner of the sofa back. The window treatments behind the sofa blended with the colors in the room. The fruit and silk flower arrangement gave life to the antique English chest and the one he used the air compressor to clean looked fresh on the coffee table in the fireplace sitting area.

He quickly glanced at the armoire and saw the urn he had purchased was placed so prominently. Jim paused as he thought of the beauty of the room and the beauty of Sarah who created this just for him. Jim smiled with satisfaction and wished Sarah to be there to share this moment.

He gasped, as he saw his grand-parents portraits hanging above the settee. Sarah had used his treasures to make his home personal. He thought of her and called her name.

In the seat of his cuddling chair was a gift box elegantly wrapped and tied with a beautiful gold ribbon. The card on top of the box said, *my dear friend. Thank You!!!* With emotions moving, he held the box to his lips and smelled her fragrance and lowered himself into his chair. He immediately called Sarah, "My darling Sarah."

She listened to his excitement. He was amazed by the changes. "If it wasn't so late, I'd ask you to come over. I've admired everything and wished you were beside me. Sarah, I need you. I need you in my life."

"My darling, I wish I were there to share this moment."

"And when I saw the gift in my chair, I called your name," Jim whispered. "Your painting of the one sweet rose touched me deeply... from the start I've thought of you as my one special rose."

"I remembered the evening you told me that. I feel I have the makings of being true to only one, and I see that characteristic in you. Your expressions to me show how much you care. Jim, my emotions are near tears. I've been lying here, thinking of the times we have laughed and cried together. I can't sleep for thinking of you."

"My dear, I touched everything in the room, because I knew you had touched it last. That's how much I want to be near you. I'm not sure I'll be able to sleep tonight."

"I look forward to seeing you soon, and I deeply wish I could have shared this special moment beside you. I love you and that's what matters," Sarah said with feelings.

"I love you also. I've realized, I don't like sitting in my chair alone, it's half empty. I'm saving this space for you. Good night and I will see you soon."

* * *

Sarah awoke with a smile as she stretched under the warm sheets. She quickly groomed herself for the day...dressed in her favorite sundress and rummaged through the beach bag. Sarah smiled as she thought of spending the day with Jim. "I know this will be a good day," Sarah said with a feeling of wanting to be with Jim.

His arrival was met with a strong embrace fueled by feelings from the night before weighing heavy in their thoughts. They left feeling the excitement of the long drive, and the closeness of spending the day together.

Their time at the O'Malley's was fun and relaxing but by mid-afternoon they felt they must leave. The excitement of the day fueled their conversation, and in no time, they reached Savannah and Jim suggested they stop for dinner.

"We enjoyed River Street before, why don't we go there," Jim said with the hope of gentle persuasion.

Lucy spotted an alluring restaurant in the restored Cotton Exchange building on Bay Street, so they stop there. The fresh seafood was delicious, and after their long day, the wine was relaxing. Their conversation brought about smiles, laughter, and flirting…sparkling glances that invigorated their desires.

They left walking hand in hand, crossed the street into a park filled with festive entertainment, and crowds of people hovering between the flower gardens. Jim and Sarah's spirits were light, and they enjoyed the romantic feeling of being together on this warm summer night. Arm in arm they maneuvered out of the park onto the sidewalk by the city street. While walking past the restaurants, bars, and hotels they enjoyed the sounds and fragrances of the city.

They passed an Inn and as the doors opened, the air filled with the sounds of a piano player flowing through the cords of Moon River. The melody was an instant reminder of the romantic evening they had recently spent in Savannah. Jim looked at Sarah, took her hand and they entered the hotel as the romantic sound of *their song* drew them into a welcoming warm retreat.

Chapter 15

David and his dad had a heart-to-heart talk concerning Sarah. "She's good to me, so thoughtful and helpful to be around. During our time spent remodeling the house I've fallen in love with her. Sarah had a rough marriage with a philandering abusive husband who eventually was involved in a deadly accident with his mistress. She has gone from being suspicious of me, to feeling somewhat comfortable and now trusting me completely. I feel confident in our relationship because I've watched it grow with undeniable respectability."

"Then Sarah's not a money hungry woman looking for a house to live out her final years."

"That's right son. If you wanted to compare portfolios, she has a lot more holdings than me."

"Dad, I just had to ask for Helen's sake."

"I understand. I know Helen has acted disrespectfully toward Sarah."

"Yes, but I'll talk to her again…I think she will eventually mellow. Sarah seems to be so kindhearted…one who listens with concern and not judgment," David said.

"She is caring, and it's been like that since the first time we met. She's not putting on. She's genuine."

* * *

Sarah worked frantically in the kitchen placing accessories. She found two beautiful Italian ceramic platters and placed one on the counter near the refrigerator. For the wall near the stove, she found three old world ceramic vegetable plaques that were the perfect color. She placed some new green plaid and floral print dish towels on the island and beside the sink, and easily installed the floral scalloped window valance. Sarah quickly changed the atmosphere of the kitchen after she plugged in a cinnamon scented air freshener near the stove.

For the kitchen island she found an iron basket underneath a cabinet, and filled it with one banana, and an apple. She added buy fresh fruit to her shopping list. Beside the fruit basket she placed a rustic urn of silk greenery accented with fruit and vegetables she had arranged at home. She sorted through a stack of books and found a Bobby Fley grilling recipe book and placed it on an easel to finish off the island vignette.

An antique French open hutch graced the wall opposite the back-door entrance. She rearranged the English Wedgewood cream china in a pattern called Patrician. Sarah added a McCoy dish of silk greenery, a few pieces of Depression glass along with a pewter candle stick on the outside corner. She also took away a few things that appeared to have been stuck there.

Sarah went into the breakfast room. The antique ball and claw foot table and chairs needed a face lift, but for now she cleaned the wood with an orange scented spray. A large faded floral print hanging over a sideboard was swapped for a mirror she found leaning against the guestroom wall. Aged antique brass candelabras were placed on each end of the sideboard. Sarah placed an antique fern stand near the large multi paned window framing a picturesque view of his lovely flower gardens. She placed a large antique soup tureen discovered in the lower cabinets of the Butler's Pantry in the center of the sideboard.

A silk flower arrangement she made at home using cream silk Gerber daisies, rusty red hydrangeas, tiger lilies, berries, and a few tags of grapes along with other fruit was placed on the table. It blended beautifully with the room's golden butter walls and the faded rust and green Persian rug. As Sarah fluffed the floral, she heard the garage door open and hurried to unlock the door.

She graciously welcomed Jim inside. When he stepped into the kitchen, his eyes were brighter than his smile. "I can't believe the changes you've made. This is beautiful and it smells so nice." He took her in his arms, and she bent like a willow as he pulled her close. "This is amazing, not only your talents as a decorator, but how you have awakened me to enjoy and appreciate the things you so kindly create for me. I have been looking forward to coming home."

She could see the appreciation of her presence in the sparkle of his eyes. Her heart softened as she smiled that little smile.

With a slightly noticeable quiver in his voice, he said, "I'm almost speechless."

Her heart melted into his as they embraced. She quickly kissed the side of his neck, and with a shaky voice as well, she said, "I love you."

While looking at Sarah humbly through his intense gray green eyes he said, "And I love you so much. You're the hardest working woman I know. Is that sexist to say?"

"No, I think it's a sexy thing to say," she said with a wink. "Now, let me show you the changes and see what you think."

They walked arm in arm around each room as he asked about all the newly discovered accessories. His hand stroked her arm as she turned to point out the new window treatments in the kitchen. Her fingertips walked across his shoulders as she led him into the breakfast room. She stood beside him as he marveled at the changes. I'm amazed at how such beautiful things were created from my hidden family treasures.

Jim didn't realize, but Sarah had thought of herself as a hidden treasure, someone who had given up and programmed herself to stay in seclusion. Sarah was gladly seeing Jim as the generous, encouraging mainstay who was turning her self-imposed withdrawal into having her hope renewed.

"I thought we could have dinner here tonight. I picked up two plates from Jane's Diner…also strawberries and whipped cream for dessert."

"You're thoughtful. Let me finish this and I'll be right there," Sarah said as she tweaked the flowers on the breakfast room table.

"We can go out to the Summer House and take a restful break from decorating."

"Perfect."

"I called Henry this morning and asked him to clean and put up the curtains," Jim said as he busily gathered the silver utensils, a couple of china plates, wine glasses along with linen napkins. He placed everything in a wicker basket for easy transport. He had given Henry detailed instructions about adding fresh candles to the candelabra, placing it on the stone server, and setting the chandelier to a dim setting. Henry also added…on his own, a white wicker basket of red geraniums.

"I noticed him working out there."

Jim walked over to look at the table, as she was putting some place mats in front of each chair. "This looks amazing." He put his arm on her shoulder before she completed placing the last mat. "I think I have everything ready to go to the Summer House."

"Let me hurry and freshen up."

"I'm looking for a small tablecloth, can you tell me where I can find one?"

"In the sideboard by the breakfast room table, second drawer," she said as she entered the hall powder room.

Sarah knows more about this house than I know, but that's a good thing, he thought as he plundered around, and eventually found what he needed.

Sarah quickly brushed through her hair, brushed her teeth, and reapplied her lipstick. She fluffed the collar to her Azalea pink blouse, as she entered the kitchen. "Hopefully, I'm a bit more presentable for dinner in the Summer House with this fine gentleman."

"My dear, you're beautiful," Jim said as she tilted her head for him to steal a welcomed kiss. "I hope I have everything we need stacked in this wicker basket."

"If we're missing something, we'll just make it work."

On the way out, Jim took a bottle of Pinot Blanc from the wine cooler. "Will you flip the first switch by the door to turn on a few outside lights?"

As they approached the Summer House, Sarah was taken aback by the magical appearance of the sheer curtains flowing luminously in the moonlight. The fragrance of the magnolia tree permeated the warm summer breeze. "This is enchanting," she said as they ascended the steps.

Jim flipped on the chandelier and Sarah was instantly overwhelmed by its endless romantic charm. Her eyes were glancing from the movement of the drapes to the warm glow that covered the area like a gentle fog. "I need to stop looking and help you."

"Just enjoy yourself. You deserve a break."

"This is thoughtful," she said as she took one side of the cloth. He placed a lantern to the side of the table as not to block his vision of Sarah and lit the candle. Sarah finished setting the table as Jim stood at the stone server and plated the food. He popped the cork on the light summer wine and filled their glasses for a toast before dinner.

"We're missing flowers on the table," he said as he eased her chair out for Sarah to be seated.

As Sarah laid her hand on her chest she said, "My heart is pounding so, and my vision is clouded like a lovely dream."

After he was comfortably seated, he reached across the table for her hand and they each spoke silent words of thankfulness.

Sarah was somewhat oblivious to the food on her plate and concentrated more on the warm glow the light cast on Jim's face as he talked about a thousand things she couldn't respond intelligently to because she was mesmerized. She ate a good portion of her meal as she laughed, smiled, or agreed with everything.

As they talked and finished their strawberries and cream Jim said, "It's getting a little cool out here. Are you ready to go inside?"

"Not really, but I know we should. This has been like a pleasing dream that I could live inside of forever like a fairytale. I love sweet surprises, and this has been the best."

"My dear, the time I've spent with you has been filled with sweet surprises. Every day has been a wonderful adventure. You have brought order, substance, and excitement to my life. Excitement to this simple man that I can't find words to describe."

She reached over, took his hand, and began to speak. "You know a lot about my past and my journey. I had no idea I would ever meet someone, and trust again, much less fall in love. I feel comfortable in your presence."

"Your words and the way you say them are sweet. Your gentle heart makes me want to love and take care of you forever." Still holding her hand, he moved beside her chair and she began to rise. Quietly they held each other with a gentle embrace. "I have to get you inside. Your arms and hands are cold."

In the gentle quietness deep in the hollow a whip-poor-will sang as Sarah continued to absorb the essence of the moment. Jim eased his grip and looked deeply into her brown eyes as they looked at each other with a smile of contentment.

Jim took her hand and in a gentle dancing movement, he twirled her around. They smiled broadly as he gave her a final dip and then brought her up into his gentle embrace.

As they passed by the rose garden, Jim cut a beautiful pink rose bud for Sarah. "This is what we were missing on the table, but I enjoyed a real rose bud sitting across from me."

They slowly entered the kitchen and put away the leftovers. They enjoyed working together washing and drying the wine glasses.

When they had finished, Jim asked, "Would you like to sit for a while?"

"Yes, I would."

"Our time together is so invigorating to me, but I'm not superman anymore."

"It's being with you that makes me happy."

Jim was captivated by her discerning humble nature and her common since intelligence. *I admire her, want, and need her in my life, and after what we have been through, I wonder if this would be the time to talk seriously. Is she ready for that conversation? In my heart I feel the time is right and I want to trust my heart.*

"You mentioned this morning you wanted to talk to me about something. Is there something wrong with the project or with me?"

"Nothing my dear is wrong with you or the project. I'm sitting here looking into your eyes and wanting to hold you forever."

Her eyes began to well up with emotion, so she hid her face on his shoulder and cried silently as she embraced him.

He exhaled and continued to massage the warm smooth skin of her arm. "I was just…Well I wanted to ask…Well do you think we…? Gee, I don't know how to ask this."

"You want to know, like if we were teenagers, can we go steady."

"Yes, my dear, that's what I want to know. I feel so committed to you, and I would like to know that only you and I together are sharing these wonderful intimate moments."

"You're special to me and have been for a long time. I've been and always will be totally committed to you. I'm that kind of person. From now until forever there will be no one else," Sarah said with seriousness in her voice.

"I would like for it to be a long, long time, but what about this guy named Bob you occasionally mention," Jim said.

Sarah burst out into uncontrollable laughter. Her body shook with delight and excitement.

"What's wrong? What did I say wrong?"

"You're worried about Bob? I love it. Bob's my dog," Sarah said and smiled that thin alluring smile.

As his eyes widened with delight he said, "You're kidding me… no, I want that to be true. Bob is your dog? He leaned back in disbelief, "How could I have not figured this out…all those nights you were taking care of Bob…what a relief."

"I was just feeding or playing with him."

"You just don't know how much of a relief it is to find out this."

With a broad smile on her face she said with emphasis, "I love you."

As he tweaked a strand of hair behind her ear and looked deep into her eyes, Jim became overwhelmed with emotions and thought, this delicate lady fought to survive her painful marriage, then struggled to regain her honor and now has moved beyond her past. She is strong and courageous…and I love her for that. As he breathed in her sweet fragrance he said, "I first noticed your quiet charm and gracefulness. I saw a lovely lady who needed to be loved. I watched you and as I waited, I fell deeply in love with you, all of you…knowing in my heart that one day you would come to know how much I love you."

As Sarah groomed his mustache with her fingertips, she looked into his eyes. "I also observed you and the gentle way you talked to me, not just the way you talked once or twice, but as you talked to me in stressful and good times. Your kindness helped me to not be afraid to speak, make decisions, and relax and feel comfortable in your presence. I'm sure you were aware of the tense uptight ways I had, but I trusted you and that trust grew into an admiration and respect for you. I silently adore you and I fell in love with you," she moaned softly. In silence, she touched his chest and felt his heart pounding, as she held him close.

In turn, in this state of romantic bliss, he laid his arm across her rapidly breathing chest, he could feel the emotions of this affectionate woman he wanted to take care of.

She cried silent tears of knowing how she adored Jim, and how she felt like a woman with assurance of their trusting relationship.

Sarah was reconciled to giving and receiving true appreciation and devotion. She was confident in her love for Jim. A bond of trust and affirmation had developed. "I will live one day at a time and make each one my best," she whispered in a tiny voice. As she held him, she felt a feeling of contentment flood over her.

Sarah knew she had to go home, but it was not easy leaving him. Jim knew how she felt and tried to make parting easier, but it was difficult for him. "When you finish feeding *my friend Bob* call me. I want to know you're ok." Knowing what was best, they kissed good night.

Chapter 16

Thursday morning, Jim was leaving on a junket to Biloxi with a group of family and friends. He wanted Sarah to go with him, but she thought it would be an anxious situation and she wasn't ready for that.

"You will be with men and couples I don't know. I don't think I would fit in. Maybe next time, besides, I'm in the final days of decorating."

"You know me and that's the only one you really need to know."

"Women are a little different in their assessment of each other. We tend to over think things. I'm not sure I'm ready for folks to know the intimate details of our relationship."

"I understand, but I can take care of that."

"I know you're trying to help, but maybe it will be best to wait until I get to know your family, before we spring going away together. Especially your daughters… I don't want to start out wrong with them. And besides, I have cold feet and snore like a…"

"You're thoughtful and modest," he said with a laugh. "I have maybe three of these excursions left on a contract. If I don't go, I'll lose about five hundred dollars on each one, but I decided if you don't feel comfortable, I'd rather forfeit the money than to leave without you."

"That's kind, but go…Bob will take care of me," she said with a laugh.

"That Bob is a wonderful friend," Jim said with a smile as his hand stroked the curve of her back. With reluctance, Jim agreed to go, this time. He didn't like the idea of leaving Sarah, but she assured him she had things to take care of at his house. "Why don't you stay here?"

"I can't stay at your house."

He looked at her with a caring expression on his face. "I don't want to leave you."

She reached around him and laid her head on his chest and said with a quiver in her voice, "It's only for a few days. You can call me as often as you like."

The next morning was bittersweet as Jim loaded his carry-on bag into the truck. With sadness, he said, "Goodbye for now and I'll see you in a few days."

The feeling of emptiness was overwhelming for Sarah and she choked as she whispered, "I love you and please be careful." With sadness in her heart and unshed tears welling up in her eyes she waved bye as he backed out of the garage and drove away.

* * *

With trembling sadness Sarah stood in the Butler's Pantry with a feeling of being lost. Her thoughts caused her to burst into tears. She questioned herself aloud, "Why didn't I go with Jim? I'm not looking forward to these days alone."

Tucked behind a platter on the counter she found an envelope and a gift box. Unexpectedly finding the note brought about sobs that welled up into a release of awareness of her deep regard for Jim. His written words brought a tearful smile as her heart was lifted. The gift box contained three delicate sterling silver bracelets which were exquisite. She called Jim immediately. Sarah could barely talk through her excited tears of appreciation and love.

They found it difficult to end the conversation as they felt the seriousness of their relationship. With an assurance of unlimited conversations while he was away, they said goodbye.

Sarah washed the china and cleaned the interior of the upper cabinets. After lunch she sat in Jim's chair and recalled his fragrance. "I must get back to work if I want this done by this afternoon." She hurried to the pantry and wiped the exterior of the cabinets and counter tops.

She found an English Rose platter to display, and a set of Haviland Apple Blossom she planned to exhibit properly behind the upper cabinet glass doors. As her energy began to fade, she methodically stacked some pewter serving pieces into the lower cabinets. With reluctance she decided to go home and rest her aching arms and back.

As she backed away from the carriage house, she noticed a silver BMW parked in front of the house. As she drove near, she recognized Helen. "Hello Helen, your dad's not here. He left this morning for Biloxi."

"I was really looking for you."

With a stark feeling of shock, Sarah wondered why she wanted to see her. "I was just leaving for home, but we can talk. Is it a question about the house?"

"No, not really, I guess it's personal."

With a fearful look on her face, Sarah said, "Ok?"

"I've been a little rude to you because I thought something was going on with my dad and you. I have been holding anger against him since my mom died. I let that anger be the reason I couldn't have a relationship with him, even though I wanted a relationship. When I saw him change and his personality brightened and his attention turn away from me and my anger, I began to wonder who was making him happy."

"I saw you with that guy having dinner last month and figured you were using my dad while having fun with someone else. I imagined a wicked villainous woman had caught his eye and was about to move into the house, so he was remodeling things for her while she was two-timing him. I never imagined the woman he had fallen in love with was real, until you comforted us during the time dad was missing, and until last week when I watched the two of you together at the house. Yesterday David talked with me about this and explained who the man is, and that dad knew all about him. I'm sorry I let my anger control me like that."

With some hesitation and question in her voice, Sarah said, "I'm not a wicked woman, but as we worked on the project, we began to care for each other…and saw ourselves as having an honest second chance in life."

"No, you're not wicked…I'm sorry I thought that. I see now with David's help how compassionate and honest you are to dad. I see how you're bringing out the best in him and giving a quality to his life that hasn't been there for years."

As she exited her SUV and walked to Helen, Sarah said, "I recognize your feelings and what you're saying. Over time, I've grown to care for your dad. It certainly wasn't overnight, because I had some issues he knew about, I had to work through. As older second timers, we have an understanding and an appreciation for each other."

"I know and with all honesty, I'm glad."

With a feeling of trust and respect Sarah and Helen hugged. "I love you. Would you like to go inside and talk?" Sarah said with gladness.

"Thank you for what you have quietly done for our family. I really must be going…have dinner ready by six, maybe another day. Love you."

"We will, I promise." *That phrase, 'have dinner by six' resonated with a flashback of my husband demanding 'dinner by six.' It sent a chill through me with the thoughts of, is this young lady captive of a similar situation. No, it's only my flashback of thoughts of my past that will probably plague me for an eternity.*

As Sarah turned into her driveway, her phone rang. She smiled broadly as she saw it was Jim. "Hello dear, good to hear your voice… just wanted to call and let you know our plane is about to leave for Biloxi. I just wanted to tell you I miss you and love you."

"My dear, I have missed you also and especially this afternoon. Some wonderful news, Helen came by as I was leaving today. She has come to realize you and I have a budding relationship that's a good thing for the wellbeing of the family."

"I'm so glad to hear that…I was beginning to think she wasn't going to mellow."

"I think she's fine. I've accomplished a lot with the Butler's Pantry and have more to do tomorrow. That's kept my mind occupied, but I miss you and wish now I had packed my bags and gone."

"My dear, throw something in a sack and hurry to the airport, I'll wait for you."

"My love…I'll be here when you get back. Darling, the bracelets and the note you left for me are beautiful and I thank you with all my heart."

"Now you take care and have fun with Bob. Love you and bye for now."

With reluctance they both pushed *end* and their thoughts began to synchronize while sitting quietly in a blinding daze hundreds of miles apart. He became melancholy at the same moment Sarah reached for a tissue to blot away tears on her cheeks.

* * *

Jim was instantly taken aback by the bright lights and the rolling pitch of the clanging sounds coming from the slot machines with an occasional ting ting ting of a winner's bell. As soon as he heard that sound, he realized, it no longer had meaning to him. There was something more important in his life and here he was eight hundred miles away from her. He dropped his head, gripped his bag, and thought, *why am I here.*

He entered his spacious room and immediately realized how alone he was. He hung his clothes in the closet and gathered his toiletries. He flipped the lights on in the bathroom and was startled by the flash of light on the mirrored walls. The prisms of the chandelier hanging over the antique French provincial dressing table were sparkling. Jim stood in amazement as he admired the ornate gold faucets at each sink, the Jacuzzi tub designed for two and the shower room with multi-water jets. "Sarah, how I wish for you," he exclaimed as he felt alone and swallowed up with melancholy.

The bedroom was just as exquisite. The drapes were a beautiful rusty red, gold, and green plaid with matching moss green sheers. "I wish Sarah could see this," he moaned as he slipped his hand over the spread and pillow. He sat on the side of the bed and his thoughts were drifting…as his cell phone vibrated…while lost with reflections of home.

His brother Paul was calling to suggest they eat at the in-house steak restaurant. Jim agreed to meet at their room around six. This gave him enough time to call Sarah, rest for about thirty minutes, then shower and dress.

"Hello little brother, come in. You look a little down and out… like you've lost your best friend."

"Well in a way I'm down, but I didn't realize it showed."

"Are you missing someone or something?"

With a little smile he said, "Yes I am. I walked around the room and saw so many beautiful furnishings and accessories and thought of a friend who's helping me with a redecorating project. She would enjoy seeing a place like this."

"Have you told her about the resort?"

"I have and she said, 'Please bring a brochure.' It won't be long, and I'll be home."

"Sounds like you would really like for her to be here."

"It does sound that way, and here I am and there she is at home."

"She's right, it won't be long," Paul said as he put his arm around Jim's shoulders. "Maybe she can come next time."

"Thanks, that makes me feel better. Now, is this threesome ready?"

"Yes, I just have to get Laura out of the dressing room. She has also fallen in love with this place."

* * *

The next morning the guys met for breakfast in the casino dining room and then off to the Blackjack tables. Playing cards in a skillful manner was far from Jim's mind, but being a participating part of the group was important to him on this junket. Jim felt lonesome and wished for Sarah.

Sarah had anxiously returned to Jim's with an aching heart. She had accomplished a good bit on her checklist, and by mid-afternoon was pleased with how the house was looking.

Into the early evening, Sarah sprawled across the guest room bed for a short rest. She covered herself with the tapestry coverlet from the foot of the bed and after a short mental fantasy of Jim's departing kisses, fell asleep.

After the guys finished watching a "Texas Hold Um Tournament" Jim excused himself. He returned to the room, unbuttoned his shirt, lay comfortably on the bed, and called Sarah.

She was lying on Jim's guest room bed sound asleep. The ringing phone startled her into a semiconscious state of mind and the first thing she said was "Its Jim, I just know it is."

"Hello dear, just wanted to give you a good night call. Did I wake you?"

"I'm awake," she said with shock. I'm at your house…I didn't intend to stay, but I'm being 'Little Red Riding Hood.' I worked all day…I got so tired…what time is it?"

"I'm glad you stayed. Just go back to sleep…I'll call you in the morning. Love you."

* * *

"Good morning Little Red…how's my lovely, brown-eyed girl this morning?"

With a laugh she said, "I've had my coffee…missed my usual oatmeal but found a granola bar. I'm sorry…I didn't intend to stay last night."

"We need to buy oatmeal and be prepared."

"I started early this morning checking things off my list, so maybe it was a good thing."

* * *

By late Saturday afternoon she felt as though her job was finished and ready for Jim's return home. She was extremely tired but pleased. As soon as Sarah took care of Bob, she went straight to the bathroom for a hot relaxing bath.

Within the hour Jim called and was anxious to hear her sweet voice, but also to give her the time he should arrive in Savannah. Sarah was in the claw foot tub when she heard the phone. She had forgotten to place it beside the tub and had thoughts of letting the caller leave a message, but in a flash, she thought of Jim and trailed water and bubbles as she cautiously made her way to the dressing table.

"I'm excited. I've worked at your house, and feel you'll love everything. I think we're almost finished," Sarah happily said.

"And ready to start another room?" Jim wishfully said with excitement.

"We'll have to talk about that…I think I need a vacation first. I'm not as young as I once was."

"Great, I know just the place," he said with enthusiasm.

"I'm taking a long bath now, imagining a warm ocean breeze and watching a colorful sun set from a gauze draped cabana…"

"I love your sweet, dreamy voice and your creative imagination. I can only lie here and wish. I can't wait to see you and I promise we will find a seaside paradise and live out your dreams."

"I'm looking forward to that. When do you think you will be home? I would really like to be at your house when you arrive, so we can walk through."

"We should land in Savannah at four-thirty and I'll be home by seven. On the way home I plan to stop for a short visit with Bill, my oldest brother.

"I'll put together a light supper for us, if that's ok."

"That sounds great, but light for me. We have eaten like hungry hounds at the feed pan all weekend. I'm looking forward to a friendly face and a warm smile and maybe something light and special to eat would be best."

"I think I can take care of that request," she said as she breathed heavy into the phone.

"I'm sure you can, my dear."

Sarah caught her breath and then exhaled. "Please be careful and know I'm waiting for you."

"See you soon…keep the water warm."

Jim was so aroused by the sweetness of her voice…knowing she had been at his house making it beautiful just for him and she would be waiting there. He fell asleep wanting her.

Sarah stepped into the shower and rinsed the soap from her body, patted herself dry and dressed for bed. As Sarah lay quietly staring at the ceiling, her thoughts of Jim drifted through her body. Sarah was so stimulated during their conversation and was now consumed by dreamy wishes. She fell asleep with a beautiful image of the two of them swirling in her dreams.

* * *

Jim was enjoying breakfast with Paul when his phone buzzed. He excused himself from the table as soon as he saw it was Sarah, "Hello my dear." After a sweet short conversation, Jim returned to the table with a gentle smile on his face. Jim asked his brother Paul to sit longer while the other guys went off to do their own thing.

"Brother, I didn't tell you the full story, I suppose because I was so down. I've met someone and during the past ten months have been getting acquainted with her. She is the one helping me redecorate. I met her about two months before I had the nerve to call. You know for the past several years I haven't wanted to settle. Nothing has ever clicked with me until this lady, Sarah."

"Well little brother, I've noticed a change in you. You haven't been going out at night and frequenting the bars. You spend more time sitting alone in deep thought or talking on the phone away from everyone…with a glowing smile on your face."

"Well, she does make me smile."

"I hope to come home for a visit soon. I want to see what you're doing with the house and maybe I can meet Sarah."

"That will work. Sarah has been a life saver with the house. After her husband died, she moved back to a weekend farm retreat they had about fifteen miles from my house. Through Lucy, I met Sarah. I barely talked to her that first night, but I watched her gracefulness and charm as she interacted with the others. Lucy helped me get to know her by having small dinner parties and visits to their river house at Barefoot Cay."

"One look at Sarah and I knew I had to change. She's different. She likes things quiet and restful. You remember Mom's Rose garden. I've been tending the roses and the old magnolia tree because Sarah loves the fragrance. She comes early each morning to the house, and we sit on the porch and have coffee just to smell the blossoms. Can you imagine me sitting on the back porch enjoying the smell of magnolia blossoms or tending roses?" Jim exclaimed with a gleaming smile on his face.

"No Jim, I can't, but maybe it's time to start smelling the roses and the magnolias. Mom always said there was a purpose for the rose garden being there," Paul said with a smile on his face.

"That's an example of the effect she has had on my life. Also, when I was lost, she brought my family together by comforting them. That meant the world to me."

"I'm happy for you because I know the ups and downs you've had in life. I'm proud you found a special lady who is giving you comfort and companionship. Remember this, love from a sweet woman in our youth was great, but the love of a sweet woman in our older days is heavenly."

"That statement is the truth. My life has a feeling of contentment. I love going home from work at the end of the day and finding her there."

"Little Brother, I think you're in love."

"I am and I honestly miss her," he said with humble shyness as his eyes began to glisten. "I begged her to come with me, but she said she didn't think it would be the right thing to do. She's an old-fashioned girl. I have a few more junkets paid for, but I would either like for her to come along or I'll stay home."

"Jim, you sound serious."

"I'm serious. I haven't let her know what I'm thinking because I'm waiting for the perfect moment. I don't want to rush her, but we have voiced our commitment to each other."

"Jim, I will support you in any way with your future with Sarah. I'm proud of you, little brother. That tournament we wanted to watch starts in forty-five minutes. We can talk as we find our way. Hope we can watch some good players because our plane leaves at two."

"I know," Jim said with exuberance.

* * *

On his way home from the airport, Jim stopped by his brother Bill's house. He told Bill about being with Paul on a junket to Biloxi. Jim said, "I really have something else to tell you. You know I have been redecorating the home place. Well, someone special has been helping me and I have grown to really care for her. Her name is Sarah."

He told Bill how thoughts of her fill his mind constantly each day. "It's thoughts of her gentle charm that warms my heart. Our cousin Lucy helped me meet her and through Lucy's help and willpower on my part I have come to know Sarah. We have gently worked through some troubling areas of our lives. Her friends speak highly of her as a sweet generous level-headed lady, and I see those same qualities. I love her, but I love her because she loves me."

"Jim, I'm so glad to hear this. I've known for a long time, you wanted someone to honestly love you and that you wanted someone to honestly love. Have you talked to your kids?"

"David has met Sarah and he has noticed a calmness in me because of her. He thinks it's a good thing. The girls have been around her twice and David has talked to them often. Helen was the hold out, but Sarah called me yesterday and said Helen came for a visit and now loves the idea of us being together. Helen's change relates to the nurturing care Sarah gave the children when I was lost and positive answers to suspicions Helen had. Mary Beth was on board the first time she met Sarah."

"You're my brother and I'm glad to see you happy and contented."

"Thank you for listening and noticing the redirection of my life. While I was away Sarah has been working on finalizing the main part of the house. She's waiting for me. The next junket is in about three weeks, and I hope we can all go."

* * *

As Jim rounded the last curve of the driveway and came into view of the house, his heart swelled, and a smile creased his face as he spotted Sarah's SUV in the driveway. *Sarah being here is a true sign of her caring and I love that,* Jim whispered with enthusiasm.

He used his key to enter and found his *Little Red* asleep in his cuddling chair. She raised her head and looked at him through droopy eyes and a sleepy smile. She started to rise, but he whispered for her to stay…he sat beside her in the chair.

"I've been waiting for you to come home, and I fell asleep."

"I'm here now…just rest. I promise I won't go off again without you."

"That's so sweet. I have dinner on the counter."

"I missed you," he softly said as he kissed her sweet lips. "I would like to hold you for a while."

"Your chair is warm and snug…I think I'm acting like Little Red Riding Hood. Didn't she fall asleep in the bear's bed?"

"I think so and it's alright for you to fall asleep here anytime. You look comfortable and feel warm. Do you remember when we bought the chair and you sat with me to try it out? I'll never forget how our eyes locked, and I think we both knew it was the perfect chair for us. We avoided it because we were afraid it would cause our emotions to run rampant, and we weren't ready for that.

Now with you here beside me and knowing how much we care for each other, I just want to hold you and enjoy being together in our chair," Jim said as she moved closer.

In a restful silence, they spoke to each other with gratefulness in a language that only kindred spirits can feel. He strengthened his hold, and she lifted her head to breathe warm breaths of air on his neck. He moved his lips downward and stroked her soft burgundy lips. His extreme desire was evident, and she responded to his movements.

"I've missed you. I tried to fill my time, but I've had some sad moments," Sarah said with sweetness as tears welled up and she reached for Jim.

"I know…so have I. My room was enormous, and I was lost all by myself. Everywhere I went I saw something that reminded me of you and home. I'm here now, and my care and love for you is stronger than the day I left."

Chapter 17

Sarah put the finishing touches on the rooms and Jim was ecstatic. It wasn't long before he started to talk about redecorating his bedroom. Her first thought was how sweet a customer wants me to continue working, but then she thought about the intimate level of their relationship and decorating his bedroom.

"Your home has been a dream project and I've loved being a part of this, but I think we should wait until after our island vacation before we talk about that."

He pulled her to him and whispered in her ear as he massaged the arch of her back. "There's another junket to Connecticut scheduled in a few weeks. I had decided not to go unless you would like to go."

"Bill and Joanne are planning, and hopefully we can all go. Think about it and we can get together with them, so you can feel comfortable with going.

* * *

Jim was making phone calls and finishing paperwork in his office the next morning when Sarah arrived a little after nine. She tapped on the door and no one came, so she let herself inside, and started the coffee brewing. Sarah found Jim's favorite cup and her cup she had purposefully left in the cabinet.

She sliced a breakfast casserole she had made the night before and arranged their squares on small plates, along with the silverware and napkins on a wicker tray. She also placed small vase of summer flowers on the tray. She hurried outside to the porch and arranged everything on the patio table. The morning air was fragrant with the heavenly aroma of the Mr. Lincoln roses and the Ginger lilies. She returned to the kitchen and found Jim slicing off a taste of the casserole.

"Good morning Sunshine," he said playfully like the little boy who was caught in the pantry with the chocolate cake.

"And good morning to you." she said with an enormous smile as they kissed with enthusiastic fervor. "Wow, what a wonderful way to start the day."

As his hands held her lower back, she leaned back to admire his smile. "I could start every morning like that," he said as he enjoyed another quick kiss.

She whispered sweetly into his ear, "Our breakfast is getting cold. I'll pour the coffee."

"Our timing has been perfect with finishing the house and this trip coming up. I'm looking forward to having a few relaxing days away with just the two of us."

"I'm looking forward to that, but I'm a little nervous," Sarah said with an embarrassing glance.

"I'll be there, and Joanne is looking forward to spending time with you."

Sarah's eyes sparkled as she said, "Joanne called last night, she's excited about our trip."

"Come here. Being together will be the best. I'm looking forward to having you alone. You're the one I want. I'm older and through my life I've been involved in things and learned a lot about living, but in that searching I never felt contentment with lasting happiness until I met you."

"I want to enjoy the simple pleasures of life with you. I want to experience the man you are."

"What a treasure. I'm looking forward to our trip."

"I'm excited. It will be a new experience, for which I'm ready," Sarah said with nervous joy.

"What a treasure..."

With Jim's house ninety-nine percent finished, Sarah was spending more time at home and found her days without seeing Jim made her feel lonely. She was looking forward to the final order of the lamp and pillows arriving so she could return to his house.

She was excited when the items came in and called Jim with plans of going back the next day to place those things. Jim was looking forward to her return.

With excitement about leaving the next day for their trip, Jim said, "I'll be at your house tomorrow morning about 6ish. I'm looking forward to our new adventure together."

* * *

Jim whistled a sweet tune as he arrived at Sarah's and found her radiant with excitement. He was smiling as he kissed her good morning and thought of being with her.

Sarah was dressed in slate gray slacks and with a silky printed blouse and deep turquoise sweater. Her graying hair was shining and neatly combed. Her make-up delicately accented her facial features. She smelled sweetly with a faint touch of Chanel No. 5 lightly touched to her body.

Jim quickly noticed her burgundy sculptured lips and held her willing body next to his excited frame. His desire was to kiss her again, but he had to refrain for now.

Sarah shyly noticed the coral oxford cloth shirt against his glowing work-tanned skin. His khaki pants were neatly pressed, and his brown loafers were buffed. Sarah smiled as she walked into his open arms and kissed him. "You look wonderful my dear."

Jim stroked his hand along her shoulder covered by the silken blouse and enjoyed the thoughts of going away with Sarah. With a desiring look on his face he enthusiastically said, "I'm over-joyed with our being together. You're a beautiful exhilarating woman who gives me energy and a zest for life. Are you ready to leave for our first amazing adventure?"

With trembling knees mixed with a dreamy feeling, Sarah said, "I'm ready for an enjoyable venture out into an unknown world sprinkled with laughter, friends, and your manly romantic charms." She put her arms around Jim and said with a pleased look on her face. "This is a big step, thank you my darling."

Chapter 18

They boarded the plane for the resort in Connecticut at eight-fifteen. While in flight he touched her fingers, as he massaged her arm and he watched Sarah relax. She leaned close beside him and in a tranquil state of mind, she settled against his shoulder.

The limousine ride to the resort through the mountains covered in fall colors was breathtaking, and the anticipation could be seen in Sarah's eyes. The resort was an outstanding architectural vision much like a Scottish castle nested in the Pachaug Mountains near Hopeville Pond.

The entrance was visually accessorized with massive pots of flowering fall plantings. The air was fresh with a heavy mist occasionally sprinkled with snow. The men took care of sorting the luggage, as Joanne looked at Sarah and they took on a feeling of two pampered ladies as the doorman opened the door and tipped his hat to them. Sarah felt Joanne's strong nature.

Sarah had never been treated to something so spectacular. The fear of the unknown crept into her thoughts, but the assurance of the others brought about a feeling of comfort.

The hotel lobby was grand with Vermont marble covering the floors and polished slabs used as wainscoting. A massive brass and crystal chandelier hung in the two-story entrance. Groupings of sofas and chairs for comfortable gatherings were throughout the grand entrance. It was designed for the pleasure and convenience of the welcomed visitors. Sarah felt relaxed, as her dancing eyes sparkled.

When she and Jim entered their room, she noticed and mentally recorded in a three-hundred-and-sixty-five-degree turn. She saw the furnishings, drapes, and colors and all in between. She laid her purse on the bed as she observed its loveliness. She turned to face Jim who was looking sweetly at her.

"I knew you would enjoy this. The place is just spectacular." He took her hand, "You have to see the bathroom."

"This is gorgeous. I have never seen such exquisite architectural features in a bathroom."

"I might have a hard time keeping you in bed. You might be awake drawing, studying, or taking pictures of all this," Jim said as he placed his arm around her shoulders.

"I might do some of that, but you have priority in my life," she said as she held his face in her hand and kissed him warmly on his lips. "I love you and thank you for coming into my life and making me a part of your life."

As he gently stole quick kisses, "Thank you for sharing your sweetness with me, my family and friends. You're a special lady."

"Do we have dinner plans for tonight?"

"Not really. We'll meet Bill and Joanne around six. We have two hours so we can stay in the room and rest, or we can go out walking around the hotel."

"Staying here sounds great."

As he took her into his arms he looked into her intense brown eyes and said with a smile, "Resting sounds good to me, also."

With a sweet agreeable smile, Sarah followed his lead and entered his magnificent arms as she cherished his embrace.

"You're lovable," he said.

Jim lifted their suitcases onto the luggage racks and they carefully laid each piece of clothing into a replica of a Louis the fourteenth chest of drawers. As their paths crossed, they touched or slipped their hands down the arm of the other. As their hanging things were put into the closet, Jim admired her colorful clothing. He fanned through the sleeves of their things and it gave him a warm feeling.

"We can rest an hour and have plenty of time to get dressed, if you would like."

"I'm a bit exhausted.

Jim pulled the covers back, changed into a pair of flannel pants and laid down in bed.

Sarah entered the room and saw him lying there, so she shyly slipped into bed and stayed quiet.

Jim reached over and touched her arm; she slipped her hand into his hand. He rolled over on his side and said, "The alarm is set, so we won't oversleep. I hope my snoring won't disturb you."

"Mine either," Sarah said with a laugh.

Jim moved closer to Sarah and kissed her sweetly as he spooned against her. "I'm glad we're together…sweet dreams," he said as he rolled over on his back.

With stirring emotions, she laid her head gently against him. As soon as she resettled beside his chest, Sarah drifted into a restful sleep.

His arms wrapped around her, loosened as he closed his eyes, and was carried into a world of pleasant dreams. The alarm startled them. They jumped and looked at each other with a shocked look and then smiled.

"That was a short nap," Jim said as he slowly rubbed his forehead.

"I was enjoying the rest. I wish in a way we didn't have to get up."

As Jim slowly rose, he said, "I agree with that."

He quickly showered while Sarah was deciding what to wear. As he was emptying his accessory bag, he watched in the mirror as she entered the bathroom, headed directly for the shower, slipped off her robe and without hesitation stepped inside. Jim observed her modesty in the mirror, and thought *what a beautiful, but shy little woman.*

Sarah dried off and exited the bathing area in a trot, and quickly put on her under garments and robe. She felt him watching her out of the corner of his eye as she returned to the dressing table. She applied her make-up and combed her hair.

He admired her tiny figure as she disrobed and dressed in patterned palazzo pants and a lovely flowing blue crepe blouse. Her jewelry was a simple sterling silver multilayered chain and the bracelets Jim had given her. She wore a small black onyx and diamond ring.

Sarah turned and saw Jim dressed in a coral Pin-Point dress shirt and khaki pants. She smiled and went to him. "You're handsome. I'm not sure I'll be able to keep my eyes off you tonight."

"My dear, you smell delicious, and you're lovely. We need to leave quickly, or else I might decide not to leave."

With a deep sigh Sarah said, "Let me get my purse, and I'll be ready."

The restaurant was crowded. "Thank you, Bill for making reservations…I'm famished after such a long day" Sarah said with appreciation. The maître d' seated them beside a large window that highlighted a lovely winter garden below them on the sixth-floor roof top.

Sparkling reflections in the mirrored walls created a starry vision to the elegant dining room. Sarah looked at Jim and smiled as she thought, *I feel mesmerized being with Jim in such a lovely romantic setting. I love sitting here watching him and feeling the warmth of his being.*

The menu had several outstanding dishes, but Sarah settled on her favorite grilled Alaskan salmon glazed with a bourbon mango sauce, and Jasmine rice as a warm side dish. Sarah drank in the room's atmosphere as she savored each taste of food, and enjoyed classical melodies performed by an ensemble playing Glenn Miller tunes.

She thought *how at peace I feel as I listened to Jim tell the story about our nap and the startling alarm as the music plays.* Sarah thought, *I'm laughing and enjoying myself with no feelings of anxiety.* She thought a little deeper…*this is the way it has been with Jim.* A feeling of contentment and joy made her smile. She looked at him soulfully as he talked. A sensation of warmth heated her core and she gently slipped her leg over and rested her knee beside his knee.

He felt her movement and pressed firmly against her as he glanced and smiled in her direction. Jim knew she was wishing because she was smiling that lovely thin smile.

After dinner they were attracted into a piano bar as a flow of ragtime jazz came pouring out of the doorway. The pianist was playing a selection by Scott Joplin and later music from several late fifties Broadway plays. Sarah immediately felt the coziness of the room and as Jim slipped his arm around her waist and pulled her close, she felt warm inside.

After they finished their night caps, Jim quickly said, "I don't know about you all, but I think it's time we old folks found a comfortable place to lie down. What do you all think?"

After a series of glances, they rose in unison and began to file out of the lounge to the rendition of the theme from "The Apartment."

Jim enjoyed the slow elevator ride to the fourteenth floor, as he kept his hand locked on Sarah's waist as he thought about being alone with her.

Bill invited them in for a final nightcap, but Jim looked at Sarah with a declining look and without her saying a word Jim said, "Let us take a rain check on that. It's been a long day." Sarah smiled and put her arm around his shoulders and snuggled her breast next to him.

"You're right. It is bedtime. How about breakfast plans around ten o'clock?"

"I'll call you around nine-thirty. Good night."

Jim turned and pulled Sarah quickly in the direction of their room. He almost lifted her feet off the floor as he turned.

She looked back and with a fleeting smile said, "Good night… enjoyed the evening."

As Jim took a quick shower and brushed his teeth, he was constantly thinking about being in bed with Sarah. He was anxious to let his tired body rest through the night lying beside her. He wanted to feel her warmth and the touch of a loving companion next to him, but he knew he must respect her shyness as their relationship was moving forward.

After a quick refreshing shower Sarah dressed into her nightgown. Brushed her teeth and completed a few nightly rituals. She entered the bedroom with a smile on her face because she thought that would disguise her anxiety, but her smile quickly changed to a questioning look when she heard Jim snoring.

She tiptoed to the bed and gently slipped under the covers and exhaled. She laid there for several minutes and replayed the day. She glowed while remembering *how comfortable she felt and how Jim smiled and eased her through some anxious moments.* She delighted in remembering *him touching her in a respectful manner on many occasions, and how each touch caused her to look into his eyes and feel warm inside.* She rolled over to face him and watched the rise and fall of his chest as he slept. She kissed his shoulder.

He gently eased her closer to his side, and in the quietness of their refuge they snuggled. Their closeness brought contentment and contentment brought security. She felt as though she belonged beside him.

* * *

They rose early with excited thoughts for the day. They spent time together and time apart with others. Their group plans were to go out for the evening, so Jim and Sarah went to the room early for a rest before dinner.

It was six o'clock and they were readying themselves for an elegant evening. Sarah meticulously groomed herself while constantly thinking of Jim.

With thoughts of Sarah, Jim carefully dressed in preparation of a special evening with his sweet lady…an evening filled with mystery and hope.

Sarah noticed the setting sun creating a dramatic fall glow and the shadows from the trees were trailing long in the setting sun. Dark boiling storm clouds rushed in over the mountains and quickly darkened the sky. Sarah smiled as she reached to close the sheers as they dressed. She noticed the shimmering glaze of melted snowflakes on the windows accentuated by the flicker of car lights rounding the mountain. As she closed the heavy drapes, she noticed the quality of the drapery fabric and let the silk fringe trim of the leading edge, glide slowly over her hand.

Sarah dressed in a simple black A-line dress with a sheer wrap for her shoulders. Her jewelry was simple with a small three diamond drop pendant neckless on a delicate sterling silver chain, a small diamond bracelet, along with Jim's bracelets. She carried a small satin flower enhanced clutch that held her lipstick, several Kleenex, and a few other personal items. Her hair was styled in a flattering cut that highlighted her small facial features. She wore his favorite perfume, which she faintly splashed on a few sensual areas of her body. Sarah was glowing with excitement.

When passing a mirror, she often checked herself. She was shocked at the vivacious woman she saw in the reflection. Sarah was amazed at her smile and observed the way she carried herself. She was even more surprised by the clothing that covered her body. She thought *it must be another person's body and dress. It doesn't look as though it should be me dressed for an evening out, but it is. I've come a long way and I feel comfortable.*

When Jim opened the doors to the dressing room, she looked at him and smiled just for him because he was handsome. They walked to each other and she laid her hands lightly on his chest and ran her fingers over his dinner jacket lapel and admired his charismatic James Bond look.

"English Leather...my favorite fragrance," Sarah said as she gently kissed his lips, then dabbed away any hint of lipstick. Sarah felt true compassion as she looked deep into his twinkling eyes.

"You're beautiful, you're beyond words," he said as he leaned forward and kissed her on the side of her neck and breathed in a long breath of her delicate fragrance. "My darling." He exhaled against her skin, and the hairs tingled on the back of her neck as she felt his warm breath against her cool skin. "You create a restless feeling...with the elegant way you look...your fragrance...your eyes. I love being alone with you, so we better go."

Sarah smiled that smile as he circled her waist and she leaned into him. As the elevator doors closed, Jim became quiet and thought, *the hostess...I hope she remembers me...this must go as planned.* They made their way to the piano bar for some quite time before they were to meet the others at the Four Seasons Restaurant for dinner.

They were seated in a plush banquette in a quite area away from the main crowd. Drinks were ordered, and they talked exuberantly about the trip. Jim asked Sarah, "Did you enjoy your morning at the spa, and being with Joanne?"

Sarah was quick to express how their morning was relaxing and stimulating. "The massage was like living out a dream, but without you," she said as she moved closer to Jim. She expressed how she enjoyed Joanne's sweet personality and how they laughed and talked all morning. "We talked about several things, but we talked about you more."

"Oh dear, I hope I'm not in trouble," Jim said teasingly.

"No, my love not at all..." Sarah said with a warm smile.

After a while Jim's voice mellowed. He began to speak in a lower tone, and more from his heart. Even the music seemed to grow softer, and he and Sarah grew in tune to each other. Sarah recognized the change in his voice and moved closer to look deep into his eyes as he spoke.

"You know I love you, Sarah."

"Yes, my darling, and I love you."

"I've known you for well over a year now. We worked together on the house, and you have gone to work with me at my job sites. I'll never forget the first kiss I stole from you at the furniture store. I didn't know if you would run out the door or if you would enjoy it enough to stay. I feel you enjoyed me because you didn't run and you're still here."

With a warm smile, Sarah said, "I did enjoy it."

Their hands were together and occasionally he kissed her fingers. Their eyes were locked on each other as he talked, and she listened.

His joy was seen not only in his words, but in his vivid facial expressions. He saw her listening intently as her head tilted and felt mesmerized by the twinkle in her eyes. He loved the sight of that intriguing thin smile as it appeared on her face, and the rise and fall of her breast, as she clung to each word he spoke.

"I especially have enjoyed our decorating adventures, the times we walked on the beach and we played together. You know I've seen you, all sweated down like when we were working in Savannah during the summer and I've seen you elegantly dressed like tonight. I loved you then and I love you now. You have grown to mean a lot to me and my family. I enjoy coming home from work and seeing the light on in the kitchen and knowing you're there. I enjoy watching you when we go out with others, and you laugh and take pleasure in being with our friends. I love your smile. You have rekindled my hope. You're a treasure."

Sarah took his hand to her lips and kissed his fingers, then moved his hand to rest on top of her heart. Her eyes were beginning to take on a glassy look and a small tear formed in the corner of her right eye.

Jim reached out and patted it away and said, "I'm so thankful for you. I could talk all night about how you have helped me…about how I want and need you in my life, in my home and waking up with you by my side."

As Sarah heard his sweet wants, she held his hand tighter to her heart, leaned closer and her eyes glassed over with tears.

His hand moved slowly across to her side. He held her gently and his thumb touched the side of her breast as he tightened his grip. His compassionate words had truly aroused her, and he could see it in the intensity of her eyes, and he loved her for her response.

Another tear formed and he quickly wisped it away and reached into his pocket for what she thought was a Kleenex, but instead he brought out a Princess cut diamond engagement ring, which sparkled in the dim light of the room.

Sarah reached for the tissue but touched the ring…looked at Jim with astonishment as her eyes widened with a feeling of questioning unbelief…then felt a surge of uncontrollable emotional joy. "Jim," as she smiled that smile.

He gently held the ring out to her. He took her hand, and with the most enduring plea straight from his heart, Jim looked into the dark brown eyes of the lady he had searched for and found, "Will you marry me?"

Quiet tears began to flow. With trembling hands, she took his hand that held the ring and said, "I have loved you for such a long time. I adored you back when you flirted and courted me from the beginning. During our first walk in the garden, the furniture store, and all those days while we worked on the house, I grew to care deeply for you. My love for you has grown from that little spark when I first met you, into an admiration that wants you near me, with me, close to me all the time. I love you and I want you and only you. I will be honored to be your wife."

With great skill and trembling hands, he slowly slipped the ring on her finger. The delicate ring graced Sarah's lovely hand and he couldn't resist lifting and kissing her fingers.

She closed her eyes and dropped her head to keep the tears of joy from flooding her face. She regained her composure and looked at her finger. "It's beautiful, it's lovely. It looks like a treasured antique."

"It is. It belonged to my mother."

"Jim it is so special. I love you. You're so thoughtful." A little tear formed, and he touched it away. He took her hand and kissed the ring and kissed her fingers, and they gently kissed.

She placed her hand softly beside his face, and *the warmth of his face was a reminder of the warmth of his heart.* "I love you in so many ways." A flashback of her life before was overthrown by thoughts of her future.

I think our love for each other, the commitment we have and our enjoyment of each other will be the building blocks for our future and will keep us on the right track."

Sarah smiled and said as she threaded her fingers into his, "You're absolutely right. We're second timers and I'm thankful for your patience as your love never failed in my struggle to overcome my past. I love you with all my heart and look forward to our future together." She slipped her arms around his neck and he lifted her onto his chest, and they embraced as the world around them became silent and she felt his heartbeat.

"I'm looking forward to that, also." He gently kissed her.

Jim's cell phone vibrated, and he said, "I should have turned this thing off."

"That's ok, it might be important."

He looked and saw it was Bill. "He wants to know if they can join us." Sarah shook her head yes, and he told them it was fine. After he put away the phone, he said, "Joanne and Bill knew about my plans to give you the ring. I had to have help on finding out your ring size and if you would even want a ring that belonged to someone else. Also, Carrie and Ben, and Lucy and Charlie helped."

Jim reached his arms around her, as she circled his shoulders, and pulled her into him. They kissed intimately with warm passion.

As Bill and Joanne slipped into the banquette, Joanne immediately hugged Sarah. "I love you, and I absolutely love you for what you mean to Jim and his family. Let me see your ring? It's beautiful and we are happy for you and Jim."

"With all my heart I care for Jim. I admired him from the beginning. This has been the best moment of my life and I thank you for your support of making this happen. I look forward, to many years of special moments together," Sarah said while choking back her tears of joy.

Jim's arm circled the small of her back and was resting on her stomach area underneath her breast. He gently eased her against himself, and Sarah moved her body more into his chest.

"How did you get here so quickly?" Sarah said.

"We were sitting near-by just watching you two and enjoying your excitement. I was crying because I could see the honest sincere feelings you have for each other," Joanne sweetly said.

Sarah smiled broadly, "Bless you, my dear," Sarah said as they hugged.

As they talked, Sarah tightly held Jim's hand in her lap. With his hand hidden by the drop of the tablecloth, he occasionally massaged her thigh.

Bill raised his glass and said, "Let me say a toast to this lovely young couple. Wish for you a beautiful life of love, laughter and adventure with family and friends to encourage you. Here here."

He magnificently toasted the couple, they freely exchanged chatter and plans concerning their future and eventually about the day's events. The guys told outrageous stories about the tournament and the girls giggling about the young handsome masseur who gave them a morning massage.

Jim's hand rested on her thigh and eventually found its way to the lace of her thigh high stockings. He felt under the lace and glided his fingers slowly across her warm skin.

Sarah could barely contain herself. She looked at Jim and touched her hand to his as it rested on her thigh. Their eyes sparkled with a sensual moment of wishing that only they understood.

Jim said, "Was he more handsome than me?"

"No, not at all, he was young and attractive, but no one can be more handsome or more charming than you my dear."

"Wow, what an answer," Jim beamed with desire.

They laughed and Sarah brought his wondering hand to her lips and kissed his fingers several times.

After dinner, the two couples walked along the promenade and window shopped. Music was playing softly as they enjoyed their stroll. The shops were elegantly fashionable with displays of furs, diamonds, ball gowns and fine living accessories. It was an adventure to walk and look.

As they strolled Jim rested his hand on Sarah's hip or held her waist accompanied by a gentle massaging motion. He would look deep into her eyes, to affirm that he knew the meaning of her touch and a smile to say they would soon be alone.

Encouraged by an erotic stimulation Sarah put her hand under Jim's coat, slipped it high on his back. She leaned into his chest as he gently pulled her into his side and she whispered, "I love you."

He slowly whispered, "You smell so sweet, and I love you."

A little after ten, some of the guys started to make additional plans for the evening, but Jim said as he looked first at Sarah and then to a friend, "It's been a long day and I think we need to turn in…we're a good bit older than most of you folks."

Bill and Joanne felt the same, so they said good night, and the foursome turned to find the nearest elevator. When they reached their floor, they hugged and thanked each other for their part in such a wonderful day. Joanne asked, "Would you like to have early breakfast?"

Jim said with a boyish grin, "I'm not sure right now. We might just sleep a little late tomorrow."

"Tomorrow morning, I might plan to get a massage from another handsome charming masseur," Sarah said as she looked at Jim and winked.

Jim quickly smiled the biggest smile, and pulled Sarah tight against him, and said, "Mmmm, I'm looking forward to that. We might skip breakfast."

Everybody laughed and Bill said, "That's my little brother."

"Love you guys and we will see you sometime tomorrow."

* * *

As soon as Jim and Sarah entered their room, he quickly took the "Do Not Disturb" sign and hung it on the outside. "I've been waiting all evening to be alone with you," he said as he closed and locked the door.

Sarah looked into his eyes and smiled. She also was looking forward to this moment. She immediately kicked off her shoes and laid her wrap and purse on the entrance hall table. She gently laid her arms on his shoulder and slipped her fingers to the nape of his neck and gracefully moved close to him.

The scent of English Leather enveloped her as Jim eased her even closer with his hands gently holding Sarah at her waist. Their eyes locked into a tranquil stare as they stood face to face. He found her to be limp as she settled and yielded to his every move, and his hands moved low on her back. He teasingly kissed her, and she playfully nibbled his ear lobe as innate passion heightened their erotic mood.

She helped him remove his jacket and gently tossed it to the wing of a nearby chair, and in a graceful waltz, they moved to the middle of the entrance hall in front of the tall pier mirror. He observed her mirror reflection and saw how her structure conformed to his stature. It was the image of a caring woman who clung to him out of true love. He saw a reflection of a companion, a loving friend he adored. It was the match he had been searching for and desperately wanted as his wife and friend.

As he turned her around, she quickly saw his reflection in the mirror as they moved to the sound of their own music. She loved the image she saw of the two of them. It was the warm gentle caring reflection she had been dreaming of in a trusting, comforting friend, and loving companion, and now her fiancé. She smiled sweetly as the dream of becoming the wife of a trustworthy husband seemed forthcoming. Sarah held him tighter as she admired his graceful charismatic charm. He wrapped his arms low across her back and gently eased her closer to his body and into his slow swaying rhythm.

Sarah clung to him as they turned and swayed around the room, teased each other with wet kisses and enjoyed the stimulation as their sensual closeness enlivened.

"I wish I had a video, so I could remember every word you spoke, and could see your expressions. I love my brown-eyed girl" Jim said with a loving smile and a gentle kiss.

With graceful elegance, they moved further to the wall at the end of the entrance hall. He leaned her against the silk wallpaper and his hands moved up from her waist to rest gently on her breast and he massaged her as she moaned with a feeling of sensual pleasure. She felt his eagerness and responded to his movements.

He reached down and began to rub her thigh and felt her laced stocking band. The tender movement surged their desires.

Her eyes glazed over. As her vision narrowed, and it all becomes dream like. She willingly yielded.

Through his wet kisses on her neck he said, "Did you have any idea about what was about to happen tonight?"

"My first thought was how sweet and romantic you are, and I clung to every word, because you were speaking from your heart. That's what brought on the first tear you dabbed away."

They kissed again with deep passion and touching. A feeling of heat surged over Sarah as she became more giving to his touch.

"When I saw your tears, I became emotional. Umm, so sweet… I'm wishing, my darling."

"…sweet because of your loving charm…umm, I'm wishing, also," Sarah moaned sweetly.

Their bodies were over-heating as he enjoyed her tenderness, and their hearts were beating faster. She unbuttoned his pristine white shirt, then unbuckled his belt and released his trousers. He removed his shirt, picked up his pants and threw them on the chair. Their eyes were locked on each other as the fragrance of loving filled their circle. They kissed again with wanting passion.

She arched her back. "With the second tear, I was struggling to hold back a flood of tears."

"My darling, I love the way you move against me." As they shifted into the coolness of the bedroom their sensual passion simmered to steady willful carnal movements.

"When you felt in your pocket, I reached forward for what I thought would be a tissue and instead your hand was holding the ring.

It really was a magnificent surprise and a beautiful moment that I will never forget, my love."

They kissed with gentle caresses and breathed heavy against the moist skin of the other. The hint of passion permeated the coolness of the room.

"I could tell by the way you looked, it was a surprise, and now I know you were expecting a tissue, but it was an engagement ring instead."

Sarah placed her fingertips on each side of his face and leaned into him as she said with boundless feeling, "Yes, a beautiful antique engagement ring…with immeasurable meaning. It's a gift from you that will bring joy to our lives for the remainder of our lives." Sarah's words and the penetrating look in her eyes were stimulating.

He eased her lower body firmly into his yearning. "…and then when you started to talk, I didn't know at first which way you were leaning. In a flash I thought what if she rejects my proposal. When you went toward acceptance, it was like a heavy load was taken away. I'm not sure if you noticed, but my shoulders dropped, and I started to calmly breathe. You made me happy when you said you would marry me," Jim said as his hand caressed the side of her face and his parted lips breathed his warm breath into her as they kissed with sensual pleasure stimulating the need for each other.

He gently unzipped her dress and laid it carefully on the chair. "You're delicate and sweet…"

She reached to unhook her lace bra, but he caressed her hand and quietly whispered, "Let me do that in bed, and keep your stockings on as well." His hand held her as he massaged and kissed her softness.

With the back of her fingers, she stroked the side of his face as she looked deep into his sparkling gray-green eyes. Sarah twitched as she felt a warm surge through her core.

He looked into her loving brown eyes and gently traced the soft curves of her body with his fingertips.

They slowly and gracefully turned the covers back. With their eyes locked on each other, no words were needed to encourage the other. It was only a natural instinctual progression of two loving souls.

He looked into her dark eyes and said, "Here we are."

"Yes, my darling here we are."

Their moments of tenderness turned into hours, changed into late night and then early morning. It was time filled with old-fashioned gentleness, enlivened by eagerness, with times of lying close in soulful renewing.

They sealed their commitment to each other, and enjoyed the peace and tranquility brought on by an antique circle of sterling silver encrusted with a sparkling diamond, that once belonged to his mother.

"Here we are."

"Yes, my love, here we are and here is where I want to be."

Acknowledgements

I wanted to thank my friends Jerrie and Sue, because they were the first to listen to a reading of the rough first draft. Even in its poor condition they encouraged me to continue.

To my friends at Hodges Antiques I am grateful because you all taught me about interior decorating which is a major part of the story.

Thank you, my friend Carol for the hours you spent reading the drafts and offered suggestions…I will forever be grateful. Your encouragement through the years kept me on track.

Thank you to Jim who shared personal information about the Vietnam War. He also shared information I used in writing about marine building. To him I am grateful as he helped and offered encouragement.

After several years, I was ready to reach out into the world of writing. My friend Brian in NYC was my answered prayer. He got me in touch with Caitlin Leffel of NYC who edited materials sent to agents. Her encouragement at a time when I was lost was a strong support. I treasure her friendship.

As I searched for a book editor, friends put me in touch with Dr. Russell Willerton, Department Chair of Writing and Linguistics at Georgia Southern University. He recommended Kristen Hamilton, a former student of his at Boise State. Kristen taught me how to take my paragraphs of telling and add color and voice. She is an outstanding editor who patiently helper my story bloom. Thank you, Kristen.

To Nita, your line-edit helped to bring closure to certain areas that gave the story a finished feel. I will forever be grateful for your discerning eyes.

My friend Marty, who help me on many occasions with my computer, especially when I upgraded. Thank you for all those questions you patiently answered again and again. I'm grateful to you and your family.

BookBaby Publishing Company, I am thankful for finding. Ramona and her team have helped me through many unknowns in the world of publishing and marketing. Thank you.

To my dad and my husband John whose years of renovating and construction training taught me the building process I used many times throughout this story. I also thank my husband for patiently working with me during the hours I've been sequestered at my writing table in the laundry room.

To the readers, if you see this as your story and from reading this you find hope, then you have found what I was wanting to convey. Thank you and I wish you many blessings.